A LONG, COOL *Rain*

THE DELANEYS OF CAMBRIA, BOOK 1

LINDA SEED

This is a work of fiction. Any characters, organizations, places, or events portrayed in this novel are either products of the author's imagination or are used fictitiously.

The author is available for book signings, book club discussions, conferences, and other appearances.

Linda Seed may be contacted via e-mail at lindaseed24@gmail.com or on Facebook at www.facebook.com/LindaSeedAuthor.
Visit Linda Seed's website at www.lindaseed.com.

ISBN-13: 978-1544675350
ISBN-10: 1544675356

First Trade Paperback Printing: April 2016

ALSO BY LINDA SEED

THE MAIN STREET MERCHANTS SERIES

MOONSTONE BEACH
LIKE THAT ENDLESS CAMBRIA SKY
NEARLY WILD
FIRE AND GLASS

For Condee, with love.

A LONG, COOL *Rain*

Chapter One

"Well, it's raining. He would have liked that." Sandra Delaney nodded once, crisply, as she looked down at the fresh gravesite where her brother-in-law, Redmond, lay.

Colin Delaney thought his mother was probably right. For as long as he could remember, his uncle Redmond had spent an inordinate amount of time thinking about rain—talking about it, speculating about it, measuring it, and bemoaning the lack of it.

Now here it was, raining, as though in his uncle's honor. Redmond, wherever he was, undoubtedly was enjoying the weather more than the assembled mourners, who were huddled under umbrellas in the gloom of a February morning.

Colin's shoes were probably ruined. If Redmond were here, he'd have been wearing size twelve Timberland work boots, most likely. The damned things were indestructible.

Only nine people were gathered around the grave: Colin's parents, Sandra and Orin; his brothers, Ryan and Liam; Ryan's wife, Genevieve; Colin's sister, Breanna; Breanna's two sons, Michael and Lucas; and himself. There would be a big gathering at the house later, and most of Cambria would probably come. But this moment was just for the family.

"I expect he went the way he'd have wanted to," Orin said,

rubbing his nose with one rough finger. His voice was thick with emotion. "Out there in the pasture, on Abby."

Abby was Redmond's horse, a big Appaloosa he'd been riding for the better part of fifteen years, though Redmond had been doing a lot less riding of late. Once he'd hit his seventies, persistent back problems had mostly sidelined him. But for whatever reason, he'd been on Abby that morning, out in the northeast pasture, when something that was probably a heart attack had dropped him from the saddle and to the ground.

"Don't know what he was doing out there," Ryan said. He shook his head and kicked at a rock in the wet grass.

Ryan had been the one to find Redmond. He'd been out looking for a stray calf and had found Abby in the far corner of the pasture, saddled but riderless. He'd found Redmond lying facedown in the grass, already gone. Already cold.

Colin could only imagine how that must have been for Ryan. At least, unlike Colin, Ryan wasn't carrying the guilt of not having seen Redmond in more than a year, of not having even bothered to call him. Colin stayed in touch with his parents, of course, but his uncle was a quiet figure in the background, someone he'd asked after but had not made the effort to reach out to. It had been a long time since they'd talked. Too long.

And now, too late.

The pastor had already said what he had to say about God and heaven and the pain of loss, and had retreated to his car and then back into town, promising to make an appearance at the house later in the day. Now, it seemed as though no one in the family wanted to be the first to leave, even though the steady drizzle of rain was soaking them.

The Delaneys were never the kind to be put off by a little weather. Most of them, anyway. Colin himself preferred shelter and warmth—just another of the many things that separated him from the rest of his clan.

If this was a pissing match with his parents and siblings to see who was the better mourner, he was prepared to lose. Hell, he was used to losing in any comparison with the rest of the Delaneys. Why should now be any different?

"I'm going to head on back," he said, his voice muffled by the patter of rain on the grass, in the trees, and on their umbrellas. "I'll see you all back at the house later."

He turned to walk through the grass of the cemetery and toward the parking lot.

Halfway there, he became aware that Ryan was hurrying to catch up to him.

"You could at least stay at the house," Ryan said, without preamble, as they walked toward Colin's car.

"I like the lodge," Colin answered, looking at his ruined shoes and not at his brother.

"It hurts Mom's feelings, you not staying there," Ryan said.

When Colin did look at him, he saw pretty much what he expected: the scorn of judgment in Ryan's espresso-colored eyes. He didn't feel like being judged right now, though he couldn't do anything to prevent it.

Colin let out a sigh and stopped walking. He peered at Ryan, tilting his chin with defiance.

"I haven't been back home in a year. Not since your wedding," he said. "And if I stay at the house, I'm going to hear about it—over and over. At least during the wake, I'll have the crowd for cover."

Ryan gave him a half grin. "I'd like to say that you're wrong, but you're not."

Sandra Delaney wasn't one to hold back her scorn when she felt her children deserved it. And right now, she seemed to feel that Colin deserved plenty.

"Don't let her get to you," Ryan said, slapping Colin on the back companionably. "You know she loves you."

"I know."

"Well, all right, then." Ryan turned to go back to where his wife stood with the rest of the group.

"Ryan?"

Ryan turned, his dark eyebrows raised in question.

"I really am sorry about Uncle Redmond."

Ryan nodded once. "I know you are. And Mom knows it, too."

Colin went to his car and got in, shutting out the pattering chill of the rain.

Colin wondered exactly how long he could hide out at the Cambria Pines Lodge before making an appearance at his parents' house. He could claim that he had to come back to his hotel room to change his soggy clothes—and that would be true, as far as it went.

But changing clothes didn't take very long. How was he supposed to account for the rest of the time, when he'd lain on the bed looking at the ceiling and thinking about Redmond? Or when he'd gone down to the bar and sat in front of the fireplace nursing a drink?

It wasn't that he didn't want to spend time with his family. It was just that whenever he did, the weight of unmet expectations pressed down on him until he felt like he could barely breathe.

He was a lawyer, for God's sake, and a good one. Since when did earning an Ivy League law degree at the top of your class and then acing the bar exam make you a disappointment to your parents?

Parent, not *parents,* he reminded himself.

It wasn't fair to paint both his mother and his father with that particular brush.

He was certain that his father would prefer for Colin to live in Cambria and work the ranch, like Ryan did. Like Liam would have done in a heartbeat if he weren't needed to manage the family's ranch land in Montana.

But Orin had long since gotten over the fact that Colin worked behind a desk down in San Diego, about 350 miles from home. He'd found peace with it, to all appearances. After all, Colin might have had a desk job, but that job was to manage the family's money, and that was no small matter. The Delaney wealth had increased substantially under Colin's care.

But Sandra wasn't going to let it go.

Every chance she got, she threw around words like *family* and *legacy* and *loyalty*. She understood why he didn't work on the ranch—his early health problems had prevented it—but in her mind, that was no reason to abandon his family home. Living anywhere but here, in her view, was just plain disloyal.

As though contributing to the family legacy in his own way was some kind of betrayal.

The thing was, no matter where he lived or what he did for a living, it wouldn't have been possible to get out from under the Delaney shadow even if he'd wanted to; it was so huge, so all-encompassing, that he could feel it following him, hovering around him, choking him in its haze of unfathomable wealth, wherever he went.

The Delaneys weren't just ranchers. They were an *important family*, and nobody, from his mother, to his brothers, to anyone he worked with day to day, ever let him forget it.

Colin took a sip of single malt scotch and watched the fire in the big stone hearth. He felt misunderstood, unappreciated. His mother didn't seem to notice that he was a critical piece of the goddamned family legacy. He managed the Delaney real estate holdings, which were vast. The investments, the tax considerations, the property management. He'd done a damned good job not just protecting the family's assets, but adding to them—significantly.

But the family had a hierarchy, and at the pinnacle of it were those who regularly mounted a horse and got their hands dirty with the cattle.

On the next rung down the ladder were those who either had already given Sandra grandchildren or who were planning to do so in the relatively near future.

Colin met neither of those criteria, so when it came to maternal acceptance, he was shit out of luck.

Comfortable and warm in front of the fire, he pulled his phone out of his pocket and checked his e-mails. He'd accumulated ten in just the past hour, at least five of which could probably be considered urgent.

Normally, he wouldn't let a thing like grief stop him from working, but today, he just couldn't get his head in the game. He composed a boilerplate message stating that he'd be unavailable for the next few days on urgent family business, and sent it to all of the relevant parties. Then he checked the time. People would be starting to arrive at the house. His family would be wondering where he was.

He signed the bar tab to his room and was headed out of the bar and toward the lobby when he heard his name.

"Colin? There you are, son."

He looked up and saw Clayton Drummond coming into the lobby from the parking lot, folding a dripping umbrella and hailing Colin with one thick, age-spotted hand.

"Clayton. I'd have thought you'd be at the house by now," Colin said. He felt a little uncomfortable to be caught out this way—seen wasting time when he should have been out at the ranch mourning his uncle with everyone else.

"Yes, well, I'm headed out that way momentarily. But first, I wanted to have a word with you."

"With me," Colin repeated, as though he might not have understood correctly.

"I heard you were staying here, and I was hoping I could catch you so we could chat in private. About your uncle's will."

Colin paused for a moment to absorb the information. Though his uncle had decided on Clayton rather than him to handle his will—a decision that had rankled Colin at the time—he couldn't imagine there was anything in there that would surprise him.

Redmond had never been married and had no family other than the people who had been gathered around the gravesite that morning. Colin figured it was a fair bet that Redmond's estate would be split up among the family, or maybe it would all go to the senior Delaney: Orin.

It was always possible that Redmond had some pet charitable cause none of them knew about, or that he'd done something crazy like leaving everything to his horse. If so, that was fine by him. Colin didn't need an inheritance. None of them did. There was more than enough money to go around, even without Redmond's share.

Colin was just about to suggest that the will could wait—they'd just buried Redmond that morning, for God's sake—but he could see from the look on Drummond's face that it couldn't. Drummond's eyebrows were drawn together in a pained look, as though his shoes were pinching him. He was fidgeting with the umbrella, which was dripping rainwater into a puddle on the floor.

"Well, all right, then," Colin said, gesturing back toward the entrance to the bar he'd just left. "Why don't we have a seat?"

At least, whatever the issue was, it would delay his arrival at the house.

That had to count for something.

When Colin and Drummond were settled in at a round wooden table near the fireplace, Colin turned to the older man.

"So, what's this about? From the look on your face, I'm not going to like it."

Drummond picked up a drink napkin that had been left on the table, folded it carefully in half, and then placed it back on the table, avoiding Colin's gaze.

"I wanted to give you a heads-up about something now, before it gets out some other way. I figure it'll be better if your family hears it from you." Drummond shifted uncomfortably in his seat.

"Well, get on with it, then," Colin said, not unkindly. It was clear that Drummond was bearing some kind of burden, and he wanted to give him permission to lay it down before the man buckled under its weight.

Drummond hesitated.

"You're not going to tell me that Redmond left his money to Abby, are you?" Colin said, attempting to lighten the mood.

"No," Drummond said, without a hint of a smile. "He left it to his son."

Colin went still.

"Redmond didn't have a son."

Drummond pressed his lips together into a hard, white line and looked at Colin with equal measures of regret and sympathy. "It turns out, he did. Young man by the name of Drew McCray. He'd be, oh, I guess about twenty-nine by now."

"Twenty-nine," Colin repeated.

"Yes, sir."

There were so many details to be filled in, so many questions to be asked. But for the moment, Colin couldn't ask them. He could only sit back in his chair and run his hands through his dark hair, perplexed by the information he'd just been given.

"Redmond never married," he said at last. "Never even had a girlfriend."

"That you knew about," Drummond put in pointedly.

"But … if he was involved with somebody …"

"She was married," Drummond said. He pulled off his glasses, which had become speckled with moisture from the rain, and began cleaning them with a handkerchief he'd pulled out of his pocket. "He didn't want to break up her marriage by going public. And he didn't want anyone to think less of him."

"This is … Jesus," Colin said. It was about all he could manage. Colin had lived in the same house as Redmond for eighteen years—had sat at the breakfast table with him every morning and at the dinner table with him every night. And never, in all those years, had Colin gotten even a hint that his uncle had a son.

Colin rubbed his forehead with one hand. "I think we'd better order some coffee, and you'd better start at the beginning."

Chapter Two

When Colin arrived at the ranch, the wide dirt road leading onto the property was lined with parked cars, and the big two-story house with its white clapboard siding and its generous front porch was humming with people and activity.

Colin found a parking place about fifty yards away, and he sat in his Mercedes for a while with the engine off, trying to muster the courage to go inside.

Drummond had told him what he knew, which wasn't all that much.

Years ago, Redmond had carried on an affair with a married woman when he'd been living in Montana working the family's ranch out there—the one Liam now managed. The affair had resulted in a son, whom Redmond had not publicly acknowledged.

Both Redmond and the child's mother had decided to break off the relationship and let the boy be raised within the marriage, thinking it would be best for everyone involved.

Redmond had sent checks to his former lover periodically for eighteen years to assist with the child's care. None of them was ever cashed.

The will named the child—now a man—as the beneficiary of a substantial part of Redmond's fortune.

When Colin had agreed to be the executor of his uncle's will, he hadn't anticipated anything like this. Questions—and potential problems—spun through his mind. Did this Drew McCray know about Redmond? Did he know that the man who raised him wasn't his father? What would he do when he found out?

Colin leaned back in the front seat of his car and listened to the rain pattering on the roof and hood. He rubbed his eyes with the pads of his fingers and let out a weary sigh.

The news Drummond had dropped on him was a lot to deal with. The first step was going to be telling his family.

He'd agreed with Drummond that the news would be better coming from him. But that didn't make the idea of dropping this bombshell on his parents and siblings any more appealing.

The longer he delayed going inside, the more shit he was going to take from his mom once he got in there. He got out of the car, opened his umbrella, and began the long, wet slog to the house.

The main house at the Delaney Ranch was part of a larger complex of structures that included two barns, a bunkhouse, a guest house, and the new house Ryan and Gen had built for themselves. The ranch itself was a large, sprawling property with a creek, areas of dense woods, rolling, grassy hills, and generous pastures where the cattle could graze under the Central Coast sun. From parts of the ranch you could see the crashing surf and hear the barking of sea lions. From anywhere, you could smell the briny ocean air.

He'd never felt quite at home on the ranch the way his siblings did. He envied them, really, because at least they knew their place in the world. Colin had never really found his place. He'd thought it would be atop a high-rise condo building in San

Diego's Gaslamp Quarter. But now he wasn't so sure. The news of his uncle's death had left him feeling empty and alone, as though an essential piece of himself was missing and now could never be replaced.

He didn't need to live in San Diego, of course. He could do his job from anywhere, as Sandra had repeatedly reminded him. He'd relocated down south initially because his family owned a considerable amount of commercial property there, and he'd told himself—and them—that it would be more efficient if he were to base himself nearby.

But he wasn't fooling anyone—not really. He'd moved down there because it got him away from here. He loved his family and he loved Cambria, but he needed to feel like his own man, and not just another Delaney.

His mother—and, hell, the rest of his family—didn't get that. They didn't get his need to be separate, independent.

And they were going to understand this thing with Redmond a whole hell of a lot less.

He climbed up the porch steps, folded his umbrella, put it into a bucket his mother had placed on the porch for that purpose, and steeled himself for what was to come.

The house was full of people, the sounds of conversation, the smells of cooking and damp wool clothes. A fire crackled in the big stone fireplace, and the front room was warm with the collective body heat of the gathered mourners.

Colin shrugged off his overcoat and hung it on the coat rack just inside the front door.

"Colin!"

Joe Dixon, a guy in his late sixties who knew Redmond and Orin from the local Rotary Club, approached Colin with his hand extended.

"Joe." Colin took the hand and gave it a firm shake. Joe, who'd been mostly bald for as long as Colin had known him, was a short and stout man, and his L.L. Bean plaid flannel shirt, faded jeans, and scuffed work boots made him look like an old, shrunken lumberjack.

"I'm so sorry about Redmond," Joe went on, still gripping Colin's hand. "So sorry. Why, I've known him for thirty years, at least. Back when me and my wife come to Cambria in the eighties, he was one of the first ones to make me feel welcome, like this could really be our home. He was a fine man. A really fine man." Joe's voice had grown thick, and his eyes were damp.

Colin felt his own eyes grow hot, and he blinked a few times as he clapped Joe on the back. "Thank you, Joe. I know he thought the world of you."

It went on like that for a while, people greeting Colin and sharing memories of Redmond. He shook hands, hugged people, and tried to hold his emotions together as he slowly made his way through the family room and toward the kitchen, where he thought his mother was most likely to be.

He was right.

Despite the somber nature of the occasion, Sandra Delaney bustled around the kitchen in her usual jeans, San Francisco 49ers T-shirt, and graying ponytail. In deference to the fact that she had a house full of guests, she'd traded her fuzzy slippers for a pair of sneakers. She was pulling a big casserole dish out of the oven and barking orders to an assortment of women that included Colin's sister, Breanna—a widow whose Marine husband had been a casualty of combat a few years earlier—Ryan's wife, Gen, and a few others who had been recruited for food preparation and distribution.

"Gen, you take this out to the table with that big serving spoon over there." She gestured with her chin toward where the spoon in question lay on the kitchen island. "Breanna, take those rolls and refill the bread basket. Your brothers just about ate everything before the guests even got here."

"Speaking of my brothers," Breanna said, looking at Colin pointedly as she walked past him with the bag of rolls in her hands.

Sandra looked up, saw Colin, and planted her hands on her narrow hips.

"Well, look what the damned cat dragged in. It's about time you got here."

As much as Colin dreaded his mother's scorn, as much as grief and the news about Redmond weighed on him, he couldn't help smiling. Regardless of what happened—death in the family included—Sandra was always just Sandra, broadcasting with her steely gaze and her no-nonsense manner that she wasn't about to take a ration of shit off of anybody.

He leaned in for a hug, breathing in her scent of Dial soap and Jergens hand lotion.

"I'd have been here sooner, but I ran into Clayton Drummond at the lodge. He wanted to have a word."

Sandra pulled away from the embrace and squinted up at him. "What about?"

"The will."

She made a dismissive sound with her breath, a *pfft* that neatly summarized her feelings. "We just buried the man. Couldn't it wait?"

Colin ran a hand through his hair and blew out some air. "Not really."

Sandra scowled at him. "Well, hell. What was in there that was so damned urgent?"

"Not now." Colin's hands still lay on his mother's shoulders from the hug. "Family meeting later."

"Well, Christ on a cracker. You mean to tell me there's some kind of bombshell in Redmond's will, and you're not planning to tell me what it is?" She looked at him as if he'd lost his goddamned mind—which he hadn't, yet.

"That's what I'm telling you. There's a houseful of people out there, and I'm not sure you'll be able to make nice with them once I tell you what I've got to say."

She looked at him as though she were going to pop off with one of her usual Sandra retorts, but instead, her brows furrowed. "It's serious," she said.

"It is."

"Well, hell."

Gen and Brianna bustled back into the kitchen after finishing their assigned tasks, and Colin released his hold on his mother and stepped away. He figured he'd better get out of the kitchen before she could grill him about what he knew.

As he squeezed past the women toward the door that led to the family room, he could feel her looking at him with scorn and not a small amount of concern.

At least this time, it wasn't because she was disappointed in him. He guessed that was something.

Colin made his way through the crowd in the front room, stopping to shake hands and receive condolences, and then went out onto the big front porch. He took a bottle of beer from the ice chest that was stationed out there for every big gathering, opened it, and took a deep drink as he leaned on the rail and peered out into the rainy afternoon.

The world was gray and filled with the smell of wet greenery. The patter of the rain on the roof and the grass, the drip of water from the leaves of the trees was soothing to him.

He heard the front door open behind him, and turned to

see Ryan coming out onto the porch. Like Colin had, Ryan bent to retrieve a bottle of beer from the cooler. Then he came to stand beside Colin at the railing.

Ryan was older than Colin by three years. About six years ago, he'd been chosen by general consensus to take over the Cambria ranch operations as Orin and Redmond retired—an arrangement that seemed to agree with him. He looked healthy and vigorous, with a hint of color from the sun in his face. Colin thought his own skin must be ghostly white from endless hours at a desk under artificial lights.

"Mom says you've got some kind of big news about Uncle Redmond's will," Ryan said, settling in beside Colin as they both looked out at the rain.

"She didn't waste much time spreading the word around," Colin observed.

"Well, she's a little irked that you wouldn't tell her what it is."

"Family meeting later," Colin said, just as he'd said to his mother.

"She told me that, too," Ryan said mildly. "Colin? What's going on?"

Colin took a deep drink of his beer and leaned his forearms on the porch railing, looking out into the gloomy day. He didn't say anything.

"Let me guess," Ryan said. "He gave everything to Shelly over at the Redwood Café. She always brings him his coffee refills before the cup's empty." Colin looked at Ryan and saw amusement in the man's deep brown eyes.

Colin thought about hanging onto the secret until he could tell everyone together, but then thought, *screw it.* It was a heavy secret for him to carry, and he wouldn't mind having someone to share the burden.

"Redmond had a son," Colin said, turning to face Ryan. "From an affair with a married woman. The kid gets all of Redmond's personal assets and a ten percent share in the family corporation."

"He … wait. *What?*"

Ryan's bewildered look mirrored what Colin felt.

"That's what Clayton Drummond tells me."

"Well … shit."

"Yep," Colin agreed.

"What do we know about the kid?" Ryan asked.

"Not much. Except that he's not a kid. Almost thirty, Drummond said."

Colin could see Ryan doing the mental math. "Redmond was in Montana back then."

"Yep."

"Well … does this son know Redmond's his dad? Does he know Redmond died? What..."

"I imagine I'll be looking into all of that," Colin replied.

"Yeah. Damn it. I expect you will."

The two of them stood side by side, drinking their beer and silently processing what Colin had just said.

"Uncle Redmond never had a relationship with a woman that I ever knew about. Tell you the truth, I always wondered if he was gay," Ryan said.

"Me, too," Colin agreed.

They considered that in companionable silence.

"Guess not," Ryan said.

Chapter Three

Julia McCray was sick of snow. She was sick of looking at snow, and driving in snow, and especially shoveling snow. She was sick of the need for snow boots, and thick gloves, and enough outerwear to effectively double a person's girth when they were fully bundled against the Montana cold.

On the bright side, it was near the end of February, and March would bring warmer temperatures—if only an increase from the midthirties to the midforties. Any little improvement would be welcome.

For now, though, it was still damned cold.

And there was still the damned snow.

This was one of those days when she was grateful that she owned her own business and could work from home. Here it was, ten a.m., and she was still in her flannel pajamas—a cheerful pink pattern with tiny corgis romping around on them. Her hair was up in a messy ponytail, and she had thick socks on her feet. Who was going to care? Who was going to see?

Nobody, she thought bitterly. Certainly nobody hot and male. And what good was it to be in your pajamas at ten a.m. if there wasn't anybody there to try to take them off of you?

Julia sighed and padded into her kitchen to make a cup of hot cocoa. When you were still in your pajamas at ten a.m., it was snowy outside, and you had a fire in the fireplace, you really needed hot cocoa.

Once the cocoa was ready, with mini marshmallows floating on the surface like icebergs in a dark sea, she went to her dining room table, where her laptop sat open beside a notebook filled with various doodles, notes, and pencil sketches.

As a landscape designer, she couldn't do a great deal of work locally during the wintertime, when the earth was shrouded in a deep layer of snow. But that didn't mean she could just sit idle, waiting for spring.

She was set to begin work for a new hotel in Bozeman as soon as weather—and the spring thaw—permitted. For now, she had blueprints of the hotel and a topographical map of the grounds, and she was beginning to create a design that she could implement once the temperatures warmed.

The hotel's owners had requested landscaping that would be eco-friendly and in harmony with the natural environment. With that in mind, she was drawing up her plans to include native plants, a reclaimed-water irrigation system, solar-powered lighting, and strategically planted trees that would provide a wind break in the winter and shade in summer.

A creek ran through the hotel's property, and she wanted to use it to maximum effect while maintaining the integrity of the waterway. She brought up a clean page on her sketch pad, drew the basic outlines of the building and the property lines, and began sketching hardscape, flower beds, a lawn that could be used for weddings and other special events, and an array of other outdoor zones for uses ranging from quiet relaxation to after-dinner strolls.

She was so involved in her work that she startled slightly when her cell phone rang.

Julia checked the screen. Mom.

She picked up the phone, rolled her shoulders to ease out the tension, and put on her game face. Talking to her mother was challenging under the best of circumstances, but even more so lately. She picked up the phone and answered it.

"Hey, Mom." Her voice sounded warm, friendly, and maybe even a little perky. It should—she'd had years of practice at cultivating just that voice, specifically for her mother's phone calls. "What's up?"

"Julia? Is this a good time?"

"Of course. How are you?"

"I can call back if you were in the middle of something."

Julia sighed and rolled her eyes. Step one in talking to Isabelle McCray was always to reassure her that you didn't mind talking to her. Which, by the time you were done, you did.

"Mom. I'm not in the middle of anything. This is fine. In fact, it's the perfect time for you to call. It absolutely could not be better."

"Well, now you sound irritated. I can call back."

Julia made a gun with her thumb and finger and mimed shooting herself in the head with it, complete with tongue lolling out of her mouth in a portrayal of sudden, violent death.

"Hey, Mom? Now that you mention it, I was in the middle of a thing for work. Why don't we just—"

"I'm worried about your brother," Isabelle said, finally spitting out the purpose of her call. "I was wondering if you'd heard from him."

"Drew?" she said stupidly, as though she had more than one brother.

"It's just … another one of those debt collectors called me this morning looking for him. I never know what to say."

"Ah." Julia felt the press of tension at the center of her breastbone. She knew the feeling well, especially in reference to her brother. "Just tell them what I tell them: 'No one by that name resides at this address.' It's true."

"Well, I suppose."

Drew, who was younger than Julia by about a year, had been hounded by collections agencies ever since his wife had maxed out their credit cards, emptied their bank accounts, and removed approximately three-quarters of their belongings from their apartment, leaving him to come home from work one evening to find a goodbye note and gaping, blank spaces where their bed, large-screen TV, refrigerator, and sofa used to be.

She'd left the book collection, an old dresser from Ikea, and the kitchen table behind—but no forwarding address.

"Could you call him and see if he's okay?" Isabelle said.

"You could call him yourself."

Isabelle let out a sigh. "You know I can't do that."

Julia began pacing over the hardwood floors, her socks making a swishing sound as she went.

"Mom. When are you going to tell me what's going on between the two of you? I can't help if I don't know what's happening."

Isabelle hesitated. "It's not my place to tell you, honey. And … I don't think you could help even if you knew."

"God, Mom. This is so ridiculous."

Something had happened between Drew and their mother three years before, shortly before their father had died of injuries suffered in a car accident. Whatever it was, it had damaged their relationship to the point that Drew no longer spoke to their mother. When Tessa, his wife, had left him a year and a half later, he had vanished from Bozeman without even telling his mother where he'd gone.

Julia knew where he was living—they stayed in touch via phone and text—but he'd forbidden her to tell their mother.

She resented the position that put her in. Drew asked her about their mother's well-being but refused to communicate with her himself. And Isabelle used her to pass messages to Drew, urging her to divulge his whereabouts.

Neither of them would budge on the subject of their falling-out, leaving Julia to wonder what in the world had happened and how it could possibly have been bad enough to keep a son from talking to his only surviving parent.

"Just … would you call him? There's something … I really think he might need your support right now."

"But *why*?" Julia threw her free hand into the air in frustration. "Would you please just tell me what the hell is going on?"

Isabelle was silent, and Julia could imagine her wringing her hands with worry.

"All right," she said finally. "All right. I'll call him."

And she was sure she would want to bang her head against a wall when she did.

Isabelle and Drew were both stubborn as hell. It was a wonder they didn't get along better, since they were so much alike.

"And what about you, Mom? Are you okay?" Whatever had Isabelle so worried about Drew had obviously taken a toll on her, as well. Julia could hear it in the tremor of her voice.

"Just call him." Isabelle hung up the phone, leaving Julia more confused than ever about how her family had abruptly disintegrated eighteen months ago, and how she would ever manage to help heal the rift.

By the end of the day, Isabelle wasn't the only one worried about Drew.

Julia had tried to call him, but he hadn't picked up, so she'd left him a voice mail message relaying their mother's concern and asking him to call back.

He didn't.

It was true that he'd become somewhat reclusive since he'd taken off from Bozeman with his clothes, his car, and the few things Tessa had left him. Julia hadn't seen him in person in all that time, because he'd made it clear that he needed his space. But he usually returned her calls, even when they were made to relay a message from their mother.

And it usually didn't take him all day, either.

She tried not to be too upset about Isabelle's cryptic expressions of concern, but it was hard. Why was she suddenly worried about him—or, to be accurate, more worried than usual? There'd been a tone in her voice—something distinctly different from the typical martyr routine she used with Julia. Something fragile, like she might suddenly shatter at the least bit of pressure.

Had something happened?

If it had, Isabelle certainly wouldn't tell Julia. Neither would Drew. As distant as Isabelle and Drew had become from each other, they seemed to have formed a tight club of secrecy and resentment, with Julia firmly on the outside.

Not that she wanted to belong to a club like that.

She went about her day and tried not to think about it. She began transferring her sketches for the Bozeman hotel job to the CAD program on her laptop. She reluctantly got dressed, including snow boots and gloves, and shoveled enough snow to get her car out of the driveway.

She drove to the Safeway on Main Street to stock up on essentials like white wine, hot cocoa, Pop Tarts, and Cap'n Crunch, and then brought her purchases home. She ate lunch—a frozen burrito she heated up in the microwave—and put the plate in the dishwasher.

With that done, she assessed the sorry state of her house and decided the laundry couldn't wait any longer, as she was already on her last pair of clean underpants. She threw in a load, and then thought that she might as well scrub the toilets while she was at it.

She'd folded the clean laundry and was beginning to think about dinner, when she realized Drew still hadn't called her back.

She plopped down onto her sofa with her cell phone and thought about what to do. After a moment of consideration, she texted him:

I'm about to call you, and you'd damned well better pick up.

Julia waited until her screen showed that he'd read the message, and then she called.

"Jules." He sounded tired.

"I tried to call you this morning. More than seven hours ago. I left a message. Are you screening my calls?"

He let out a sigh and didn't answer, and that was as good as a yes.

"Drew, jeez. What's going on? I get a phone call from Mom this morning, and she sounds all quivery and upset, saying she's worried about you. And then you shut me out. Like always. Is everything okay? And you'd better not give me some bullshit line just to placate me, either."

"Jules, don't worry about it. I'm—"

"I *said* I don't want a bullshit line." She was using her bossy big sister voice, which she had employed often and to good effect during their childhood.

"Okay. Something did happen, and I'm … a little thrown. But I'm not ready to talk about it, and I promise that I'm going to be okay."

"You're *going to be* okay," she repeated. "Which means

you're not okay now."

"Julia …"

"Something happened that Mom knows about, and that has the two of you upset, but you won't talk to each other about it, and neither of you will talk to me." She neatly summarized the events of the day, feeling hot tears coming to her eyes.

He didn't say anything.

"I'm your *sister,* Drew."

"I know you are."

Those burning tears threatened to spill over as she seesawed between worry and anger. She stood with one arm pressed tight across her chest, as though the defensive posture could protect her from her hurt.

"You've changed." Her tone was accusing. "You and Mom both. At first I thought it was grief over Dad, but it's not that. It's not. The anger and the silence and the secrets …"

"Julia? You need to respect the fact that there are things I don't want to talk about," he said.

"Yeah. Sure. Right." She swiped at her eyes with the back of her hand. "And you need to respect the fact that I used to have a family." Her voice broke. "I used to have a brother and two parents, and … and we all loved each other, and we were *here* for each other. And what do I have now, Drew? What do I have now?"

She hung up before he could answer, and then threw her cell phone onto the sofa, where it bounced once before coming to rest.

It was a goddamned good thing she'd thought to buy beer and junk food. She was going to need them.

She took the beer, along with a jumbo bag of Cheetos, over to Mike's house later that evening, though she hadn't been invited and likely would be interrupting some essential male function, like lounging in sweatpants and watching football highlights on ESPN.

Mike Norton, a rough-hewn, weathered guy in his midfifties who was the go-to general contractor on Julia's biggest jobs, answered the door in sweatpants, just as she'd predicted. But there was no TV noise coming from his living room—just the whine of the smoke detector blaring throughout the small, 1950s-era house.

The smoke alarm was accompanied by the distinct smell of something burning and a light haze of gray smoke.

"What the hell, Mike?" Julia pushed past him and into the house, carrying the beer in one hand and the Cheetos in the other. She set the items down on the coffee table and proceeded into the kitchen, waving one hand in front of her face as though that might be an effective method of clearing the smoke from the air.

"Just let yourself right in," he said dryly, following behind her. "It's not like I was in the middle of anything."

In the compact kitchen, she found a formerly frozen pizza sitting on the counter. The edges of the crust were charred into a black and smoking ruin, and the forlorn little pieces of pepperoni looked like some kind of irradiated debris from the surface of Mars.

Obviously, waving her hand around wasn't going to cut it. She heaved open the window over the sink and began flapping a dish towel in the general direction of the kitchen smoke detector.

"Jeez, you're opening a window?" he groused. "It's twenty degrees out there."

"It's either that or suffer from smoke inhalation."

They had to yell at each other to be heard over the screaming of the smoke alarm.

As Julia continued flapping the dish towel, to little effect, Mike pulled a step stool out of a utility closet, climbed onto it, and disconnected the smoke alarm. The sudden, blessed silence was sweet relief.

Mike climbed down from the step stool with the silent smoke detector in his hand, and they both looked at the blackened pizza.

"You can build a gazebo big enough to seat twenty out of nothing but lumber and a dream," Julia said, looking at him in wonder. "But you can't manage to cook a frozen pizza at four hundred degrees for twenty minutes?"

"I guess I got distracted." He scratched the gray stubble on his chin. "Kinda forgot it was in there."

"Distracted by what?" She grabbed a pair of oven mitts off the counter, picked up the smoking, black pizza, and threw it into the garbage can sitting on the floor near the refrigerator.

He shrugged, looking embarrassed. "I was on the phone with Emma."

Emma was Mike's ex-wife, whom he harbored great, persistent dreams of winning back one day. The problem was, she had already remarried and moved to Arizona, where she and her new husband had a house, complete with a swimming pool, a sunroom, and a dog.

"Oh, Mike." Julia looked at him with equal measures of pity and scorn.

"Yeah, yeah." He waved her off. They'd had this conversation many times before—the one where she told him he was wasting his time and doing unnameable damage to his heart by refusing to move on—and they both knew that it wasn't going to do any good.

"Well." Julia let her shoulders sag in defeat. "What are you going to do about dinner?" She changed the subject and gestured toward the trash can, which now smelled like charcoal and burned cheese.

"I saw you brought Cheetos," he suggested.

Julia and Mike had a kind of routine they went through every time one of them showed up at the other's house. If Mike was the one to come to Julia's place, he had to pretend he was there to render some essential manly service out of paternal concern. He'd grumble that somebody had to clean out her rain gutters, since there was no way she would ever get around to doing it herself, and then, either while he was completing the task or afterward, he would bring up whatever it was he'd come to talk about.

If Julia was the one to go to Mike's house, she had to pretend that she was there to consult him on some question related to the landscaping business. There had to be some kind of pretense that the visit was related to an important chore or work-related issue. Otherwise, Julia would have to admit that she had no female friends, and Mike would have to admit that he was lonely without his wife and wanted someone to talk to.

Since admitting those things would have required more introspection than either of them was comfortable with, they danced around an awkward fact that was, nonetheless, as true as the North Star: They were each other's best friend.

An outsider might have called the routine pointless or even absurd, but the two of them had grown comfortable with it, and they relied on it like one would any other of life's rituals, like brushing their teeth or drinking morning coffee.

"So, you didn't come here to bring me Cheetos," Mike said, stuffing a handful of the bright orange snack food in his mouth. "Why *did* you come?"

"I wanted to find out what your schedule looks like in August."

"August," he repeated.

"Yeah. I'm bidding on that restaurant job."

"It's February," he pointed out.

"Of course it is."

They ate some more Cheetos and drank some of the beer she'd brought, and then she launched into the real reason she'd come. "There's something going on with my mom and Drew."

Mike took a swallow of beer to wash down the Cheetos. "This isn't exactly news," he informed her.

"Yes, but this is something different. My mom called me this morning and said she was worried about Drew, but she wouldn't say why. Then I call him up, and he sounds like hell. Really awful. Like maybe he's been awake for the past forty-eight hours, living on coffee and cigarettes. Which would not be unprecedented for him. But he won't tell me what's wrong. What am I supposed to do? What am I supposed to think?"

"You could stay out of it," Mike suggested. He was lying back in his La-Z-Boy, in full recline mode. "Maybe try minding your own business for a change."

"I would!" She threw her hands into the air, forgetting that one of them was holding a Cheeto. The orange corn nugget flew two feet to the left and landed beside her on a sofa cushion. "I'm not the one who brought me into this, remember. My mom called *me*. I was happy! I was just ... living my life! And now I can't just be happy and live my life, because there's some big, mysterious thing going on with Drew. He might not want to talk about it or even see me"—she let out a ragged breath, suddenly overcome by emotion—"but I love him, Mike. And I want him to be okay."

"Of course you do." He put his chair into the upright position and leaned forward, resting his elbows on his knees. "You know, kid, you're a good sister and a good daughter." He looked at her pointedly. "But if they won't accept what you've got to give, there's not a hell of a lot you can do."

It was uncharacteristically touchy-feely advice, coming from him, and so she felt compelled to nod thoughtfully. As though there was even a rat's ass of a chance that she was going to just walk away from her family's problems.

"I'll think about it, Mike," she said. "I really will."

"Ah, that's crap," he said mildly, leaning back in his chair again. "You're going to do what you always do. You're going to piss and moan and feel bad, and then you're going to obsess, then you're going to come back here and bitch about it again in a few days."

"Probably," she admitted. She finished off her first beer. "Are you going to eat the rest of those Cheetos?"

Chapter Four

"So, Clayton thought it would be better coming from me," Colin concluded.

After the last of the mourners had left the ranch, Colin had called the family meeting. Sandra had complained that she was too busy with all she had to do—cleaning up after a gathering for two hundred was no easy feat, and it wasn't like the dishes were going to wash themselves—but her grousing was all for show. She'd likely been stewing all day, wondering what he had to say.

As a lawyer, Colin had a lot of practice remaining stoic while delivering unwelcome news, but this time was a particular challenge. He laid out the information he'd been given in an even tone, sticking to the facts. When he was done, his parents and siblings, all gathered in the family room, stared back at him in stunned silence.

"Wait. Just … wait. You're saying that our uncle Redmond has had a son for thirty years … and he never said a damned word to anybody about it?" Liam was the first to respond to what Colin had told them.

"That appears to be the case, yes," Colin said, still in lawyer mode.

"Well, I guess he told Clayton Drummond about it," Sandra

said, her lips pursed, her eyebrows nearly knit together in the center of her forehead. "Clayton Drummond! The man's good enough as a lawyer, I guess, but he's not family."

"I suppose that was the point," Ryan said. "It was safe to tell Drummond because he's *not* part of the family."

"Well," Sandra grumbled.

"I don't get it." Orin shook his mostly bald head. "I just don't get it. Redmond never had much use for women. I mean, he had some girlfriends back in high school, but since then ..." He spread his hands, his unfinished thought drifting in the air among them.

"Maybe there were no other women because none of them were her," Gen suggested. As the newest member of the Delaney family, Ryan's wife was the only one who didn't seem shell-shocked by the information. Instead, she seemed interested. If pressed, Colin would have to admit that he was pretty damned interested, too, now that the surprise was wearing off.

"And this guy's getting an inheritance?" Liam went on. "This guy who we don't know anything about, who Redmond never even met?" He shook his head, his face showing exactly how half-assed a notion he thought that was. Liam could never disguise his feelings, Colin thought. Since they were kids, Liam's every emotion had shown on his face as though he were wearing a sign that said HAPPY or EXCITED or PISSED.

"Well, 'this guy' is his son," Ryan said, rubbing at the back of his neck.

"We don't know that. Not for sure," Liam said. "All we know is that Clayton Drummond says so."

"Because Redmond told him so," Orin pointed out.

"Yeah, but did *he* even know for sure? I mean ... I can't imagine they ever did a DNA test. Does he just have the mother's word for it?" Liam said.

"That's a valid point." Colin brought everyone's attention back to where he stood at the head of the room. They were all gathered together on sofas or hard-backed chairs, the chaos of a recently completed get-together still surrounding them. The flames in the fireplace crackled softly. "But, unfortunately, it doesn't actually have any bearing on the will. The document refers to Drew McCray by name. There's nothing in it stipulating that the inheritance is contingent on McCray actually being Redmond's son."

"Then this guy could be taking all of us for a ride," Liam said.

"If that were the point—if this were some kind of scheme—we'd have heard from him by now, wouldn't you think?" Ryan added, not unreasonably.

"That brings up my next point," Colin said, again sounding like a lawyer. "Drummond hasn't contacted this Drew McCray yet. Neither about the will, nor …" He paused, the words he was about to say bringing an unexpected lump to his throat. "Nor to inform him that his father is dead."

"If Redmond was even his father," Liam was quick to interject.

"He was." Orin's eyes were red, and he cleared his throat roughly. "At least, Redmond must have been sure that he was. Otherwise, he wouldn't have done this. Redmond wasn't a man who did things lightly."

That, at least, was God's truth.

Colin couldn't remember Redmond ever making a decision without first considering the options, weighing his choices, discussing it with his brother or his nephews, moaning and dithering over the right thing to do, and then waiting what seemed like an unnecessarily long time before finally making a decision. *Impulsive* was not a word one would use to describe the man. There was no way he had put Drew McCray into his will without considerable deliberation—even if he'd hidden it from his family.

"In any event," Colin said, "I asked Drummond not to do anything. I think the first contact should come from us. From the family, and not some lawyer nobody outside of Cambria has ever heard of."

Colin had a number of reasons for that. But it seemed like everybody had their own interpretation of his motives.

"I think that's wise. It's going to be easier for him to hear all of this if it's coming from one of you." Gen shook her head, her concern for a man she'd never met written in the tilt of her brows, in the crease of her lips. "Can you imagine how he's going to feel if he's been living his whole life thinking someone else is his father? If he's about to get hit with the news that not only is his dad not his dad, but that his biological father is dead? And that doesn't even touch on what the inheritance is going to do to his life."

"It's not like the inheritance is going to be some kind of burden," Liam said, scowling.

"It might be," Gen said. "It's upheaval, and any kind of upheaval—positive or negative—can take a toll on a person."

Liam, who was perched on a sofa arm next to where his mother and father were sitting, crossed his arms over his chest, his face dark and brooding. "I'm sure Colin's more worried about what all of this is going to do to the family." He nodded at Colin. "Hell, yeah, we need to be the ones to tell him. I want to look this guy in the eye. We've built something for ourselves here, starting with the first Delaney who settled on this land, coming right down to us today. We've got a stake in it, and that comes from our own sweat. If this … this *stranger* thinks he's going to come in and take what we've all worked for—"

"He doesn't think anything." Breanna spoke up for the first

time since the discussion had started. "As far as we know, this is going to be as big a surprise to him as it was to us. Bigger, probably. Let's just dial it down a little until we see what's going on."

Liam, who apparently didn't appreciate being told to dial it down, scowled at his sister, who simply glared at him in response. It was the familiar, nonverbal language of siblings who'd shared a lifetime of daily battles, but who had matured too much to actually hit each other and call each other names like they had when she was eight and he was three. This way was no less effective.

"You've got contact information for the man?" Sandra asked, bringing things back around to the practical.

"I have an address and phone number for the mother," Colin said. "But Drummond tells me it might not be current. It's the last address Redmond knew, but there's some reason to believe she's not there anymore."

"Why's that?" Orin asked.

Colin cleared his throat. "According to Drummond, Redmond tried to send a letter to that address a few years ago. It was returned unopened."

"All right. Well, has anybody tried the number yet?" Ryan asked.

"I'm going to do better than that," Colin said. "I'm going out there."

"'Out there' where?" Liam wanted to know. "Where are we talking about?"

Colin paused, then said, "Bozeman. She never left there, as far as we know."

"Well, hell." Liam got that stubborn look that Liam often got, the one that harked back to his boyhood, when he'd refused to clean his room or eat some green thing that appeared on his dinner plate. "I should do it, then. It's my home territory."

"No, Colin's going to do it." Sandra hadn't said much up to this point, but her tone was clear and sure, letting her sons know she would brook no backtalk. "He's the executor. And anyway, Liam, you're too damned hotheaded. You go out there, you're going to scare the man to death. We don't need that."

Liam started to say something, but his mother talked over him. "No, we don't need that," she repeated. "Colin keeps his head in a crisis. Always has. Ryan and Breanna, too, but the two of you are needed here." Ryan was needed because he ran the Cambria ranch operation, and Breanna because she had two young sons who needed to be taken to school, harangued to do their homework, and generally kept in line.

The implication didn't escape Colin's notice—that the others were needed here, but he wasn't. Well, that was no surprise, he thought with some bitterness. That was no great shakeup of the status quo.

"It's settled, then. I'll get a flight tomorrow. If he's not at the address I've got, then I'll just have to do some sleuthing and find him," Colin said.

"You've been working on that land development down in Palm Springs," Breanna said. "Are you going to be able to get away right now?" She was the only one who'd thought about that, apparently, and he was grateful that she'd taken the time to consider how this shitstorm might affect his life and the various business deals he had going on.

"He'll work it out," Sandra said, and then she got up from where she'd been sitting and stalked off into the kitchen to begin the cleanup she'd so reluctantly put off.

He guessed he'd work it out, at that. God himself couldn't drive Sandra Delaney off her course. And if He couldn't do it, then neither could Colin.

◆◆◆

As convenient as it would have been to take a flight out of San Luis Obispo, that was out of the question, because the airfares from there to Bozeman were astronomical. Colin's parents had made it clear from the time he was a child that coming from a wealthy family didn't mean you could piss away your money just for the sake of it.

In fact, they'd been side-eyeing his Mercedes and his Italian loafers since the day he'd returned to town. The car and the shoes mattered, though, even if Sandra and Orin couldn't see it. Nobody took seriously a lawyer who wore forty-dollar shoes and drove a Ford Fiesta. They respected someone who projected an aura of success.

Of course, none of that mattered once people knew Colin was one of the Cambria Delaneys. Once they realized that, they'd defer to him even if he was wearing plastic flip-flops and driving a Schwinn.

He thought about the benefits and drawbacks of his family name as he drove up Highway 101 toward the San Jose airport with his suitcase in the trunk and the window open to the clear, cool, February day.

Coming from money was a double-edged sword, and Colin had regularly used one side and felt the sting of the other. He wanted the people he did business with to respect him not because of who his parents were, but because he was damned good. But that hadn't stopped him from playing the Delaney card whenever it would be to his advantage.

He drove past patchwork plots of farmland under a sky of cloudless, startling blue. The paper Starbucks cup in the cupholder had been empty for at least twenty miles.

The hell of this whole thing was that amid the surprise of Clayton Drummond's revelation, Colin hadn't had much time to think about Redmond.

Grief was a funny thing. You thought you had it under control—might even have congratulated yourself on your stoic acceptance of the inevitability of death—only to be brought down by the sight of an empty pair of slippers next to the person's favorite chair, or the sight of someone in the grocery store who looked a little like him at the right angle, from behind.

It happened to Colin when a Garth Brooks song—"Friends in Low Places"—came on the radio. Not that Redmond had liked the song, or even Garth Brooks. In fact, he'd resented the very existence of country music, because, as a lifetime rancher, he was expected to like it.

Well, I guess I'll listen to whatever kind of music I damned well please.

Colin felt the sting of tears in his eyes, tried to will them away, and then pulled the car over when it became clear that the tide of his emotion was not about to ebb. He sat in the Mercedes on the side of Highway 101, the engine running, and cried into his hands, his head hunched over the steering wheel, his nose running. His shoulders shook with the unbearable weight of his loss.

When the worst of it had passed, he fumbled in his glove box for a stack of napkins he'd picked up from some fast food joint, and used them to wipe his eyes and blow his nose. He took a deep, ragged breath.

"Goddamn it, Redmond," he said, to no one.

Then he put the car in drive, pulled back out onto the highway, and drove to catch his flight.

Chapter Five

Julia was on the treadmill when the doorbell rang. She'd been on the machine she kept in the spare bedroom, running at six miles per hour at a two-degree incline, and her face was red with exertion and damp with sweat. Her hair had started out in a relatively tidy ponytail, but motion and effort had combined to leave it tousled, with strands of hair that had escaped from the ponytail sticking haphazardly to her forehead.

When she heard the chime of the bell over the whirring of the treadmill and the slap-slap-slap of her sneakers on the belt, she considered not answering it. If some salesperson was foolish enough to brave the snowy roads just to try to sell her carpet cleaning or a security system or meat from the back of a truck, then they deserved to be ignored.

If it was her mother, then that was even more of an argument in favor of pretending she'd never heard the bell.

But what if it's Mike?

She could imagine a scenario in which he needed to be talked down after another disastrous conversation with Emma. If she didn't come to the door, he might do something stupid, like tell his ex-wife he still loved her and wanted her back.

She turned off the treadmill, waited for it to come to a slow halt, and then went to the front door on rubbery legs.

Julia had imagined salespeople. She'd imagined her mother. She'd imagined Mike.

But she hadn't imagined a mouthwateringly handsome man in his late twenties with wavy dark hair and piercing blue eyes. Nor had she imagined that the man in question would be carrying Mrs. Newmeyer's dog.

A blast of cold air from the open door chilled Julia's sweaty, lightly clad body, and she grabbed a coat from the rack next to the door and pulled it on.

She'd meant to say *Yes?* or *May I help you?* or possibly, *I don't accept sales solicitations.* There was always, *Would you marry me?* But instead, she said, "Why do you have Mrs. Newmeyer's dog?"

The man, whose expensive overcoat was now lightly frosted with dog hair, looked down at the animal as though he'd almost forgotten he was holding it.

"Oh. So, you know where he belongs? Good. He ran up to me when I got out of the car. I thought maybe he was yours. I was worried about him because he seemed lost, and it's cold outside."

"Here, I'll take him." Julia reached out for the dog, and the guy transferred the fuzzy, warm body into her arms. "You know you're not supposed to be outside," she scolded the dog. "Your mom's going to be mad." She rubbed the dog's head affectionately.

She turned to the guy on her front porch, figuring now that he'd done his duty as a good Samaritan, he'd want to get on his way spreading the word of the Lord or selling vacuum cleaners, or whatever it was that he was doing out here. Still, she couldn't exactly imagine someone this sexy selling solar panels. What did he want? She felt a little butterfly thing going on in her stomach and cursed the fact that she was losing her composure over a particularly handsome face. And those incredible blue eyes.

"I'll take him home. Thanks for bringing him," she said. That was her cue to close the door, but she didn't seem to be doing it. She just seemed to be standing there looking at him.

"I was actually coming to speak to you. I'm looking for Drew McCray. Does he live here?"

That certainly threw some cold water on her attraction to the stranger at her door. She hadn't pegged this guy as a debt collector, but apparently she'd called that one wrong.

She scowled at him. "No one by that name lives here." It was her standard line, the one she'd urged her mother to use. True but evasive. She began to close the door.

"But you know him," the guy said. "I can tell by the way you're glaring at me. I really need to talk to him. It's urgent."

Julia sighed, the dog growing heavy in her arms, and looked at him pleadingly. "Can't you guys just leave him alone? His ex is the one you should be going after. He can't pay you what he doesn't have." Her eyes grew hot, but she wasn't going to cry in front of this guy she didn't even know. Even if he was a lowlife collections thug.

"Hold on," he said. " 'You guys' who? I'm not sure what you're talking about."

"You're not a debt collector?"

"Uh … no. I'm an attorney. I'm here from San Diego. There's a legal matter that requires his attention."

Her face shut down again. An attorney. That explained his expensive coat and upscale haircut. With that face, he probably did well in court. "God, you people. Who's suing him? I told you, it's his ex you should be going after. I also told you he's not here."

And she closed the door on him.

Well, that was interesting.

Colin stood on the front porch, thinking about all he'd just learned. Drew McCray had apparently gone through an acrimonious breakup that had resulted in lawsuits and debt problems. And the woman he'd just spoken to was trying to protect him. Was she the new girlfriend? New wife? Whoever she was, it was clear he'd come to the right place.

He rang the doorbell again, but she didn't answer. He thought about what to do. Call to her through the door? Slip a note through the mail slot? Leave and come back later?

As he considered the situation, he realized that she would have to come out to take the dog home—or the neighbor would have to come over to get it. When that happened—and it would likely be soon—he could try again.

He got into his car, pulled his coat a little tighter around him, and settled in to wait.

Julia ignored the doorbell when it rang again. She put the dog down on the floor, and he sat on his butt and looked up at her.

"This sucks, Duke," she told him. "Don't ever marry the wrong woman. It'll only lead to heartache."

Duke wagged his little stump of a tail encouragingly.

She waited until she heard the hottie lawyer's footsteps going down off of the porch, and then peeked out the window to see if Mrs. Newmeyer was home. She saw her neighbor's Toyota in her driveway, pulled her down parka around her, and scooped the dog up into her arms.

"Come on, Duke. I'm going to take you back to your mom."

Duke licked the underside of her chin with his pink tongue, and Julia grimaced a little at the thought of where that tongue might have been.

She opened the front door, stepped out on the porch—and realized, too late, that the hottie lawyer had never really left. He got out of his rental car and started toward her purposefully. Julia kept her eyes on Mrs. Newmeyer's house and strode forward toward her destination, trying to ignore the guy in hot pursuit of her as she crunched her way through the snow.

"He doesn't live here," Julia said.

"But you know where he is."

"I'm not going to help you. He's had enough trouble."

"What kind of trouble?"

"I don't have to tell you that."

"I'm not here to cause problems," he said from somewhere close behind her. "I'm here about his inheritance."

If he'd intended to shock her into stopping, it worked. Julia froze halfway between her house and Mrs. Newmeyer's, and she slowly turned to face him. Duke whined softly in her arms.

"His inheritance?"

The guy nodded, a grim look on his face. "It's substantial."

Julia stared at him for a moment, considering what he'd said.

Who in the world could be leaving Drew a substantial inheritance? Nobody in their family was above middle class, and as far as she knew, no one had died recently. She supposed it was possible there was some great aunt she didn't know about, but why would the mystery aunt be leaving money to Drew?

She knew, also, that debt collectors routinely used deception to locate their marks. That had to be it. This guy—heart-stoppingly delicious as he was—had to be lying.

"Nice try." She headed off toward Mrs. Newmeyer's house again. "I don't believe you. Now, please get off my property."

"I'm not on your property. I'm on Mrs. Newmeyer's property," the guy said.

It was true, he was. Damn it.

She continued across the snowy yard, clomped up the front steps in her sneakers, which she hadn't thought to change since her workout, and rang the front doorbell. Nobody answered, but Mrs. Newmeyer had a bad habit of forgetting to lock her front door. Julia tried it, found it unlocked, opened it just enough to put the dog inside, and then closed it again and turned to go back home.

The problem was, the guy was standing at the bottom of Mrs. Newmeyer's porch stairs, blocking her exit.

"Would you move, please?" Her arms were crossed protectively across her body as she glared down at him.

"I need you to listen to me."

"Look, Mr. …"

"Delaney. Colin Delaney." He tried to hand her a business card, but she didn't take it.

"Mr. Delaney, with all due respect, I don't actually care what you need me to do." She walked down the steps, shoved her way past him, and then headed toward her house.

"Hey!" he called after her, still following her across the yard. "Whoever Drew McCray is to you, it seems like you care about him. Do you really want to stand between him and a really quite impressive inheritance?"

She stopped so suddenly that he almost ran into her back. She turned and shot her best *go screw yourself* look at him.

"I don't believe there's an inheritance, and I don't believe you're a lawyer. Or, if you are, then you're here because you're somebody else's lawyer—someone who wants to hurt Drew. So I'm going to need you to get off my property"—she looked pointedly around them to indicate that he was, in fact, back on her side of the boundary—"before I call the police."

She marched up the steps of her own front porch and

through the front door, slamming it and locking it behind her. She moved the curtains on the front window aside just enough to see him walking unsteadily through the snow and back toward his car.

Well, that went perfectly.

Colin sat in the driver's seat of his rental sedan, wondering what to do next. If he went back up to the house and rang the doorbell again, it seemed likely that she really would call the police. But it also seemed likely that if he could just persuade her that he was who he said he was, then she might tell him what he needed to know.

He considered his options.

He could try to find Drew McCray without this woman's help. An initial search of the Internet hadn't turned up anything useful, but he could always hire a detective to track him down. He could start calling McCrays in Bozeman in the hopes that someone else in the area might know the man's whereabouts.

Or, he could just go home and let the whole thing be. He could say he'd tried and failed to find him. If Drew McCray ever presented himself, then he could collect his inheritance. Until then, life would continue as usual for his family, without the shakeup this new cousin would bring.

But, really, that last one was crap. He was too curious about Redmond's secret life to let this go. He was too heartsick about Redmond's death to let his final wish go unfulfilled.

And then there was Colin's sense of justice.

Here was this man, this Drew McCray, living in fear of debt collectors and lawsuits, unaware that he was part of a family that had more money than any of them could spend in ten lifetimes. He'd been denied his rightful place, denied his family. He'd been unclaimed by his father, and God only knew what kind of damage that could do to a man. Had he been lied to his entire life about his parentage? Did he even know the truth about where he'd come from?

Redmond had done the wrong thing during his lifetime, in Colin's opinion, letting his son live a lie, cut off from his blood. But through the will, he'd intended to set things right.

Colin couldn't do anything about the fact that he'd drifted away from his family over the past few years, couldn't do anything about the distance that had formed between him and his uncle, a distance that was now too late to bridge.

But he could do this. He could make sure his uncle's will was fulfilled. He could bring Redmond's son into the family where he belonged. He could give him his birthright.

He could take this one injustice, one in a world of many, and make it just a little bit closer to right.

He sat inside the car, looking at the house.

This was the last known address for Redmond's son, the one Redmond had told Drummond about. And the mailbox still said McCRAY.

The woman inside knew where Drew was, and she cared about him. If he could just convince her that he was honest in his intentions, then she could help Colin to find him.

And there was another reason he wanted to try again.

He wanted her to think well of him. He didn't know why, but he did. The way she'd looked at him, with anger and contempt, had stung with the pure unfairness of it. He wanted her to look at him with something else in her eyes—earnestness, or interest, or even compassion. He wasn't sure why that was important to him—why he cared about the opinion of this woman with her tousled hair and her face red from the cold and the exertion of the exercise routine he'd interrupted.

But he did care. When she had first opened the door and

they'd locked eyes, he'd thought he saw … something. Before it had all changed. He wanted to know what that something was, and what it might mean.

He needed to take another shot with her.

But not today. Today, she was defensive and angry. Today, she wouldn't listen to him, wasn't primed to open her ears and hear what he was saying.

He started the car, turned on the heater, and waited while the air began to warm. Then he pulled the car out onto the snowy road and headed back toward his hotel.

Chapter Six

Julia finally let out her breath when the lawyer—or whoever he was—started his car and drove away. It was creepy the way he'd just sat there in the driver's seat, watching the house. What did he want? Because she was sure it had nothing to do with some big, mysterious inheritance.

What kind of trouble had Drew gotten himself into now?

She stepped back from the window, where she'd been peeking out the curtains to make sure he left. She thought about whether to call Drew again to ask what he knew about all this, but of course, that would be futile. He wasn't going to tell her—if he even knew.

Julia had a strong feeling that her mother knew what was going on and why, though she couldn't have said how, since Drew hadn't talked to their mother in three years. But that call in which she'd said she was worried about him—that wasn't about a mother's usual concern for her children. That was about something specific, something Julia knew nothing about.

But confronting her mother would be just as pointless as confronting Drew.

The whole thing made Julia want to bang her head against a wall. How was she supposed to protect her family when no one would even tell her what she was protecting them against?

She took off her coat, hung it on the rack, and headed back down the hall toward her treadmill to finish her workout. On the way, she passed a mirror mounted on the wall over a hall table. She caught a glimpse of herself, and froze.

Only then did it occur to her that she'd been talking to one of the sexiest men she'd come across in years with her hair askew, her armpits soaked with sweat, and her face blotched from the effort of exercise. And she was wearing tattered sweatpants that should have been thrown out months ago.

Well, shit.

What was the world coming to when you had to worry about how you looked while working out in your own home, because a hot, wavy-haired, blue-eyed guy with an expensive coat and designer shoes might turn up on your doorstep?

Honestly, life was too hard already without that kind of pressure.

The drive between Bozeman and the Delaney ranch land up near Billings was more than two hours, and Colin knew he wasn't done here. So, instead of staying at the family's house—which was empty right now, since Liam hadn't yet returned from California—he'd checked in at the Lindley House in downtown Bozeman.

The B&B, built in 1892, had a homey feel with its wood floors and exposed brick, its quiet, tree-lined neighborhood now covered in snow. The whole place only had four rooms, and Colin's included a queen-sized bed, a small and sleek bathroom, and views of the white-dusted Bridger Mountains.

He'd only taken the time to check in and drop off his bags before going to the McCray house, so now, with his coat off and his feet beginning to feel warm again, he began the job of unpacking—though he hoped he wouldn't be here long.

With any luck, he'd be able to locate Drew McCray, tell him about the inheritance, and persuade him to come to California to meet the family he might not know he had, all in the next day or two.

If not, he supposed he would have to get comfortable, because he wasn't going home until he'd done what he came for.

He unpacked his things, thinking how inadequate his clothing was for the Montana weather. And why wouldn't it be? He'd lived in San Diego for a few years now, and the daytime temperatures there rarely got below the midsixties. And before that, he'd grown up in Cambria, which wasn't exactly known for its severe climate.

He wished he'd at least thought to bring some boots. He looked ruefully at his leather loafers, which would likely never be the same after his trudge through Mrs. Newmeyer's front yard.

Once he'd gotten his things reasonably in order, he settled onto the bed with his back against the headboard and opened his laptop.

He Googled the name McCray, along with the city of Bozeman, and hunted around a little to see what came up. Of course, he'd done that before he'd left California. But then, he'd been Googling Drew McCray specifically. Now, he was searching to see what he could find out about the woman who'd answered the door earlier this afternoon.

At the thought of her, he couldn't help picturing her face and the way she'd looked at him, both before she'd concluded that he was the enemy, and after. He'd seen a stark vulnerability there that intrigued him.

He found himself hoping that she wasn't Drew McCray's wife or girlfriend—and then he chided himself for it. He was being stupid. And his mother would be the first one to tell him so, if she were here.

Online, he found the usual items one would expect: obituaries, White Pages listings, LinkedIn profiles, a few Facebook entries. None of it jumped out at him. Then he thought to click on IMAGES. He scrolled through a few pages of randomness: maps, places, people, businesses.

And then, there she was.

On page three, he found a photo of the woman from the house. She was standing in a group of people at some sort of ribbon cutting ceremony. She was smiling. Thick auburn hair, pale skin, a smattering of freckles across her nose. She was dressed in some sort of skirt suit, makeup done, that glossy hair gathered at the nape of her neck.

He clicked on the photo and followed the link to the source page.

The page was an article from the local newspaper about the opening of a shopping center just outside of Bozeman. The caption for the photo Colin had found listed representatives from the developer, the construction crew, and some of the anchor stores. It also listed the landscape designer for the property—Julia McCray.

Okay, so she was family. *Was* she Drew's wife? The idea of that rankled him.

Now that he had her name, he Googled that—JULIA MCCRAY, BOZEMAN MT—and got several pages of hits. He found her business page, detailing her services as a landscape designer to homes and businesses throughout the state. He found her Facebook business page, and then her personal page, which was set to private. There were numerous articles about jobs she'd done, including hotels and resorts with names he recognized.

When he pulled up a magazine article—one of those deals profiling local women in business—he started to make some headway. In the article, which had been published only a couple of months before, Julia talked about her education, her family, and her efforts to build her career.

And the challenges of doing it all as a single woman.

Okay, so she wasn't Drew's wife. Then who was she?

He went back to his Google search results and kept scanning for anything useful. At the bottom of the third page, he found an obituary, dated three years earlier. Andrew McCray, dead at fifty-seven as a result of injuries suffered in a car crash. And down at the bottom, there it was:

He is survived by his wife, Isabelle, and his two children, Julia and Drew.

Julia was Drew McCray's sister.

A few questions ran through his mind. Was it possible she was Redmond's child, too? If so, Redmond apparently hadn't known about her, because she hadn't been mentioned in the will.

He needed to talk to Drew's mother—Redmond's former mistress—but the only address he had for her was the house where Julia lived. Did Isabelle live there with her daughter? If not, where had she gone?

Colin hunted around online and found a site where he could check someone's public records for a small fee. He entered ISABELLE MCCRAY, BOZEMAN MT, used his credit card to pay, and then waited for the results.

It turned out to be worth the $29.99.

Isabelle McCray had remarried in 2016 and was now Isabelle Bryant. And the site had an address for her, right here in Bozeman.

Julia probably would have Googled Colin, if she'd cared enough to do it.

But she didn't. Not at all.

It was so much easier to assume that he was some lowlife out to make Drew's life more miserable than it already was. Then, she could just ignore him, shut him out, slam the door and pretend he'd never showed up at her house with his brooding good looks and Mrs. Newmeyer's dog in his arms.

That was the theory, anyway.

But in fact, it wasn't so easy to forget about that afternoon's incident.

She let the whole thing nag at her as she finished her workout, showered, dressed, and then tried to get something done on her sketches for the hotel project. With Colin Delaney's face and voice in her brain, she couldn't focus on what she was doing. Sitting at her desk with a pencil in her hand and her sketchbook in front of her, she found herself losing her train of thought and staring at the blank page.

What if Drew was really in some kind of trouble? What if he wasn't, and he really did have an inheritance coming to him? A *substantial* inheritance, the guy on her porch had said. It had to be a lie, but what if it wasn't?

Around four p.m., she gave up and poured herself a glass of Chardonnay and took it into her front room, where she flopped onto the couch. It had been snowing steadily for the past couple of hours, but now it had stopped, and some blue sky was peeking out through the gloom.

When she heard a car's engine outside on the street, she peered out through the curtains, worried that this Colin Delaney had come back to try again. Instead, she saw Mike's truck, and then Mike himself as he got out of the driver's seat and went to the bed of the pickup to retrieve his snow shovel.

When she got outside, Mike was already shoveling the front walk.

She grabbed her coat from the rack, put it on, and went out

onto the front porch.

"Mike. What are you doing?" she called to him.

"What does it look like? I'm baking some goddamned cookies." He scooped up a shovelful of snow and hurled it into the yard.

"You don't have to shovel my snow," she said.

"Who else is gonna do it? You'd just leave it until you had to tunnel out of there." He kept working, and didn't look up.

Julia looked around and sighed in exasperation. "What did we get today, two inches?"

"Doesn't mean you can just ignore it," he grumbled.

The idea of ignoring the snow reminded her of everything else she was ignoring.

"I've got wine," she said.

He looked up at her, askance, from under the hood of his coat. Then, shovel in hand, he trudged up the walk and onto the porch. He propped the shovel up against the side of the house and unzipped his coat.

"Red or white? You know I hate that red crap."

"You're telling me Drew's gonna get some kind of big inheritance?" Mike peered at her skeptically, a glass of the Chardonnay in his hand. He was doing the man spread on her sofa, one arm draped across the back cushions, knees wide.

"No! You're not listening! It was kind of a … a scam to get me to tell the collections people where he is! God. I told you that already." Julia was sitting on the edge of a chair facing the sofa. She was leaning toward Mike, her elbows on her knees, her face earnest.

"From what I'm gathering, you don't know that," Mike pointed out. "You're guessing."

"Well …" She waved her hands around in an effort to defend herself from his logic. "I'm guessing based on experience!"

"Sure." Mike nodded.

"But this Colin Delaney—supposedly he's this lawyer from San Diego—just wouldn't back off! I wouldn't be surprised if he *stole* Mrs. Newmeyer's cocker spaniel just as a way to get me to let down my guard."

She didn't really think that, but she sensed she didn't have Mike's full sympathy, and the dog scenario was a desperate bid to get it back.

Mike was looking at her, doing this sucking thing he did with his front teeth when he wanted to show skepticism. He pulled his smartphone out of his pocket.

"Colin Delaney? From San Diego?" He looked to her for confirmation.

"That's what I said. But that probably wasn't even his real name."

"Uh huh," Mike said absently as he tapped on his phone.

"Am I boring you?" Julia wanted to know. "Is this conversation failing to keep your attention? Because I have to tell you—"

"What's this guy look like?" Mike said, interrupting her.

"What?"

"This Delaney guy. This fake lawyer. What does he look like?" He continued to tap on the phone.

"Well …" Julia was flustered by the question, mainly because the way he'd looked was still so prominent in her mind. "Uh … He was tall. Dark hair. Blue eyes. Medium build." *With a face like Henry Cavill,* she thought but didn't say. *And a body, under that coat, that probably looks like it's sculpted out of marble.* She had no way of knowing that last part, but a girl could take advantage of a vivid imagination. "He was just … a guy," she lied, for Mike's benefit.

"Uh huh," Mike said again. He turned the screen of his phone toward Julia. "Did he look like this?"

And there, on Mike's screen, was Colin Delaney, looking startlingly dapper in a dark gray suit, his cobalt eyes brooding at the camera.

Julia's eyebrows drew together. "That's him. Where did you find that photo?"

Mike cocked his head to the side and looked at Julia with a mixture of pity and weary patience. "I got it from the *Fortune* magazine website. Let's see … 'The Twenty Most Eligible Bachelors in Business.' They put him at number ten, if you're curious."

Julia gaped at the picture on the screen.

"He's not a debt collector," she said.

"No, he is not. Don't you know how to Google?"

"Give me that." Julia grabbed the phone from him and began to scroll through the article. Colin Delaney's family, it turned out, owned a cattle ranch on the Central Coast of California, as well as extensive real estate holdings throughout that state and several others. The family's collective wealth, the article said, totaled somewhere in excess of one billion dollars.

With a *B*.

"Holy shit," Julia said.

"You still wanna stonewall this guy, or you think maybe you should find out what he wants?" Mike asked dryly.

"But … but why would this California billionaire be out here looking for Drew?" Julia couldn't get the concept straight in her mind.

"I'm sure you'll wanna ask him that," Mike said, reaching out to take back his phone.

"An inheritance," Julia said, shaking her head in wonder. "From whom? And why? And … and why wouldn't a California billionaire lawyer *send* someone out here to find Drew, instead of showing up on my doorstep himself?"

"Life's a real kick in the ass," Mike observed, looking at her as though he still thought she might be acting like a fool.

Julia picked up her wineglass, looked at the contents, and then drained the glass in one large gulp. "I have to call this guy. This Colin Delaney. I have to call him and find out what's going on. I have to … *shit.*"

Mike raised his eyebrows questioningly.

"I slammed the door in his face before he could give me his contact information."

"Oh, I imagine he'll be back," Mike said.

She didn't want to wait to find out whether Mike was right. If the man who'd shown up at her door holding Mrs. Newmeyer's dog had answers about what was going on with Drew, then she needed to get those answers from him.

And, considering how she'd looked when he'd seen her the first time, it wouldn't hurt if she was wearing something cute when that happened.

Chapter Seven

Colin supposed it would have been the polite thing to do to call Isabelle Bryant first before just showing up at her house. But considering the sensitive nature of the situation, he thought he might get stonewalled. What if Isabelle hadn't told her current husband the truth about her son's paternity?

No, it would be better to show up unannounced. If he had surprise on his side, she might be more willing to talk to him.

So, that evening, Colin entered the address he'd found for Isabelle Bryant into the app on his iPhone, got into his rental car, and headed across town to confront Drew McCray's mother.

The Bryants lived in a single-story house on Arrowhead Trail in the Four Corners neighborhood, on a sizable parcel of land dotted with white-dusted pine trees. Spruces and cottonwoods stood starkly in the winter landscape.

Colin made his way up the long driveway, which had recently been plowed, and parked near the brick-colored wood frame house, which looked like it was built in the 1980s.

The Ford Bronco that sat just outside the closed garage door indicated that someone was home; Colin hoped it was Isabelle and not her husband. If the husband was home, and he didn't know the truth about Drew's origins, then it seemed likely that Colin would get a door closed in his face even more decisively than he had earlier in the day.

And that would be saying something.

On the way over, he'd tried to create a cover story he could use if the husband were the one to answer the door, but he hadn't been able to come up with one. Deception had never been his strong suit, which was probably the reason he'd never become a litigator. He would just have to say it was a private matter between him and Mrs. Bryant.

If that led to an uncomfortable conversation between the Bryants later, well, that wasn't his problem.

He got out of the car and made the walk to the front door across the icy ground.

The woman who answered the door had to be Isabelle; she looked like Julia, except that age had softened her, adding a sprinkling of gray to her hair and etching fine lines at the edges of her eyes. She opened the door a crack and looked at him with benign expectation.

"Isabelle Bryant?" he asked.

"Yes?"

"Ma'am, my name is Colin Delaney, and I'm here to talk to you about my uncle, Redmond Delaney. I believe you knew him."

Her face blanched and her eyes widened.

"Yes. I did," she said finally. "A long time ago. But I don't know what there could possibly be to talk about now."

"Ma'am, you're going to want to hear what I have to say," he told her. "It's about Redmond's will."

Isabelle hesitated, and she seemed to be considering her options. A range of emotions crossed her face, starting with surprise and ending with sorrow. She said, "I think you'd better come in."

Isabelle knew about Redmond's death, because there'd been a piece on him in the *New York Times* obituaries, which she read each day as a matter of course. She'd taken it hard, she told Colin as the two of them sat on the sofa in a living room that looked, with its dark wood paneling and its floral-upholstered furniture, as though it hadn't been updated in twenty years.

"He tried to write to you," Colin said. "You returned his letters." There was a cup of coffee on the table in front of him that he didn't really want, but that he'd accepted as a ritual of courtesy.

Isabelle pressed her lips together, deepening the lines that feathered out around them. She spread her hands in a gesture of helplessness. "You have to understand, I was married. If my husband had found the letters ..." She let the thought stir the air, unfinished.

"He wanted to provide for his son," Colin said.

"And I wanted to keep my son's family together." Her hands were clasped tightly, the knuckles white.

Colin simply nodded to acknowledge the point.

"I'm sorry about your uncle. About Redmond," she said. "But I don't understand why you're *here*."

Colin cleared his throat and rubbed the palms of his hands over his pants.

"I'm trying to locate Drew. I went to the address Redmond had for you, and I spoke to your daughter."

A hand flew to Isabelle's mouth. "You spoke to Julia? What did you tell her?"

"Only that I needed to locate him, and that it had to do with an inheritance. I didn't tell her about ... anything else."

Isabelle let out a shaky breath. She leaned forward and picked up her own coffee cup, probably for something to do with her hands. She held the cup in her palms but didn't drink.

"She doesn't know that Andrew wasn't Drew's father. I didn't tell her." She looked into the cup, avoiding Colin's eyes. "Even when Drew found out on his own. Even then, I still didn't tell her. I couldn't." She shook her head. "What would she have thought of me?"

"She might have thought you were human," he said. "That you had things in your past she couldn't understand, because she wasn't a part of them."

Isabelle shook her head again, her eyes far away. "I couldn't. She knows there's something, some secret between me and Drew that drove us apart. But …" She didn't finish the thought. She didn't have to. "I told Matt—my second husband—before we got married. I didn't want to enter into a new marriage with secrets. But … I couldn't tell Julia."

"So, Drew found out on his own?" Colin prompted her.

"After Andrew's accident, when he needed blood. Drew tried to donate, but his blood type …"

"Andrew couldn't have been his father," Colin concluded, so she wouldn't have to finish. "Is there any chance that Julia…?"

"No!" One of Isabelle's hands flew to her throat in surprise. "Oh, no. Julia is Andrew's daughter. I hadn't even met Redmond when she was born."

"All right." Colin considered what he'd learned. "How did Drew react when he found out the truth?"

Isabelle let out a ragged sigh. "When I told him—about Redmond—Drew was so angry. So hurt. He felt that I'd betrayed both him and my Andrew. And I suppose he's right. I did." She put the cup back down on the table in front of her and clasped her hands together tightly.

"Ma'am, I'm not here to cause trouble for you. Or for anyone. I just need to find Drew. Redmond left him a sizable inheritance, and I need to make sure he gets it." There was more to it, of course. Colin needed to meet Drew, to look into his face, to see Redmond there, alive and vibrant again. He needed answers about the uncle he'd thought he knew. And he needed to set things right for Drew, this angry, fatherless son.

"I'd like to tell you where to find him." Isabelle spread her hands in helplessness. "I would love to see him get whatever Redmond's left him. Lord knows he needs the money. But I don't know where he is. After his marriage ended, about a year and a half ago, he left the area, moved away to God knows where. By then, he hadn't spoken to me in more than a year." Her eyes had grown red and were beginning to pool with tears.

Colin spoke to her in a gentle tone.

"But Julia knows where he is."

Isabelle nodded silently. "She says she doesn't, but I know she does. I know he talks to her sometimes."

She plucked a few tissues from a box on the table beside the sofa. She dabbed at her eyes, and then at her nose, which was beginning to turn red.

"Ma'am … Mrs. Bryant," Colin began. "I'm going to need to talk to her again. And I'm going to have to tell her the truth. I don't think she'll help me otherwise."

Isabelle looked at him with something like fear, and then her expression changed, and she nodded.

"Just give me a day, would you? Give me twenty-four hours. I'd like to tell her myself."

"Of course," he said. "Of course I will."

He didn't want to wait twenty-four hours, or even four hours. Now that he'd set out on this mission, he felt compelled to follow through as quickly as possible. For one thing, he had business to attend to at home; he'd been working on a land purchase near Palm Springs, and the timing of all of this was unfortunate. But there was nothing to be done about it. This was going to take as long as it took. He went back to the B&B, looking forward to getting out of the cold.

Julia stared at her mother in disbelief.

When Isabelle had called the next day and asked Julia to come to her house for something important, she'd though it would be her mother's usual brand of *important. Have you talked to Drew? How is he doing? Tell him I love him. Tell him it isn't fair that he's doing this to me.*

Well, it *had* turned out to be about Drew. But not the way Julia had expected.

"What do you *mean* Dad wasn't Drew's father?"

When she'd heard what Isabelle had to say, Julia had the odd sensation that she'd been transported to some alternate universe, somewhere that made her feel sick and dizzy, somewhere where nothing made sense and everything was out of kilter. She felt certain that she'd misunderstood somehow, and that if she could just clear her head, she'd realize that her mother had said something else, something normal. Something about her vacation plans or her thoughts about a new hairstyle.

Not a revelation that Julia's entire life had been a lie.

"Julia, honey, you have to understand. Your father and I were going through a rough time, and I was lonely. So lonely. And Redmond—"

"Did Dad know?" Julia broke in. Suddenly, that question seemed like the most important thing in the world.

"No! No. I couldn't tell him. I don't know what he would have done. He might have left, and I couldn't do that to you children." Isabelle's eyes were puffy and red, as though she'd been crying before Julia had arrived at the house.

"So you lied to him all those years? And to me? And to Drew? Oh, God, Drew." Suddenly it was clear why he'd refused to talk to their mother for so long, why he refused any contact from her, why he wouldn't even allow her to know where he lived. "He already knows." It wasn't a question.

Isabelle nodded. "He found out when your father was hurt. When he tried to give blood."

"Oh, my God."

Julia could imagine Drew trying to deal with their father's accident, and then his death, while at the same time learning that his father wasn't his father. How much worse must the pain of loss have been? How much more confusing?

"He's been dealing with this alone, all this time," Julia said. "He wouldn't tell me what was going on. He didn't cut me off completely, but he sure as hell cut me off from knowing the truth."

"I think he didn't want you to ... to hate me." Isabelle's voice broke.

So many thoughts were rushing through Julia's mind. And then a terrible idea struck her.

"Mom ... what about me? Am *I* ..." She couldn't finish the thought.

Isabelle reached out to put a hand on Julia's arm. "You're Andrew's daughter, you have to believe that."

Did she believe it? Her mind cast around to look for signs of a lie. But deep inside, she knew it was true. She had her father's fair skin, his hair color. She had his stubborn streak, and his extra-wide feet. And when she'd donated blood after the accident, no such red flag had been raised.

So, it was just Drew, then. Just her brother, who turned out to be her half brother. And whose real father was—oh, God—part owner in a billion-dollar real estate fortune.

"The man who came to see me yesterday. He said …"

"Redmond's nephew. He said there's an inheritance. I don't know how much. All I know is that he needs to find Drew to let him know."

Julia stood up from the sofa and began to pace the small living room. "That's why you're telling me all of this. Not because you thought I had a right to know, but because you need me to tell you where Drew is. If I didn't have something you want, then you'd have left me in the dark forever."

"Julia—"

"Does Matt know?" Matt Bryant, Isabelle's second husband, would be at work right now. Was he being deceived, too?

"He knows, honey. He's always known."

At least she'd been honest to someone.

"I have to go." Julia gathered up her coat and her purse and headed toward the door without even bothering to put the coat over her shoulders.

"Oh, honey. If we could just talk about this—"

"You had years to talk to me about this, Mom." Tears were beginning to blur her vision, and she wiped her eyes with her fingertips. "I just … I can't right now. I have to go."

She stepped out onto the porch with the coat in her arms, and the cold slapped her with a shock that was almost welcome, because it brought her out of her head and back into her body—something she could manage.

She struggled into her coat and slung her purse strap over her shoulder as her mother stood at the door, trying to coax her back inside.

"Julia, please. If you'd just—"

Julia ignored her and stalked down the porch steps and to

her car. She got inside and slammed the door shut, closing out her mother's protests. She pulled away from the curb and drove off, wondering if she'd ever really known her mother at all.

Chapter Eight

Julia didn't know what to do. Drew had made her swear that she wouldn't tell her mother where he was living, and she hadn't. Did the same apply to Colin Delaney? Was she sworn to secrecy when it came to him, too?

She tried to call Drew as soon as she got home, but he didn't pick up. That was no surprise—he'd been accepting her calls less and less frequently. What if she reached him, and he didn't give her permission to pass on his contact information to Colin Delaney?

And what if he did?

Either way, this wasn't something she wanted to handle over the phone. She needed to see him face to face, to talk to him about what she knew and how it was affecting him. She needed to find a way to get her brother back.

At home on a cold Tuesday afternoon, she sat at her kitchen table with her laptop, checking her bank balance, investigating available flights, and considering her options.

She could just show up on his doorstep, the way Colin Delaney had showed up on hers. But what if he didn't want to talk to her? What if he didn't even let her in? Their telephone conversations had been awkward and perfunctory since he'd left, and the unfairness of that pissed her off. She wasn't the one who'd lied to him his entire life. She wasn't the one who had dropped a bombshell on him when he'd been mourning the loss of the man he'd thought was his father.

He should have been able to turn to Julia for support when he'd been struggling to deal with the truth about his life. But instead, he'd somehow lumped her in with their mother, as though Julia and Isabelle were an inseparable unit.

Julia was being unfairly blamed for something she'd had nothing to do with, something she'd had no knowledge of. Part of her wanted to react by turning her back on both Drew and Isabelle. She was angry and hurt, and if Drew didn't want her in his life despite her innocence in all of this, then he didn't deserve her. But a bigger part of her felt compassion for all he must have been going through these past years, without anyone to talk to about it.

She wondered if he'd talked to Tessa about it, back when it had first happened. Back when they'd still been married. She wondered if he'd shut her out, too, and if that had anything to do with the breakup of their marriage.

God, this was all such a mess.

She could fly out to see Drew today, if she decided to go that route. She'd be harder to push away if she were standing right there, a real person instead of a voice on the other end of the phone or a name on the other end of a text message.

Then she could decide what to do about Colin Delaney.

Isabelle had said Delaney was planning to contact Julia again in the next day or so, once she'd heard the truth from her mother. He'd passed his business card on to Isabelle, and she'd given it to Julia.

Julia looked at the card, which sat on the table next to her laptop.

She figured it wouldn't hurt to be fully armed with all of the information before she went flying off to confront her brother.

She picked up the card, felt its texture between her fingers.

At least five times since she'd talked to Isabelle, Julia had picked up her cell phone and started to dial before stopping herself. She couldn't shake the feeling that she'd be betraying her brother, going behind his back to talk to a stranger about the most sensitive secrets of Drew's life.

But he was already blaming her for a betrayal she hadn't committed. It seemed like calling Colin Delaney to get the rest of the story could hardly be any worse.

Somehow, she didn't want him in her house. Him, and the turmoil he represented. She knew she was likely doing the same thing to him that her brother had done to her—blaming an innocent bystander for someone else's misdeeds. Still, she felt the way she felt.

They decided to meet at a diner—a place with wood paneling and mounted fish on the walls, where you could get a cinnamon roll as big as your head. Julia sat at a Formica table across from Colin, each of them with a thick, white ceramic mug of coffee in front of them. The place smelled like hamburger grease and damp shoes.

Julia shoved the laminated menu aside and looked at the man across from her.

Chiseled jaw, a clean shave, an expensive haircut. And his well-cut clothing—just slightly inappropriate for the weather conditions—reflected the fact that he came from a warmer climate and an environment that was considerably less rugged than this one. She thought about what it would be like to sit across a restaurant table from him under other circumstances, but then pushed those thoughts aside. The idea of dating someone this rich and this gorgeous was absurd, especially for her. Because

Colin Delaney looked the way he looked, and Julia looked … well. Like herself.

More absurd than that thought was the fact that she was even thinking that way at all. She needed to be thinking about Drew. And thinking about Drew was pretty damned uncomfortable at the moment.

In contrast to her own intense feelings of awkwardness, Colin appeared to be at ease. She supposed that in his line of work, he had plenty of experience talking to people about things they might prefer not to talk about.

"Your mother told you why I'm here," he said, cutting into her musings. His hands were wrapped around his coffee mug, either to give them something to do, or for the warmth of the mug. They were strong-looking hands.

"She did." Julia could feel the tension in her mouth, around her eyes.

"I'm sure it's got to be a shock, if you didn't already know about your mother and Redmond."

"It's fair to say I was surprised."

His blue eyes focused on her with an intensity that made her even more uncomfortable. "I can imagine."

"So … where do we go from here?" She hoped he had some ideas, because she certainly didn't. "When you first showed up to talk to me, I thought you were a debt collector. Now …"

"Now you know I'm not."

She nodded. "Now I know you're not, but I still don't know what to do."

He spread his hands, and she found herself focusing on them. They were smooth, uncallused. The hands of a man who worked with his mind.

"I have to talk to him," Colin said. "Your mother says she doesn't know where he is, but you do."

She looked at the tabletop to avoid his gaze. "He made me promise I'd respect his privacy. And I always have. If you show up …" She left the thought unfinished.

"I'm not here to make trouble for him. He's got an inheritance coming, and he can't receive it if we can't locate him. It's a significant inheritance. And if you thought I was a debt collector, I'm guessing he could use this kind of news right about now."

Considering what she'd learned about the Delaney family, she wondered what exactly he meant by *significant.* She couldn't bring herself to ask, partly because it wasn't her business, and partly because she thought she might not want to know.

"I tried to call him, but he's not picking up," Julia said. "And it didn't seem like the kind of thing I should tell him about in a voice mail message."

"You're his sister, and he doesn't take your calls?"

Julia lifted one shoulder in a reluctant shrug. "Our relationship has been … complicated … for the past few years. Ever since he found out our father is not his father. Of course, I didn't know that was the reason until I talked to my mother."

"That had to have been a shock." Colin was looking at her intently, and she thought she saw concern in his eyes.

She nodded—it had been a shock, all right. "But at least now I know what's going on. All this time I knew there was some kind of secret between the two of them—Drew and my mom—and that it had driven everyone apart. But I didn't know what it was. It's better to know." She nodded decisively. "I think it's always better to know."

Colin thought it was better to know, too. That was why he had to meet Drew and get to know him, learn about who he was and what that meant for Colin's family. Also, the more he learned about the situation, the more he thought it would be better for Drew to know all there was to know—about the Delaneys, about Redmond, about his biological father's relationship to his mother, and about how he fit into everything in the aftermath.

He could imagine what all of these revelations must have done to Drew, but that's all it would ever be—Colin's imagination. He couldn't truly know how something like that felt. But he had to think if it were him—if Orin turned out not to be his father—he'd need to know everything he could learn about the truth. While that wouldn't heal things, couldn't reverse the damage, it could be a step in that direction.

And as someone who'd never really seemed to fit in himself, Colin felt that any step forward for Drew would probably be a good one.

"Please tell me how to get in touch with him, Julia. It's time to get things out in the open, don't you think?"

"I suppose it is." An expression crossed her face that he couldn't quite place. Contemplation, reluctance, pain. "But I'm not just going to tell you and have you show up there and drop this bomb on him." She seemed to consider something, and then nodded. "I'm going out there to tell him in person."

Colin cocked his head slightly. "Where is 'out there'?"

"Canada. Drew is on Salt Spring Island."

"Huh. I've never been there, but there's no time like the present."

Julia looked at him with alarm. "I didn't mean—"

"Relax," Colin said with a half grin. "I'm a pretty good travel companion. At least, I haven't had any complaints yet." He raised a finger to get their server's attention, and the waitress, whose hair seemed to be sprayed into an immovable mass atop her head, reached into her apron pocket for their check and headed his way.

"We're not going *together,*" Julia said, exasperated.

"Well, I'm going and you're going," Colin said amiably. "It would just be friendlier to go together, don't you think?"

Of course, meeting Drew was his first motivation. But if he were being honest, he'd have to admit that the idea of spending more time with Julia—getting to know her a little—would be a bonus. She wasn't at all the type of woman he was usually attracted to, and yet there was something about her that drew his attention and made him want to know more. There was something vulnerable in her face, something honest and intriguing. Sitting next to her on an airplane for a few hours would give him an opportunity to find out just what that was.

Two birds, one stone.

He paid the check, gathered up his coat, and waited patiently for her as she gaped up at him from her seat at the table.

"I'll make the travel arrangements and call you later today with the details," he said. "Thanks for agreeing to meet with me. Drive safely. The roads are icy."

He turned and walked out of the diner, feeling her gaze on his back. He nodded to himself. As a real estate lawyer, one thing he knew how to do was close a deal.

Chapter Nine

Some things just didn't make sense.

For example, it didn't make sense to Julia that she'd somehow ended up on a plane to British Columbia with a man she'd just met days before, on the way to see her estranged brother about his giant inheritance.

It didn't make sense that the words *giant inheritance* were in any way connected with her brother.

And it didn't make sense that the man sitting next to her—a man who was, by all accounts, hugely wealthy, and who had bought the plane tickets—was crammed into economy class, with his knees pressed up against the back of the seat in front of him.

"I'd have thought the Delaneys traveled first class," Julia remarked as the plane taxied toward the runway at Bozeman Yellowstone International Airport. She, herself, didn't mind traveling economy, as it was all she'd ever known. But seeing Colin crammed into a seat that could barely accommodate his height seemed incongruous with what she'd always believed about the lives of the rich and famous.

Colin let out a soft grunt. "You haven't met my mother."

"Well, no," Julia said.

"She reuses plastic sandwich bags."

Her eyes widened. "You're joking."

"No. No, I'm not. I went through all of elementary school with my ham and cheese sandwiches smelling like the previous day's PB&J." He grinned at the memory. "Partly, it's because my mother grew up poor before she married my father. And partly, it's a matter of principle. *You don't show your gratitude for everything you've got by wasting it all willy-nilly*, she likes to say."

The wistful smile on his face told her of his deep love for his mother, and Julia felt the sweetness of that like a warm glow in her belly.

"You're obviously not as thrifty as your mother, though." She gestured at his shoes. "Are those Ferragamos?"

He looked at her with surprise. "You know shoes."

"I'm a girl, of course I know shoes. Not that I ever get a chance to wear good ones in my line of work, and living in the frozen tundra."

There was his grin again, the one that made her feel a little soft and gooey. She didn't really want to feel soft and gooey about this particular man, considering the chaos he was bringing to her family.

"Well." He shrugged. "I have more expensive tastes than the rest of my family. But the plane tickets come under the heading of Delaney business, not my own personal expenses. So ..." He waved a hand to indicate the appalling lack of leg room. "Sorry it's not more comfortable."

"Don't apologize. I didn't want you to pay for my ticket in the first place."

It was true. When Colin had called Julia to say that the tickets had been bought, she'd told him that she would pay her share when they met at the airport. He'd argued with both parts. He wouldn't accept her money, he'd told her, and he'd insisted on picking her up in his rental car. At the time, that last gesture had seemed gallant. But now it occurred to her that he might just have wanted to keep an eye on her to make sure she wouldn't run off to Canada without him.

Which, honestly, she might have done.

As the plane reached the runway, she faced forward in her seat, grabbed the armrests, and stared straight ahead.

"Hey, I didn't realize you were mad about the plane ticket," he said.

"I'm not," she said through gritted teeth.

"Then …"

She reached out, grabbed his hand, and clutched it in a death grip as the plane accelerated for takeoff. "Just shut up until we're in the air."

"You're afraid to fly." He sounded as though he'd maybe heard of full-grown adults with that particular affliction, but had never seen one up close.

"I said, shut up. Can you do that? I have to concentrate on not dying."

"Sure." There was humor in his voice, and she'd have been pissed about it if she hadn't been so busy willing the plane not to crash.

She squeezed his hand as though he were the only thing keeping the plane aloft, and she kept squeezing it—threatening both his circulation and hers—until the pilot announced that they'd turned off the FASTEN SEATBELT signs. When she finally loosened her grip and let him go, he flexed his hand and shook it out.

She thought he was just being theatrical until she spotted the little red half-moons where her fingernails had made indentations in his skin.

"Oh, God. I'm sorry about that." She could feel her face reddening with embarrassment.

"I guess I'll live." He shot a look at her. "Are you okay now?"

The feeling of dread and impending doom in her stomach was beginning to fade, and her thoughts of leaving behind her family, her friends, and all of her unfulfilled dreams eased.

"Yeah. Mostly," she said. "It's just takeoffs and landings."

"So, I'm going to go through this again?" He shot her a teasing grin. "Don't get me wrong, I'm up for it. I just wish I'd brought protective gloves."

She smacked his shoulder with the palm of her hand and couldn't help smiling, despite the heart-pounding anxiety that was just now releasing its grip on her. Something about him was immensely reassuring, though it shouldn't have been. He was the one who'd brought upheaval and uncertainty into her life, after all. Then she corrected herself: No, he hadn't. He'd simply brought the reason for the upheaval and uncertainty to light. And surely having their family secrets out in the open was a good thing.

At least, she hoped it would be a good thing.

She glanced at Colin in the seat beside her and thought that she'd have to be careful with him, she'd have to watch herself. He was immensely sexy and more than a little charming. Add in that slightly brooding thing he had going on, and she could easily be a goner.

But he wasn't here for her, she reminded herself. He was here for Drew.

And she was here to protect her brother from whatever threat might come his way.

It was best to stay focused on that, no matter how much she liked the feel of Colin Delaney's hand in hers.

Colin couldn't have said why Julia's fear of flying made him like her even more, but it was true. Her phobia made him want to protect her, as though his own good thoughts could somehow keep the plane and its passengers safe.

And he wouldn't have minded if she'd wanted to keep holding his hand—though maybe a little less tightly this time.

He wasn't sure where that feeling had come from. She'd set herself up as an adversary, first refusing to disclose Drew McCray's whereabouts, and then making it clear that she was suspicious about Colin's intentions.

But he could understand all of that. He'd have done the same for his own brothers, or for Breanna.

Maybe that was the connection he was feeling. Or maybe it was the way her hair fell onto her shoulders, the way her full lips curved into a sardonic grin. The way her face showed a slight sprinkle of freckles across the nose. The way her pale skin seemed to glow.

And, damn it, he needed to stop thinking like that. He needed to stop thinking about her hair, or her lips. Or the way it had felt to have her shoulder brush against his.

In an effort to get his thoughts back where they belonged, he said, "So, tell me a little bit about what's going on with Drew."

She shot him a suspicious look.

"Hey, I don't want you to reveal his inner pain. I just ... you know. Thought we could make conversation. It's a four-hour flight." He smiled at her hopefully. The guy in the window seat next to Colin was focused on the in-flight entertainment, ear buds firmly in place. Their conversation would be private, as much as it could be under the circumstances.

She side-eyed Colin for a moment, and then her expression softened, and she sighed.

"The money problems ... the thing about the debt collectors …" She gave her head a little shake. "He's not a flake. He's not some out-of-control spender, or … or some deadbeat who doesn't work. None of it was his fault."

"Okay," Colin said encouragingly. "So what happened?"

Her eyes narrowed. "His ex-wife. Tessa. She ran up the credit cards and cleaned out the bank accounts before she left. Drew's been trying to pay off the bills, but it's taking time. More time than his creditors want to give him."

"He could pursue legal action," Colin said, now on familiar ground. "She can't just escape responsibility for bills that are in her name as well as his. And if they had joint accounts—"

"He's not going to pursue legal action," Julia said, a weariness in her voice that said she'd been over this, if only in her mind, many times before. "He's insisting on taking care of everything himself, if it takes him the rest of his life. Which it might."

"It won't," Colin said. While Julia didn't know the amount of the inheritance her brother stood to collect, Colin did, and no matter how much debt Drew's ex-wife had racked up, it wouldn't be a drop in the ocean of the man's future wealth.

Colin hoped like hell that Julia's account of the situation—that the debt and financial mismanagement was all the ex-wife's doing—was true. Because if Drew had screwed away his own money, that would be one thing. But Drew was going to become a voting shareholder in the family's corporation, and that meant he'd be in a position to screw away money that belonged to the Delaney family. While there was nothing any of them could do once that power was in Drew's hands, it wouldn't sit well if he turned out to be an irresponsible ass. And certain members of the family were going to lose their shit if this newly discovered heir took the money Redmond had worked hard for all his life and started throwing it around like confetti.

Liam, for instance.

Colin shuddered to think how his brother would react if Drew started buying Teslas and beachfront mansions, or if he went on some kind of party binge in Vegas. The shitstorm that would result would be epic in its range and scope.

But Colin couldn't control his brother's actions any more than he could control Drew McCray's.

McCray was entitled to the money because Redmond had decided he was. That was all it came down to, really. And if this was what Redmond wanted, well, they'd all just have to go with it and hope for the best.

"So." Julia shot him a tentative look. "How much money are we talking about?"

"It would be inappropriate of me to say without talking to your brother first." Colin had anticipated the question, and he'd prepared the answer.

"Of course." Julia nodded. She'd likely known what he was going to say before he said it.

"It could be enough to wipe out his debt, though?" she asked hopefully.

Colin's grin was apologetic, as though his family's wealth were a matter of some embarrassment. "It could be enough to wipe out the debt of a small country."

"Oh, shit." Julia paled, her jaw slack. "I mean … oh, shit."

"It's going to be a lot for him to deal with," Colin acknowledged. "When you've grown up in that environment, it's one thing. But having it drop into your lap can be … unsettling, I imagine."

"You think?" Julia said sarcastically.

They both considered that for a moment, then Colin said, "What do you think the problem was in the marriage?"

"I have no idea. And how is that even relevant?"

"It's not, I guess." Colin shrugged. "But it's a long flight, and we have to talk about something."

"Then let's talk about books or music. Or the weather."

"Fine. The snow in Bozeman should be letting up soon, right? I mean, it's almost spring."

She glared at him like talking about the weather was the stupidest idea she'd ever heard, even though it had, in fact, been her own idea.

"He wouldn't talk to me about it, but looking back, I'm guessing it had something to do with our father."

"The marriage, not the snow," he clarified. She smacked him again, and he grinned.

She settled into her seat, the best she could in a tiny, uncomfortable space with inadequate padding and no leg room, and sighed. "When my mother finally told me what was going on, she said Drew found out when my father was in the hospital. That was about three years ago. Tessa left maybe a year and a half after that. I don't think the timing was a coincidence."

"Anger and depression—if that's what it was—can be hell on a marriage," Colin acknowledged.

"I'm sure it can. Not that any of that makes it okay the way Tessa left. She took everything. Not just the money, but almost all of their belongings. She cleaned him out."

"Makes me glad I never got married." He said the words casually—just an offhand comment. But it was more than that, he had to admit to himself. He wanted Julia to know he was single. And what was that about? He knew he shouldn't get involved with her. There were too many complications. But on the other hand, it didn't hurt to get the information out there.

He faced forward and slipped the in-flight magazine out of the seat-back pocket, flipping through articles about Asian getaways and the best restaurants in Austin, Texas. He could feel her looking at him, though, and it wasn't entirely unpleasant.

A couple of hours later, when the pilot announced the plane's imminent landing in Victoria, Colin wordlessly reached out and offered Julia his hand.

She looked at it, then looked at him, and then grabbed on gratefully.

She gripped it tightly, her fingernails jabbing into him, all the way down, and she kept holding it, though a bit more gently, until they came to a complete stop at the gate.

Even then, it was her choice to let go. He didn't pull away.

Chapter Ten

Once they got off the plane, they were both starving, so they grabbed a quick sandwich at the airport before they got their bags and caught a cab to the Swartz Bay ferry terminal. The ferry to Salt Spring Island, where Drew was living, left Victoria every couple of hours in the afternoon, so they had no problem catching a boat for the thirty-five-minute trip to the island.

Once they arrived at Fulford Harbor, they called a taxi and got a ride to a car rental place—a necessary step, considering the dearth of public transportation options on the small, sparsely inhabited island.

Before they'd left Montana, Colin had reserved two rooms at a bed and breakfast in Ganges, the only place on the island that could really be considered a town. He navigated the winding, pine-shaded roads of the island and located the B&B. He parked the car, and they began pulling their luggage out of the trunk.

He could see Julia's discomfort growing. The line of her mouth was tight and hard.

"Are you okay?" he asked her as he took her suitcase from her hand and began carrying it up the walk to the B&B's front door.

"I'm fine," she said. "And you don't have to carry my suitcase."

"Yes, I do." His lips quirked up into a half smile. "My mother taught me always to carry a lady's bags. She's mad enough at me already without adding lack of courtesy to the mix."

She stopped walking. "Why is she mad at you?"

"Let's get checked in," he said brightly, leading her up the walk. "Not a bad looking place."

"You avoided the question," she pointed out.

"Yes, I did. But I still think we should get checked in," he said over his shoulder as he continued toward the building.

Once they were checked in and Colin had carried Julia's bag to her room—over her objections—he gave her little more than a half hour to unpack and unwind from the flight before he knocked on her door and asked about going out to see Drew.

"Now?" She was standing in the doorway, holding onto the doorframe, looking at him as though he'd lost all sense. "We just got here. I need some time to … to decompress."

"I don't see any sense in wasting time," Colin said. "You could give me his address and phone number, and I'll go out there myself. You could—"

"No." She crossed her arms over her chest in a display of stubbornness. "You're not going without me."

"Fine. So, why don't we—"

"Damn it, Colin. I'm not ready yet." And suddenly, out of nowhere, there were tears pooling in her eyes, threatening to spill over.

"Hey, hey." He put a hand on her shoulder. He wasn't certain whether it was okay for him to do that, but after the airplane hand-holding incident, he figured it was fair to assume he could. "It's okay. Just … let's sit down a minute, all right?"

She nodded tearfully, and they went into her room and sat down side by side on the edge of her bed.

He didn't prompt her to talk about it; he didn't ask her what was going on, or why she was crying, or why she wanted to delay seeing Drew. Instead, he simply sat there, his shoulder lightly touching hers, and waited.

The room, all blond wood and white bed linens, seemed to wait patiently as well, as though a person could have any feelings they wanted here and would be soothed and comforted in the end.

"I haven't seen him in a year and a half," she said, finally, when she was ready. "He wouldn't let me come visit him. I can barely get him to take my calls. What if he closes the door in my face? What if he …"

She shook her head to dismiss the thought, then wiped at her eyes with her fingertips.

Colin reached for a box of tissues on the table beside the bed, pulled a few out, and handed them to her.

"Thanks." She took the tissues and dabbed at her eyes, then blew her nose in a way that seemed improbably quiet and ladylike.

"How can he blame you for what happened?" Colin said. "You had nothing to do with it. You didn't even know."

"It's not that," she said. "At least, I don't think it is. It's … He probably felt like he couldn't tell me what was happening because he didn't want me to think badly of our mother. I can see that. And then, since he couldn't talk to me about the thing that was most on his mind, he just didn't talk to me at all."

"I can sort of get that," he said.

"So can I. But it sucks, Colin. It sucks. I lost my father, and then my mother started being all quiet and weird, and then I lost my brother."

"And none of it had a damn thing to do with you," he added.

"No! It didn't!"

"That must feel pretty unfair."

He watched her face as she pulled herself together, as she carefully arranged her features in an expression of calm repose. Her skin was smooth and pale, her hair a thick, waving cascade to her shoulders. He wanted to reach out and pull her into his arms, and he told himself that feeling was simple compassion.

But he knew it wasn't.

"Well." Julia primly patted her knee with one hand, her other hand still holding the wadded-up tissues. "That's enough of me feeling sorry for myself. And there's no sense in delaying what we came here for. Just give me a few minutes to pull it together, and I'll be ready to go."

"Just knock on my door when you're ready," he told her.

She nodded and gave him a brave smile.

He didn't want to leave her. Reluctantly, he did.

Once Colin had left the room, Julia cursed herself for being such a girl.

Why had she cried in front of him? Why had she fallen apart that way? That wasn't how she'd intended to handle things. That wasn't the composed, take-charge person she wanted to be.

She thought about what that person—that take-charge Julia—would do.

For one thing, she wouldn't let some near stranger dictate the terms of her reunion with her brother. As appealing as that stranger might be.

She yanked a few more tissues from the box on the bedside table, went to the mirror that hung over the dresser, and carefully wiped under her eyes to eliminate the black smudges of eyeliner and mascara that were beginning to form.

As she repaired the damage, she thought about how dumb it was that she was wearing makeup in the first place. She didn't like makeup, and she never bothered with it unless she was preparing for a business meeting.

Or unless she was on a date.

This was neither of those things, so why did she have smudges of mascara and eyeliner to remove in the first place?

Oh, can it. You know why.

There was no use denying that she'd worn makeup because she'd wanted to look nice for Colin Delaney—and it would be stupid to pretend she hadn't liked holding his hand on the plane, hadn't noticed the way he'd looked at her a few minutes ago as they sat together on the bed.

And, God, this situation—this painful, awkward situation—would be so much more bearable if she could distract herself with an afternoon of fun, uncomplicated lust in this very same charming bedroom.

But, by definition, lust with Colin Delaney could not be uncomplicated. Not when she considered why they both were here.

And that brought her thoughts full circle. Colin was here to oversee and control and micromanage the confrontation she needed to have with her brother.

Take-charge Julia wouldn't allow that.

She checked herself in the mirror one more time, scooped up her purse and her coat, and slipped quietly out the bedroom door. As she passed Colin's room, she didn't even pause.

When he hadn't heard from Julia in a half hour, he started to wonder whether she'd ditched him. That seemed unlikely, though, since he had the only keys to the rental car.

When forty-five minutes had passed, he knocked on her

door and got no answer. Suspecting that maybe he'd been played, he went downstairs, found the innkeeper puttering around in the kitchen, and asked her if she'd seen Julia.

"Why, yes." The elderly woman had a crown of white curls on her head and a floral apron around her middle. "She asked me to call for a taxi, and she left about twenty minutes ago. I thought it was odd, since you'd both arrived in a car."

"Damn it," he muttered. "Did she say where she was going?"

"No." The woman looked concerned, and she wrung her hands atop her blue and white apron. "I know it's none of my business," she said after a moment. "But I find that flowers always help."

"I don't … what?" He rubbed his forehead with his hand.

"If you've had a fight. Flowers always smooth things over. I know a good florist right here in town."

"If anybody ought to get flowers in this situation, it's me," he replied.

Julia felt a little bit bad for ditching Colin, but not bad enough to turn around and go back. Besides, she was too consumed with nerves about seeing Drew again to worry very much about her manners toward Colin.

"Mike? I'm freaking out. Seriously. I'm freaking out to such an extent that I'm not even going to pretend I'm calling for some other reason." Julia held her cell phone to her ear as the taxi wound its way along Fulford-Ganges Road, past a landscape thick with pine trees, toward the southern tip of the island. She didn't even care that she was probably spending enough on international roaming charges to pay for this month's groceries.

"Take a breath," Mike told her, his voice more gentle and less gruff than usual. "Are you doing it?"

"Yes."

"No, you're not. I mean it. Take a damned breath."

Julia closed her eyes and took the overheated air inside the taxi deep into her lungs.

"Did you do it?" he badgered her.

She let out the breath in a slow sigh. "Yes. I really did this time."

"Good. Now, remind yourself what this is about. Your mother screwed around on your father and lied to your brother, and he's pissed as shit about it."

Julia grinned at Mike's typically blunt assessment of the situation.

"Now, whose name didn't I mention in any of that?" he prompted her.

"Mine."

"You're goddamned right. Because none of this is about you. Say it."

"It's not about me," she repeated dutifully.

"And if he kicks you out on your ass when you get there, that won't be about you, either."

Julia had been doing her best to get into a zone of calm, her eyes closed, focusing on maintaining some sort of unflappable Zen equilibrium before arriving at Drew's place. But now her eyes snapped open, and her eyebrows bunched together in angst.

"What do you mean if he kicks me out on my ass? Do you think he's going to kick me out on my ass?" she demanded.

"No, I do not," he assured her. "I'm just saying, *if*."

"Well, don't! You're supposed to be giving me a pep talk! Keep your *ifs* to yourself!"

Maybe Mike was being of some help, though, because Julia was so preoccupied with her outrage that she barely noticed when the cab pulled up in front of a rustic wood-frame house with some sort of outbuilding, roughly twice the size of the house itself, situated about twenty yards behind it. The house looked tidy and reasonably well-kept, though it appeared to have been built at least a few generations before. The house was nestled in a clearing amid towering pines, with little patches of snow on the ground that were in the process of melting away.

"Is this it? Are we here?" she asked the taxi driver, trying to keep the rising anxiety out of her voice.

"Yes, ma'am. This is it," said the driver, a stout middle-aged woman wearing a knit cap and an old, hooded sweatshirt.

"Okay," Julia said. "Okay." She put the phone back to her ear. "Mike? I'm here. Oh, God."

"He's your brother, Jules," Mike said, as though that should put a definitive end to all of her concerns.

"I know he's my brother," she snapped at him. "This is not new information. You're not helping."

"Ma'am?" The cabdriver turned around to gaze at Julia questioningly over the front seat.

Julia put the phone down on the seat beside her, with Mike still on the line, and fished around in her purse for the fare. She pulled out some Canadian currency, passed it to the driver, and said, "Could you wait for a few minutes, please? I don't know if he's home." A ten-year-old Toyota sat on a patch of dirt in front of the house, but who was to say it was Drew's? Part of her hoped it wasn't, and that she could avoid this confrontation one more day.

"He *is* your brother, ma'am. I'm sure he'll be happy to see you," the driver said.

Julia picked up the phone and said, "Mike? I have to go. I'm doing this." She hung up without waiting for his response.

She tucked her phone into her purse, clutched the bag in front of her like armor, the way she'd seen her grandmother do countless times over countless visits during Julia's childhood, braced herself for whatever was about to happen, and got out of the car.

"Ma'am?" the driver called to her through the passenger side window, which was just now sliding open.

Julia peered into the car. Had she underpaid by mistake?

"Good luck," the woman said, smiling in a grimly encouraging way.

Julia nodded at her with what she hoped was steely resolve, and turned toward the house.

Chapter Eleven

Julia had been scared to see Drew again, scared that he would reject her, that he would send her away. That he would, somehow, no longer be her brother, who had seen her through so many of life's challenges before he'd retreated into whatever kind of solace he found out here on this small island.

But she need not have worried.

When he opened the front door and found her standing on the porch with her purse, looking small and frightened, he simply reached out and pulled her into his arms.

"Jules," he breathed into her hair.

"Drew." She was already crying; she couldn't seem to help herself. "Are you all right? Mom told me what happened. Finally. Why didn't you tell me? Why did you just leave?"

She had so much to say to him that it all just seemed to spill out.

"*Shh*," he whispered, holding her, rubbing her back with his hand. "It's okay. Don't cry, Jules. I'm all right."

"Are you?" She pulled away from him so she could look into his eyes. He had the same fair skin as she did, the same auburn hair that they'd both inherited from their mother. But he looked tired, and too thin. The lines on his face were etched too deep for a man so young.

"Did she also tell you that he died? My biological father?" Drew hugged himself, his elbows cradled in his hands.

"I know." Her voice was the same soothing tone their mother had used when they were children and they were sick or scared. "Drew, I know."

She waved the taxi driver away, and they went inside. His house was small but warm. The furniture appeared to have been bought secondhand—or maybe he'd rented the place already furnished.

He led her into a compact kitchen with yellowed Formica countertops and linoleum that was peeling up at the edges of the floor.

"You want coffee?" he asked her. "Or I've got tea. I could—"

"I don't need anything," she interrupted him. "I just needed to see you. To talk."

He'd greeted her so warmly, but now he appeared to be retreating into himself a little at a time. He leaned against the countertop with his long legs crossed, his arms folded over his chest, as though his very posture could lock her out, keep her silent.

"There are some things I have to tell you," she said. "Maybe we'd better sit down."

Once she'd laid out everything that had happened—Colin approaching her about the inheritance, their mother coming clean about Drew's parentage, and then Colin accompanying Julia to Salt Spring Island—Drew looked not just tired, as he had before, but stunned.

"You've got to be shitting me," he said.

Drew was sitting on the sofa in the small living room, and Julia sat perched on the edge of a chair beside him. She didn't say anything, because she didn't think he needed or wanted her to. For now, he just had to absorb what she'd told him.

"I don't … How could this even be happening?"

He raked his hands through hair that had the same thick, wavy texture as Julia's. It would have been impossible to tell that they weren't full siblings; apparently, their mother's genes were strong.

"I knew he was rich. Of course. Once Mom told me about him, I Googled him—I mean, who wouldn't? But he never tried to contact me all those years, so I just thought …"

"He sent money to Mom."

Drew just stared at her.

"He sent checks, regularly, for eighteen years," Julia went on. "But Mom just threw them away. She didn't want you to know about Redmond. Didn't want Dad to know."

He bent forward, elbows on his knees, and rubbed his eyes with his hands. "He cared, then. At least a little. So, I could have known him if Mom hadn't shut him down. I could have had him in my life all that time."

"That would have killed Dad," Julia said softly. "To know that you weren't his son, to know that you wanted a different father?"

"I didn't want a different father," Drew said sharply. "You know I loved Dad. And he's still my dad. He always will be. I just wish I'd had the truth."

She reached out and put a hand on his knee. "Of course you do."

"But it's not entirely her fault. You know? I've known about Redmond Delaney for three years now. I could have gotten in touch. I could have gone out to California. I could have…" He shrugged, to indicate the enormous potential of all of the things he could have done.

"But he died," Julia said.

"Yeah, he died. Just like Dad." Drew shook his head and gazed at the floor. "I told myself that I didn't want to contact him because he didn't want me. Didn't love me. Because he didn't try to see me for all those years. But the truth is, I was scared."

Julia watched him, watched all of the emotions play across his face, and her heart hurt for him. But this wasn't something she could help him with. This was something he had to go through alone. And that was why he'd come here, away from her, away from everything he'd known.

She noticed, of course, that they weren't talking about the money. She suspected that the subject was simply too shocking, too enormous, for Drew to process right now. But he would have to try, because she had to bring Colin here to see him.

"Colin Delaney—Redmond's nephew—needs to see you. To talk to you about the inheritance. Is it okay if I bring him out here? I know I shouldn't have let him come to the island with me without speaking to you first, but—"

His expression hardened. "Why did they send his nephew out here? Why didn't they send a letter, or a lawyer, or …"

"Colin is the family's lawyer."

"Colin? You're calling him by his first name? You're awfully friendly with the Delaneys now."

He was glaring at her, staring her down with accusation, and Julia didn't like it.

"We've been traveling together all day. It would have been odd to call him Mr. Delaney, don't you think?" She didn't care much for the defensiveness in her own voice, but she couldn't seem to help it.

"I just want to know whose side you're on here," he said, his gaze still hard.

"Whose *side*? I'm on the side of you getting your inheritance, Drew. I'd have thought that was clear."

He sighed and seemed to sag a little. "It is. I'm sorry. It's just … that family. Ignoring me all this time, like I didn't even exist …"

"They didn't know." Julia reached out and put a hand on his arm, and he tensed at her touch. "Drew, they didn't. They only found out when they read the will."

He let out a bitter laugh. "I'll bet they're thrilled to be handing over some of their fortune to their uncle's bastard son."

"Drew, don't." Julia scolded him in her big-sister voice. "Just talk to him. Talk to Colin. It's not like you couldn't use the money right now."

His eyes narrowed. "Right. Thanks for reminding me that I don't have a goddamned pot to piss in. That I need *charity*"—he spat out the word like some foul-tasting thing—"from some West Coast rich people who didn't want a goddamn thing to do with me until their dead uncle forced them to."

"Drew, that isn't—"

"I think you'd better go," he said.

She blinked at him. His tone and the way he was looking at her planted a hard pain in her gut. "You don't mean that."

"Yes, I do, Julia. I want you to go."

"I'm not going anywhere until we talk this out." She mimicked his stance—arms crossed over her chest, chin raised in stubborn defiance.

He stared at her a moment and then nodded. "Fine. Suit yourself."

He grabbed his coat from a hook by the front door and shook it on. Then he snatched up his car keys from a side table, went out the front door, and slammed it shut behind him. As she stood there in stunned silence, she heard his car start up and pull away.

She didn't move for a moment as tears stung her eyes. Then she pulled out her cell phone and called Colin.

"I need you to come and get me," she told him, and gave him the address.

Colin wanted to be angry at her for ditching him at the B&B, for leaving him feeling naïve and gullible while she went off to pursue her own agenda. But she looked so sad sitting there in the passenger seat of the rental car that he couldn't quite manage it.

"I'm sorry it didn't go well," he told her. "That must have been hard."

"Hard?" She was holding wadded-up tissues in her hands, her eyes red, her nose stuffy from crying. "My brother just tried to kick me out of his house, he and my mother have been lying to me for years, nobody in my family is talking to each other, and my father is dead! That's pretty freaking hard!" She honked into the tissues.

"Fair enough," he allowed as he navigated the car through the tree-lined roads of the island and back toward the B&B. After a while, he added, "You know, he's not really angry with you."

"Oh, shut up," she snapped. "You sound like Mike."

He shot her a glance. "Who's Mike?" Did Julia have a boyfriend? He knew she wasn't married, but was there a significant other? The thought troubled him more than he would have expected.

"He's … it doesn't matter."

"Your boyfriend?" Now that the thought was in his head, he found that he needed to know the answer.

"No. God. No. He's the general contractor I work with in

my landscape business."

"But … why does your general contractor have an opinion on your relationship with your brother?" It seemed like a logical enough question to Colin.

"Because!" She threw her hands up into the air, the tissues still clutched in her fists. "He's … You could say he's a friend. We give each other advice. We help each other out. We eat Cheetos."

"Cheetos," he repeated.

"Sometimes, yes. Or frozen pizza, when he doesn't burn it."

"Okay." Colin figured it would all make sense in time, if he didn't try to force it. Sometimes life was that way.

"But, yes. Mike says that none of this is about me. And I know that. I know it. And yet, I'm the one who just got rejected by my brother, aren't I?"

"Yes. Yes, you are."

"See?" She looked at him in triumph, as though all of her most basic points had just been proven.

He drove the rest of the way back to the B&B in silence, because that seemed like the best bet, given her volatile mood. Not that he blamed her for it, but still, it seemed like a good idea to let the storm dissipate somewhat before navigating his little boat back out onto her waters.

He parked the rental car on the street in front of the B&B. It was dark now, and the evening chill pressed against him as they stepped out of the car and into the street.

"Are you hungry?" he asked her as they both stood on the sidewalk in front of the inn. "If you're not, I get it. You're emotional, and sometimes—"

"I'm ravenous," she said. "I could eat everything they've got at one of those Las Vegas lobster buffets. Everything." She looked at him. "Even the silverware."

It wasn't the answer he'd expected, but it was one he could work with. He gestured toward a steak and seafood place a couple of doors down from the B&B. "Shall we, then?"

She looked at him, looked at the restaurant, and then stalked down the sidewalk ahead of him. "God, yes."

Chapter Twelve

He'd thought she was speaking in hyperbole when she'd said she could eat an entire Las Vegas buffet. But looking at her now as she attacked the surf 'n' turf special, he wondered if maybe she'd meant it literally.

"Why are you watching me eat?" she demanded as she buttered another dinner roll. With real butter, he noted, and plenty of it.

"I'm reevaluating what I know about women," he said. "The last woman I took out to dinner ate a small salad with no dressing. Then she said she was stuffed."

"She wanted to sleep with you." Julia pointed her butter knife in Colin's direction. "Women don't eat in front of men they want to sleep with. At least, not at first."

The revelation was both interesting and disappointing to Colin. Interesting, because it was a tidbit he might find handy in the future. Disappointing, because the zeal with which Julia was eating must therefore mean that his chances of sleeping with her were pretty much nonexistent.

Not that he wanted to. Except, he found that he *did* want to, more and more the longer he knew her. He silently scolded himself for the very thought. Trying to sleep with someone as plagued by emotional turmoil as Julia was right now would be unwise, to put it mildly.

"So, did she?" Julia asked, interrupting Colin's thoughts.

"Did she what?"

"Did she sleep with you? I kind of want to know now. Since the poor woman had to go without a meal to make it happen." She took another lusty bite of her roll.

"Ah ... no. I took her straight home after dinner. Peck on the cheek at the door."

"Ouch. The date must have sucked. In my experience, a peck on the cheek at the door is a man's way of saying, *Hey, let's do this again as soon as hell freezes over.*"

Julia was exactly right about how the date had gone and about what Colin had meant with the goodbye kiss. But it would have been ungentlemanly to say so.

"So, if a woman doesn't eat in front of a man she wants to sleep with ..." He trailed off and gestured toward Julia's plate, which looked like it had been attacked by a pack of starving wolverines. He knew he shouldn't be going there, shouldn't be raising the idea of the two of them together, but he couldn't seem to help himself.

She followed his gesture, looking down at her plate with confusion. Then she looked back at him questioningly, before understanding dawned in her eyes.

"I'm just saying, I guess this means I don't have a shot with you." He gave her an amused half grin that he had reason to believe was charming. At least, he hoped it was.

"Do you *want* to have a shot with me?" She looked vaguely stunned, as though his flirtations had come out of nowhere. But they hadn't; not really. Not after the hand-holding on the plane that had gone on long after she had stopped being afraid of a fiery death.

Had he just imagined something there?

He didn't think so. But now, considering the way she was looking at him in surprise, he wasn't so sure.

It was too much.

After all she'd been through that day, she didn't have the emotional energy to deal with getting hit on by an epically hot, spectacularly rich man whom she wasn't sure she could resist. It was too much pressure, too weighty with possibility. And there was too much potential for excitement and joy—and there was no way she could feel excitement and joy right now, with everything else that was going on.

"Would it be such a bad idea?" he said, in answer to a question she'd almost forgotten she'd asked.

Of course it would be. The idea of having what likely would be mind-blowing sex with a man who made her palms sweat, combined with the anguish of her family's implosion, would give Julia emotional whiplash on a scale she hadn't experienced since seventh grade, when Jason Atwood asked her out on the same day she woke up with a zit the size of a walnut on her forehead.

It would be too much pleasure and pain. Too much yin and yang. Just too much everything.

"For God's sake," she said. "I'm going to the bar for a drink." She slung her purse over her shoulder, picked up her coat, and then, as an afterthought, grabbed another roll from the basket on the table and took it with her as she stalked out of the dining room and to the bar.

It was possible that Colin had made a tactical error. He'd thought that getting his growing attraction to Julia out in the open would be a good thing—either she would be open to seeing what might happen between them, if anything, or she would shoot him down and he could move on. But his tentative inquiry had just seemed to piss her off, and now he was left alone at the dinner table with a decimated surf 'n' turf plate and his own sense of regret.

He called for the check, paid it, and then considered his options. Should he join her at the bar? Return to the B&B and leave her to walk the twenty yards back by herself?

Thinking about all he knew of Julia, an admittedly limited amount, he called the waiter back and ordered a dessert to go. When it arrived and he had paid, he carried the small, square, Styrofoam container to the bar and perched on a stool beside Julia.

By the time he got there, she was most of the way through a martini.

"Why did you have to do that?" she barked at him.

The look he gave her was all innocent surprise. "Do what?"

"Oh, you know what."

She must have been someone who didn't drink a lot, or who didn't usually drink hard alcohol; the martini had already softened her edges, made her a little looser, made her voice a little louder. Unless it was the stress she was under, which he had to acknowledge was considerable.

"Maybe I do, but enlighten me."

"Bringing up the thing about … you know …" She waved a hand vaguely. "*Sex*. Because that's really all I need right now. To think about you, and me, and what that would be like, when I was *already* thinking about you and me, and what that would be like. And I don't have time for that! I have to think about Drew." She shook her head. "God. Men." She said it as though men were the single greatest source of exasperation and sorrow in the female universe. Which, he supposed, they might be.

"You were already thinking about it?" he prompted her.

"That's not the point!" She took another slug of the martini, finishing it off, and then put the glass back down onto the bar with a slap.

He grinned—he couldn't help it. The idea that she'd been thinking about him, and as more than just the asshole who'd brought turmoil into her life, warmed him inside, and the smile just wasn't something he could suppress.

She was not like any other women he'd dated—not that he was dating her, although that thought was appealing.

He'd made his way through a number of women down in San Diego, mostly of the upscale, overly polished variety, the kind of women who wore a size two, got their hair expertly colored and deep-conditioned every six weeks, and worried about the grooming of personal areas that, in his opinion, did not require grooming.

Julia was different. She knew how to eat, for one thing, she dressed for comfort, and she had a natural glow about her that had nothing to do with expensive cosmetics or skin treatments. He didn't know her well—not yet—but she seemed to be just … herself. When had that trait in a person become a rarity? And was it a rarity among everyone, or just the people he seemed to socialize with these days?

Even as he asked himself the question, he knew the answer.

The Delaneys—the rest of them, anyway—were just themselves, always, and to hell with the consequences. But Colin had left that world behind when he'd gone to an Ivy League school, and when he'd settled in a city that valued appearances about as much as it valued waterfront property and a good fish taco. Part of him enjoyed his adopted environment—he liked expensive shoes and well-cut suits as well as anyone, and certainly more than any of the other Delaneys—but another part of him could see what he'd been missing, could see why his family shook their collective heads at his choices.

Julia raised her hand to order another drink from the bartender, and he remembered the dessert box in his hand.

"I brought you this." He put the box on the bar and shoved it toward her.

"What is it?" Her voice held a suspicious edge.

"Look."

She opened the box and peered inside. Her eyes widened.

"It's double chocolate lava cake. I didn't know if you liked chocolate, or if you had any food allergies or anything. I took a chance."

It was bad enough that Colin Delaney seemed to be offering Julia sex. But now he was also offering her chocolate, and that was just playing dirty. How was she supposed to stay strong and resist her animal impulses when he kept appealing to them so expertly?

"Damn it," she said. "Really, just … damn it. You're too much."

"Well …"

"And there's no fork."

He got up from his barstool, walked over to a server's station near the bar, and returned holding a clean fork aloft triumphantly. He handed the fork to Julia.

"I guess you might as well get another fork for yourself," she said grudgingly.

She'd thought to bury her sexual impulses in a grave made of molten chocolate. But it didn't quite work out that way, as sharing warm chocolate cake with Colin turned out to be nearly as sexual as actual naked fondling would have been.

"My God," she moaned as she slid a forkful of cake, dripping with chocolate sauce, into her mouth. She let out a low, throaty sound that was involuntary—and that was also a tactical error, apparently, since it caused him to stare at her with desire.

He hadn't had any alcohol that evening, but now he raised his hand to the bartender and indicated, with a flick of his finger, that he wanted one of what she was having, plus a fresh drink for Julia.

The bar wasn't busy, so it took only a moment for two fresh drinks to be placed in front of them. They both drank and ate until the martinis and the molten chocolate cake were gone.

She liked a good glass of wine in the evenings, but usually, that was it. She'd only ordered a martini because they looked good when people drank them in the movies. Now, she understood that people didn't drink them for the sophistication of the little olives on their little toothpicks inside the glass. They drank them to get drunk off their asses.

She wasn't quite drunk off her ass, but she definitely felt more effect than her usual glass of Chardonnay had ever managed to produce. She hadn't felt like this since college, when she'd mistakenly had some punch at a frat party because it had looked refreshing.

Live and learn.

When she got off her barstool so they could head back to the B&B, the room spun a little, so she had to grab onto the edge of the bar for purchase.

"Whoa, there," Colin said, taking her arm to steady her.

"Jeez. I don't usually drink martinis," she said as she stood still for a moment to steady herself.

"The travel and the stress probably also have something to do with it," he said. "It's been a hell of a day for you."

The reminder of just what she'd been through that day—of Drew's accusing look when he'd told her to get out of his house—made tears spring to her eyes without warning.

"Hey, hey," he told her. "Let's get you back to your room."

Chapter Thirteen

He'd walked her all the way back to the door of her room because it was the gentlemanly thing to do. She was woozy from the martinis and emotional from the events of her day, and he couldn't very well leave her to fend for herself in the unfamiliar wilds of British Columbia, could he?

But when they got to her room, when she had the key in her hand, she didn't just unlock the door and go inside, the way they both knew she should have. Instead, she turned to him, leaned back against the still-locked door—*sank* into it, really—and gazed up at him with sleepy, half-closed eyes.

He had it in mind to take the key from her hand and unlock the door for her, see her inside, and then go to his own room, where he would indulge in whatever harmless sexual fantasies presented themselves. But instead, God help him, he put one hand against the door on either side of her body and leaned in.

"I never answered your question," he murmured, his voice foggy with desire.

"Which question was that?" her own voice was a whisper.

"Whether I wanted to have a shot with you." He trailed one finger gently down her cheek. "Well … I do."

She let out a low moan. "Colin …"

Before she could finish whatever it was she was going to

say, he moved his mouth to hers and touched her lips briefly, softly, with his, before drawing her lower lip gently between his teeth.

A number of thoughts *whooshed* through his head. First was that he shouldn't get involved with someone who was so inextricably linked to his own family turmoil. Second was that his mother would deeply disapprove if he took advantage of a woman's overly enthusiastic alcohol consumption. And third wasn't a thought so much as a general buzz of excitement that rushed to his nether regions and urged him to ignore points one and two.

"Uh … Colin?" She pulled away from him reluctantly.

"Hmm?" His eyes were closed as he breathed in her scent and imagined what she would look like in bed amid rumpled white sheets.

"I'm maybe a little drunk, and I—"

"Let's go in your room. Or mine." He nuzzled her cheek lightly with his own and felt her let out a weighty breath.

He was just about to go in for another kiss when she put her palms against his chest and pushed him back a couple of inches.

"I can't," she said. "I mean, I want to … I *really* want to … but not like this. Not when I'm drunk and upset and—"

"Oh."

He opened his eyes, took a deep breath, and realized that he didn't like the way he was acting. She was right; she was a little bit drunk and a lot upset over everything that had happened that day. If he talked her into bed under these conditions, he'd feel like an asshole in the morning. More than that, he'd actually *be* an asshole.

"I get it," he said, clear-headed now. "I do. You're right; it's not a good idea."

He stood there as she put her key in the door, unlocked her room, and went inside. She gave him an apologetic look, then closed the door. He could hear the *snick* of the lock sliding into place.

He paused in the hallway to gather himself, then headed to his own room.

What had he been thinking? When had he become that guy? And, more importantly, what made him think he deserved a woman like Julia McCray?

Don't drink and dial, Julia told herself. *It never leads anywhere good.*

But she had to talk to someone about what had just happened, and it wasn't that late—not even ten p.m. She envied women who had girlfriends they could talk to, someone you could call when a hot guy made a move on you and you were kicking yourself for saying no. But since she didn't have that, she flopped down on the bed, cursed herself for what she was about to do, pulled up her contact information, and called Mike.

"What?" he barked at her. The greeting—if you could call it that—didn't put her off. It was standard Mike, and she was used to it.

"I … need your advice on that hotel project out by Springhill Park."

"You do." She could hear the skepticism in his voice.

"Yes. And … Colin Delaney hit on me."

"Who am I, Dear Abby?" Mike growled.

"That's pretty much who I need you to be right now, yes," she acknowledged.

He sighed his usual exasperated Mike sigh, but she knew that was just for show.

"So, this guy hit on you," he prompted her. "And?"

"And, I turned him down. Because I was kind of drunk, and him hitting on me was all tangled up in the feelings I was having about Drew, and it was all just too much."

"Sounds sensible." She'd heard the TV in the background, and now she heard him turn it off. "So, what's the issue?"

"The issue is, I didn't want to turn him down! I wanted to … to *not* turn him down! And now he's right across the hall, and I want to go over there, Mike! I really want to go over there and—"

"For God's sake, do *not* go over there," he said. "Because if you do, I'm going to have to hear for the next week about how you shouldn't have gone over there. And I've got to tell you, I'm not exactly comfortable hearing about the sex you had, or didn't have, or wish you'd had. Watch some TV or take a hot bath—women seem to like hot baths—or get yourself a piece of paper and a pencil and write *I will not screw my brother's cousin* a hundred times. Whatever it takes. But do not go over there."

"Okay." She nodded with fresh resolve. "Okay. But … what about the awkwardness? Tomorrow, I mean? I'm going to have to face him, and—"

He made a kind of *pfft* noise. "He's the one who got shot down like a mallard during hunting season. He's the one who's going to feel awkward. You've got the high ground."

She hadn't thought about it exactly that way. "Huh. You're right."

"Of course I'm right. Now get some sleep. And, Julia?"

"Yeah?"

"Do *not* go over there."

Colin lay on his bed in his room and wished Julia would change her mind and come over. She could just knock on his door, and then he could stop imagining what it would be like to be with her and find out for sure.

He was lying there looking at the ceiling, thinking about whether he'd acted like an ass, and whether *she* thought he'd acted like an ass, when his cell phone rang.

He wasn't surprised, even though it was a little late for a phone call. Various family members had been texting him all day to get an update on the Drew situation, but he'd ignored them. He hadn't had anything to tell them, anyway.

Now he checked the display on his phone: Liam.

Perfect. Liam, more than anyone else, had been hostile about the very idea of Drew McCray from the start. All Colin needed right now was another tirade about how their newly discovered cousin was a threat to their very livelihood.

Colin considered letting the call go to voice mail, but that would just delay the inevitable. He took the call.

"What the hell, Colin?" Liam opened the conversation with his usual good cheer. "I texted you three times today."

"I'm aware."

"Then why didn't you answer? You didn't want me to come with you on this, so the least you could do is keep me up to date."

Colin rubbed his eyes and sighed. "I've been pretty busy traveling to the middle of nowhere and tracking down our mystery cousin."

"The middle of nowhere?" Liam repeated. "What are you, about thirty miles from Victoria?"

"That's not the point," Colin said. He sat up on the bed. A conversation with Liam demanded that one be upright.

"Well, anyway, you're not busy now. Did you find him?"

"I found him." Colin got off of the bed and went to the little minibar in the corner of the room. A conversation with Liam also required scotch, if it was available. He hunted around amid the tiny bottles, and found that it was.

"Well? Are you going to tell me what the fuck happened?" Liam demanded.

Colin put the phone on speaker, set it down on the dresser, opened his tiny bottle of scotch, and poured the amber liquid into a glass he found on the nightstand. He picked up the phone and settled back onto the bed with his drink.

"Not much," Colin said. "I haven't talked to him yet."

"What? Why not? You said you found him." Liam's voice was accusing, as though he were personally offended by Colin's lack of progress.

"Yeah, well … it's a long story. His sister talked to him, and it didn't go well. He got pissed and walked out. I figure I'd better give it a day and then try again."

"His sister," Liam said.

"Yeah, his sister. Half sister."

"His sister is there with you? How the hell did that happen?" Colin had updated Liam on the fact that he'd met Julia, and that he had traveled to British Columbia to look for Drew. But somehow, he'd left out the detail that Julia had come on the trip with him. He wasn't sure why he hadn't wanted to tell Liam that part of it—probably a brotherly instinct that Liam would give him shit about it.

Which he did.

"She wouldn't tell me where he was unless I brought her along," Colin told him, and then braced himself.

"What? This isn't some kind of game. This isn't some … some vacation you're taking just for the hell of it. What is she playing at? And what were *you* thinking, going along with it? Goddamn it …"

"I was thinking that I wanted to find out where Drew McCray was without having to hire a damned detective," Colin said. He took a sip of the scotch, thinking he would need an economy-size barrel of the stuff if he stayed on the phone with Liam much longer.

"Well, if she saw him, you should have been right there with her. You shouldn't have let her go without you. You should have—"

"Give it a rest, Liam, would you? It's been a long day." He could have told Liam that Julia had sneaked out of the B&B to see Drew, and that's why he hadn't gone with her. But he knew Liam would hold his blunder over him for the rest of his life, and he didn't need to deal with that on top of everything else.

"Well … but you're seeing him tomorrow, right?" Liam demanded.

"I will if he hasn't fled town."

"Goddamn it, Colin …"

"I'll see him tomorrow, all right? I'm here to find this guy, and that's what I'm going to do. Maybe give me a little credit for some basic competence."

Liam was silent for a moment, a rare occurrence. "I never said—"

"Look. It's late, I'm tired, and I just got shot down by a woman, so if you could just can it, I'd really—"

"Oh, yeah?" Liam sounded interested now. "Who shot you down?"

Colin was silent, mentally kicking himself for letting it slip.

"Colin? Who shot you down?"

Silence.

"Ah, Christ. It's her, isn't it? The sister? I knew we shouldn't have let you—"

"Liam."

"For all we know, she's Redmond's kid, too. She could be your … what? Your half cousin."

"She's not."

"Well, even if she isn't, she's—"

"I'm hanging up now. Goodbye. And, Liam? Don't tell Mom."

He disconnected the call, thinking how absurd it was that, at his age, he was still asking his brother not to tell on him.

His phone beeped with a text message. Liam.

If you sleep with the sister, you bet your ass I'm telling Mom.

Colin smirked. Liam would do it, too. That alone was enough to keep him in his own room and away from Julia McCray.

Chapter Fourteen

The thing about turning a guy down for sex—especially when you really wanted to have sex with him—was that it was hard to know how to act when you saw him in the breakfast room the next morning.

While Julia was gathering up her coffee and her blueberry muffin in the little sun-filled dining room downstairs at the B&B, part of her hoped that Colin would happen to come downstairs at just that moment and join her, so they could continue with the sexual chemistry that had ignited the night before.

But part of her hoped that he wouldn't come in, hoped that he would have breakfast in his room or get something in town so there'd be no chance of early morning awkwardness. After all, she didn't know his state of mind. Was his pride injured? Would he do that defensive man thing, where any woman who said no was suddenly dead to him? Julia had come across that type before—she suspected every woman had—and it would make for rough going until this thing with Drew was sorted out.

She really hoped he wasn't that kind of man, because when she'd said *no* the night before, what she'd meant was, *not yet.* She'd wanted him last night, and she wanted him now. She just didn't want him when she was drunk and emotionally fragile.

If he couldn't understand that, she decided, then she didn't want him at all.

She finished her muffin and went back for a carton of yogurt, having pretty much decided that he wasn't coming. Maybe he was a late sleeper. Maybe he was on his laptop, already dealing with the many unfathomable demands of managing the Delaney wealth. Maybe he was such an early riser that he'd already come and gone.

Or, maybe he was avoiding her.

In any case, she was starting to relax as she finished her yogurt and then refilled her coffee mug. A handful of people were having breakfast around her, eating toast and Danishes and hard-boiled eggs in the cozy room with its hardwood floors, its lace curtains, and its smells of hot coffee and fresh baked goods. She could hear the murmur of conversation from an elderly couple at one table, and a mother and child at another.

Gradually, her tension eased. The B&B really was a pleasant little retreat, and the island was beautiful and serene. She wouldn't mind coming back here sometime under less fraught circumstances. Maybe in the spring.

She was just musing about the possibility of canoeing and hiking when a familiar form filled the doorway.

Julia wasn't sure whether to feel excitement to see him or intense discomfort after all that had passed between them the night before. So she just went right ahead and felt both.

Colin was wearing jeans and a blue sweater that was probably cashmere, layered over a white T-shirt that peeked through under his sweater's V-neck. His shoes looked expensive and inappropriate to the surroundings, as they always did. She wondered whether he even had any sneakers or hiking boots, or if he bought all of his footwear from designer boutiques.

He waggled his fingers at her in greeting, a shy smile on his face.

Not defensive, then, but a feeling a little awkward. Well, she could relate to that.

He came to her table and stood there with his hands stuffed in his pockets, waiting for an invitation—which she couldn't help thinking was pretty damned cute.

"Sit down," she said. He pulled out the dainty chair across from her and settled into it.

"Listen. About last night …" he began.

Julia wondered how many difficult early morning conversations, over the history of mankind, had begun just that way. Thousands, certainly. Millions. Perhaps billions.

She held up a hand to stop him. "I'm not going to make you have this conversation before you've even gotten your first cup of coffee. God knows what you might say. And anyway, it would just be cruel." She gave him a little half smile, and he grinned gratefully.

"Good point," he said. "Hold that thought."

She waited while he went to the buffet table, filled a mug, and doctored the coffee with milk and sugar.

When he was back, again seated across from her, he leaned closer so the others in the room wouldn't hear.

"Just to make it clear where I stand," he began, "I'm not sorry I hit on you last night. I hope to hit on you again sometime soon. But I am sorry that I did it when you'd had such a hard day, and when you'd had too much to drink, and when you were dealing with so much difficult stuff. I won't make another move if you don't want me to. But if you do want me to, I promise to work on my timing."

She felt a bloom of warmth in her chest. Maybe he wasn't feeling as shy and awkward as she'd thought.

"I rehearsed," he said, and a bubble of laughter escaped her lips.

"All right." She nodded, still grinning. "So you'll know where I stand, I do want you to make another move. Sometime. Just not while I'm so … stirred up about everything."

"Fair enough. It's good to be on the same page." He said it in his lawyer voice, the one he probably used when he was wrapping up a contract or a negotiation.

"Now," he continued, still in business mode. "Are we going back out there to see Drew together, or should I go alone?"

Of course they went together, because there was no way Julia was going to let him go out there alone, and there was no way Colin was going to let her give him the slip again.

They decided it was best not to call Drew first, because given his state of mind the day before, there was always the chance that he would take it as a warning and leave the house to avoid them.

Why anyone would want to avoid learning about an enormous inheritance, Colin didn't know. But he supposed the whole thing was so wrapped up in Drew's various emotions that it would be pointless to try to make logical sense of anything the man might do.

Colin and Julia were mostly quiet as they got into the rental car and drove amid the pines and ferns, and the occasional deer sprinting across the roadway, toward Drew's house on the south side of the island.

Colin could sense Julia's tension, and he wanted to give her space. Besides, his own feelings about meeting Drew McCray were complicated at best. Drew represented an entire life that Redmond had lived that neither Colin nor any of his family had known about. It had always seemed to Colin that Redmond was as steady and knowable a man as any could be. Everyone had a hidden emotional life, he knew that. But Colin had always believed Redmond to be a man of plain and simple values and integrity. To realize that Colin had never really known him at all seemed to tilt the earth on its axis.

Still, Colin had a mission, and he meant to achieve it. He was here to make sure justice was done, that a right was wronged. Drew McCray had been cut out of his rightful family for nearly thirty years. Colin meant to restore the man to the place where he belonged, no matter what upheaval that might set into motion.

When they arrived at the house, they parked the car and walked to the front door under a light drizzle of rain. The sky was a foreboding gray, and the cold pushed in against Colin despite the shelter of his overcoat.

Huddled under the cover of the front porch, they knocked on the door and got no answer. The place had the feel of being occupied, though. Drew's car was parked on a dirt patch of the lot, and they could hear the faint sounds of human activity from somewhere on the property.

"Let's try the workshop," Julia said, pointing to a large outbuilding behind the house.

Colin peered around the corner of the house at the big, rectangular building made of weathered wood. "Workshop?" It occurred to him that he didn't even know what Drew McCray did for a living. "What kind of workshop?"

"He builds boats," Julia said. "At least, he used to. In Montana. Custom fishing boats."

Colin's eyebrows rose. "There any money in that?"

"Not so far."

Colin began to head down the front porch steps, but Julia was trailing behind, hesitating.

"You okay?" he asked her.

She took a deep breath and shoved her hands into the

pockets of her down coat. "I will be," she said. "Let's go."

They found Drew in the workshop, a space heater blowing to make the room habitable, the shiny, gleaming sides of what would be a twenty-foot fishing boat perched atop a network of sawhorses in the center of the space. He was sanding the panels when they walked in, but now he turned off the sander, put it aside, and stood with his arms crossed over his chest as though he were preparing himself for a confrontation.

Which, Colin supposed, he was.

Colin approached Drew with his hand extended.

"Drew?" Colin kept his voice neutral, even pleasant. "I'm Colin Delaney. I'm here—"

"I know why you're here." Drew remained in his defensive pose and refused to take the hand Colin offered to him. "Julia told me."

Colin left the hand out there long enough for it to become intensely awkward for both of them. Finally, he let it fall.

Colin thought about trying to make icebreaking small talk—something about the boat, perhaps—but he knew he wouldn't be able to pull it off. A failed show of friendliness would just make things worse.

"Is there somewhere we can talk?" Colin said instead.

Chapter Fifteen

If Colin's mother had brought a stranger into her home, she'd have offered him coffee. Orin would have offered him a beer. Colin himself would have offered any visitor a choice of whatever beverages he had on hand. It wasn't about the drink itself, and it sure wasn't about hydration. It was about hospitality, a gesture that indicated the visitor was welcome in your home.

That was probably why Drew McCray didn't offer him anything—not even a seat.

Drew perched his butt on the edge of the sofa in the living room of his little house and left Colin and Julia standing there awkwardly. At least, Colin thought it was awkward. Julia, as Drew's older sister, simply scowled at the man as older sisters are known to do.

"Colin, please sit down," Julia said, throwing Drew a judgmental look out of the corner of her eye.

Colin nodded and sat in a chair facing Drew. Julia sat on the sofa a foot from Drew—where she could either comfort him or bring him into line as the situation warranted, Colin imagined.

With his wet overcoat draped over the side of his chair—Drew lacked even the social skills to offer to hang it up—Colin launched into the purpose of his visit.

"If you know why I'm here, then you know about the inheritance." Colin thought it best to start with the money—no one could remain cold and distant to someone who was offering them wealth beyond their greatest expectations. At least, he didn't see how they could.

Drew managed it.

"I don't want your money," he said.

"Drew, don't be stupid," Julia said. There was that big sister–little brother dynamic at play.

"I don't want it, Jules," Drew said, turning to her. "Redmond didn't acknowledge me while he was alive, so I don't want anything to do with his money or his family now. I can take care of myself. I don't need my so-called father's money."

"Because you've been doing a stellar job of taking care of yourself this far," Colin put in. It was a bold play, but, hell. The situation called for boldness.

"What did you tell him?" Drew demanded, glaring at Julia.

"She didn't have to tell me anything," Colin said. "When I showed up at her door, she thought I was a debt collector. That pretty much said it all."

The defiant look in Drew's eye changed into something that might have been shame.

"I've had some financial problems. Some setbacks. But I'll get back on my feet."

"Sure," Colin said. "It'd be quite a bit easier to get back on your feet if you had an inheritance to boost you up. Wouldn't it?"

"I don't want it." The steely, *screw you* glare was back, and something about it made Colin want to help Drew whether he was willing to accept that help or not. Because the glare had a story behind it, and Colin thought that story might have something to do with what it meant to be a man.

"I haven't even told you how much," Colin said.

That got through.

Drew's eyes narrowed. He didn't want to ask, Colin could see that clearly. But he couldn't help himself. Hell, who could?

"All right. How much?" A muscle in Drew's jaw ticked.

"I'll have to liquidate some assets, in accordance with Redmond's will. There's some real estate. And the shares in the family's corporation fluctuate in value according to the markets. But I can give you a ballpark figure." He named the figure.

Drew's face blanched.

"Holy fuck," he said.

Colin leaned back in his chair and folded his arms over his chest. "You still want to turn it down?"

Drew put a hand over his mouth, then rubbed at the stubble on his chin. "Holy fuck," he said again.

Julia looked as pale as her brother, as though she might topple off of her seat on the sofa. "I knew it was a lot, but … I didn't … Oh, my God."

Colin seemed to be the only one in the room still fully in charge of his faculties. The Delaney money wasn't news to him, and neither was the fact that the very concept of it was a lot to take in if you weren't used to it.

"Look," he said, leaning toward Drew with his elbows propped on his knees. "The money, the property, the shares—it's all yours. Redmond left it to you. If you don't want it, there's nothing that says you couldn't give it back. Or give it to someone else. Or donate it to charity. But you might want to sleep on it."

Drew seemed frozen in place. He didn't respond to what Colin was saying to him; he simply sat there, looking like he might suddenly puke on his area rug.

Colin stood. He retrieved a business card from his wallet

and placed it on the coffee table in front of Drew.

"When you recover the power of speech, you might want to give me a call. There's going to be a lot to think about, and I can help you." He put his coat on and shoved his hands into the pockets. "And for the record, if you think my family didn't want anything to do with you, that's just plain wrong. We didn't know about you. Redmond knew, and he didn't claim you, and that's on him. But the rest of the family had no idea you existed. If we had, we sure as hell would have wanted to know you. I still do."

Colin nodded at the card on the table.

"Think about it, and call."

He looked at Julia. "You ready?"

Julia, who still looked stunned, nodded. "Uh … yes. Yeah." She stood, grabbed her coat, and put it on.

They were about to leave when Julia stopped, rushed back to where Drew was sitting, and impulsively grabbed her brother into her arms. Drew clung to her and murmured something into her ear.

Colin turned away, not wanting to intrude on what was obviously a personal moment between them.

After a while, she released her brother, and she and Colin went back out into the light and steady rain.

Julia didn't speak on the way back to the B&B, and Colin didn't push it. The figure he'd named had effectively short-circuited her brain, Colin figured, and it would take a while to get the neurons firing again.

When they did, she'd have a lot to process. So would Drew.

Of course Drew was going to accept the inheritance, regardless of the show he'd made of being a self-sufficient man who could solve his own problems. He had his pride, but he wasn't crazy. At least, Colin didn't think he was.

But integrating Drew into the family financially was one thing, and it probably wasn't even the important thing.

Colin wanted to know him, even if the guy had pretty much acted like a dick so far. This was his cousin; this was Redmond's son. Colin wanted all of them—Drew and all of the Delaneys—to find a way forward as a family. Redmond had made that hard through his decades of silence. But that didn't mean it was impossible. That didn't mean it was too late to make amends.

When Colin and Julia arrived back at the B&B, Julia stood on the sidewalk in the rain, unmoving, as Colin headed toward the shelter of the inn.

"You coming?" he asked her.

She was silent for a moment, the gentle rain coming down on her, soaking her.

"Can I … Do you mind if I borrow the car?" she said. "I just … I need to be alone for a little while. To think."

Colin fished the keys out of his pocket and handed them to her.

"You're going back to talk to Drew," he said. It wasn't a question, and she didn't answer.

He placed the keys in the palm of her gloved hand.

"Let me know when you're ready to talk," he said, and walked up the front path and into the B&B.

When he got to his room and checked his phone, he had two text messages from Liam, one each from Ryan and Breanna, and three missed calls regarding the land deal in Palm Springs. Colin sighed, dropped his coat onto a chair, sat down on the bed, and prioritized everyone who was on his ass.

He thought about calling Liam, then decided he'd rather remove his own appendix. Instead, he called Ryan—the calmer, more rational brother. Ryan could relay the information to the rest of the family, thus saving Colin from having to deal with Liam's angry, blustery bullshit.

It was a good plan.

Ryan picked up on the second ring, and Colin gave him the short version: Drew had at first claimed that he wanted nothing to do with the Delaneys or their money, but had wavered when he'd heard the figure.

"Well, I can't say I blame him for being pissed," Ryan said. "If I suddenly found out Dad wasn't my father, I guess I'd have questions." Ryan's mild understatement made Colin smile.

"Yeah, I get that, too. He'll come around, though."

"I guess he will," Ryan agreed.

They chatted some about what Colin planned to do next, and how Ryan would pass the information along to the others. Colin asked after Breanna and the boys.

When all of that was dispensed with, Ryan said, "It's a hell of a thing. Redmond, I mean. I sure didn't see this coming."

"None of us did," Colin said.

"Why do you suppose he thought he couldn't tell us?" Ryan asked the question that had been on Colin's mind, and likely on everyone else's, too.

"Hell, I wish I knew," Colin said.

And now, with Redmond gone, he probably never would.

Chapter Sixteen

When Julia arrived back at Drew's place, the house was empty and she could hear the sounds of the power sander coming from the workshop. She followed the dirt path from the house to the big outbuilding and stood in the open door, watching him.

She hadn't noticed it before, but she could see the Delaney in him now. The shape of Colin's jaw was repeated in Drew, the angle of his nose. There was something around the eyes, too. She hadn't wanted to believe that any of this was true, but now, she could see that it was.

Drew was hunched over one of the side panels of the boat he was building, working the sander, his focus on his work so complete that he didn't see Julia standing there.

When he turned off the sander and ran his hand over the wood, she said, "Drew?"

He looked up, and didn't answer for a moment.

"What are you doing back here?" His tone was mild, without the contempt she'd worried she might hear.

"I wanted to see if you're okay." She walked into the room, her shoes crunching on a fine layer of sawdust.

He shrugged. "I ought to be, I guess. I'm a multimillionaire."

"The debt Tessa left you, the stress of that—it's all over," she said.

"I guess." He shrugged again, as though none of it mattered, as though inheriting an immense sum was just one irritating detail in an otherwise routine day.

"You've had a few years to absorb the news about who your father was," Julia said. She hugged herself for solace, if not for warmth, since the space was comfortable enough with the heater Drew had running. "But this is all still hitting me." She shook her head. "God."

He avoided looking at her and busied himself around the workshop while he spoke—putting away the sander, fiddling with rags and tools.

"It's been hard enough having to adjust to the fact that I'm some cattle tycoon's bastard," he said. He grabbed a broom and began sweeping up sawdust from the floor. "But this? When I read the news that Redmond had died, I thought, fine. I missed my chance to talk to him, to meet him, but that was okay, because he didn't care about me anyway. He didn't care if I was alive or dead, so what did it matter?" He paused in his sweeping and looked at Julia, the broom in his hands. "But now, with the money …"

"He did care," she said. "He did."

He nodded slowly. "I guess he must have. Enough to give me his money. Enough to let everybody know I was his."

He began sweeping again. He looked at the floor, not at Julia, but his voice was fierce. "If he cared, then why the hell didn't he find me? Why didn't he get in touch with me, when we still could've …" His voice trailed off, and he shook his head. "Ah, hell. I don't know what we could've done. Dad was my dad, you know?"

"Yes." Julia could feel the emotion welling up inside her. "If you'd had a relationship with Redmond, it would have hurt Dad. And I know you wouldn't have wanted that."

"Mom didn't mind hurting Dad though, huh?" The bitterness in Drew's voice cut through her.

"Why didn't you tell me what was going on between you and Mom? For three years, you just let me wonder."

"How could I tell you, Jules? How could I tell you that Mom cheated on Dad, that she … I wanted to protect you from it."

"You didn't protect me from anything. I didn't know why our family fell apart, but I knew it did. Maybe I could have helped you. Maybe I could have been there for you."

He didn't respond to her, and the room was silent except for the sound of the gentle rain falling on the roof.

"Did all of this have anything to do with your divorce?" she asked finally.

He let out a bitter laugh. "I guess you could say that, yeah. I was angry—angry about all of it. I was pissed off pretty much all the time. She got tired of dealing with it, I guess. I don't really blame her."

"That's why you just let her do it. The money, the credit cards. You could have hired a lawyer, but you didn't."

"Yeah, well." He propped up the broom in a corner of the room. "I figure she deserved something, after all I put her through."

She went to him and put a hand on his arm. "You deserve something, too. Take the inheritance, Drew."

"Yeah. I don't suppose I'm going to turn down money like that, am I?"

"And …"

"What?"

"I think you should go out there. To California. You should

meet the Delaneys."

"Ah, Jesus. Julia—"

"They're your family."

He moved away from her touch, his face hard. "You're my family. Not them."

"They didn't know, Drew. They didn't know about you. Colin—"

"You seem like you two are kind of close. What the hell is that about?"

He was changing the subject, and she couldn't let him. She needed to get him to face what was happening, to deal with all of it instead of turning away like he had been. Instead of running off and hiding with his anger and his boats.

"You need to meet them. For better or worse. Whatever happens, at least you'll have your questions answered."

For all of the show he was putting on, despite the brooding, she knew her little brother, and she knew he was scared.

"I could come with you," she said. "If you need a friendly face."

"I just … It's a lot to process. I need to think. I need to … let it soak in."

"Of course you do." Her voice was soothing.

She pulled him into her arms. He was stiff at first, refusing to accept the comfort she was offering. Then he relaxed and wrapped his arms around her.

"I don't know what to do, Jules."

"We'll figure it out," she told him. She stood there with the rain on the roof and the sweet smell of sawdust surrounding her, and savored having her brother back, if only for the moment. "Don't worry, Drew. I'll help you. We'll figure it out."

Once she left him, she didn't know what to do next. She

felt restless, unsettled. Usually, when something was bothering her, she liked to talk it out with someone—most often, Mike. But this time, she found herself wanting to be silent, to be alone, to work out everything within her own mind before opening up to anyone else.

The rain eased to a light mist, so she followed the signs for Cusheon Lake, parked at the side of the road, and walked a short distance to a small public dock jutting out over the water. She sat down on the dock, the dampness from the wet wood seeping through her jeans, and dangled her boot-clad feet out above the calm surface of the lake. She listened to the sounds of water dripping from bare tree branches, someone having a conversation on the other side of the lake, something rustling around in the brush at the water's edge.

She pulled her coat around her against the cold.

She knew she'd been right—Drew needed to go to California to meet the Delaneys. He needed to face them, face the family he'd never known, whatever that might bring. But what if they were cold, suspicious, even hostile of this newcomer who'd be taking on a large chunk of what they might consider rightly theirs? What if they shut him out, or even put up a legal fight to prevent him from inheriting? Colin seemed to have a genuine desire to see Drew get what was his. But what if the rest of the Delaneys didn't feel the same way?

What if she was urging her brother to go into a situation that would confirm all of his worst assumptions about his biological family? What kind of damage might that do?

She knew it was a chance he needed to take, though. He had to know. Though it wasn't her life, and it wasn't her call, she felt certain that he wouldn't begin to heal until he ripped off the Band-Aid and faced them.

And she meant what she'd said about going with him. He

didn't have Tessa now, didn't have someone who could hold his hand while he rode out the emotional upheaval the journey was certain to bring. So, she would do it for him. She would hold his hand. She would be his advocate, someone who would be on his side no matter what happened.

After a while, when she was wet and cold and when the silence of the lake had settled her mind a little, she got back up and walked to the car. She was ready to do whatever had to be done.

But first, she had to talk to Colin.

When Julia got back to the B&B, she saw no sign of him. She knocked on the door to his room, but got no answer. She was chilled from the wet weather, so she went to her room, stripped off her cold, damp clothes, took a hot shower, and then dressed in warm, dry jeans and a cotton sweater. When she was dressed and had pulled her hair up into a messy bun, she ventured out of her room and downstairs to the breakfast area, where the food from the morning had been cleared away but there were still urns of coffee and hot water for tea.

She made herself a cup of strong coffee with cream and sugar, wrapped her hands around the white ceramic mug for warmth, and then settled into an overstuffed chair in the downstairs sitting room to wait for Colin. He couldn't have gone far, she reasoned, since she'd had their only car.

He came in the front door about fifteen minutes later dressed in sweatpants, a hoodie, and running shoes, breathing fast, his hair damp from the light rain and from exertion.

She couldn't have said what it was, exactly, but something about seeing him all casual, tousled and sweaty—a sharp change from the lawyer persona he usually presented—left her momentarily speechless. For a split second she wondered what it would be like to kiss him right now, while he was breathless and tasting of salt and rain.

She silently chastised herself and shoved the thought away.

"You run?" she said, because it seemed like a better opening than licking him.

"Yeah, usually." He ran a hand through his wet hair. "I've been missing it lately because of everything that's been going on. The travel, and Drew, and … But I had some time today, since you were out, so …"

He was rambling. It was cute that he was rambling.

"We need to talk," she said as he stood in front of her, dripping on the floral rug.

"All right." He nodded. "I'll just run up and shower. I'll see you back here in ten." He jogged up the stairs—old, wooden stairs that creaked under his weight. She watched him go and thought about kissing him again.

Get a grip on yourself, Julia.

She took a deep breath and focused on her coffee. Coffee was always safe.

When he came down, all freshly showered and smelling of soap and some light, spicy aftershave, he already knew what she'd wanted to tell him.

He went to the coffee urn, poured himself a cup, and returned with it to sit in the chair beside her in the downstairs parlor.

"Drew wants to come to California," he said. "He left a message on my cell phone."

"That's what I wanted to talk to you about," Julia told him.

A fire was crackling in the fireplace, and the room was cozy and warm. The innkeeper was fussing around with the coffee urn in the next room, and they could see her through the open doorway refilling the sugar container and putting out fresh mugs.

"I'm surprised he wants to come," Colin said. "Glad, though. Everybody's got a lot of questions, on both sides. It'd be good to get them answered, as much as we can with Redmond gone."

"I'm coming with him," she said.

Colin gave her an appraising look, as though he were evaluating all of the many reasons she might want to follow Drew out to Cambria and the Delaney Ranch.

She told herself she didn't have a reason other than wanting to protect her brother. But even as she thought it, she knew it was utter crap. This thing with Colin was like a drop of clean, refreshing water amid her long drought with men. What might happen if she chose to immerse herself completely, to dive in for a deep, satisfying swim?

She wasn't going out there for him. She was doing it for Drew.

But in the process of supporting Drew, she might get a few of her own questions answered—questions about Colin Delaney, and what lay underneath his smooth and very appealing exterior.

If a trip to California turned out to be a multipurpose deal, would that be so bad?

"He mentioned in the voice mail message that you might," Colin said, the barest hint of a grin on his freshly shaved face. "Well, we've already traveled together, so we know what that's like."

"I've never been to Cambria," she said.

"You're going to love it." Colin nodded with certainty. "And your brother's about to own a big chunk of it, so there's that."

The words hit Julia hard as she worked to adjust to this new reality.

"Well, I guess it would be good to see it, then."

Julia felt fortunate that all of this was happening at a time when she didn't have to be at work on a job site. That was the thing about the winter season for a landscape designer; whatever you had to do, you could do on paper. The hands-on work wouldn't start until the snow melted in Montana and the ground thawed, so she had a certain amount of freedom to go traipsing around, hunting down her brother in Canada and then following him to California.

Once she'd made the decision to go, she called Mike and asked him to check her mail, make sure her pipes hadn't burst, and otherwise take an occasional peek at her place until she came back.

"This isn't your deal, Julia," he grumbled at her. "It's Drew's. I get that you want to help him out, be there for him and all that. Just … try to keep some distance. Don't get too caught up in it."

"What are you now, some kind of self-help guru?"

"Don't be a smartass," he said.

She was packing her suitcase as she talked to him on her cell phone, tucking her toiletries into the front compartment. "Sorry. I know you're right. But I can't help worrying about him."

"You're his sister, not his mom," Mike said.

"Yeah, because look how well Mom has handled things so far," she added dryly. "And anyway, it's not just about protecting him. This whole thing … it's just so *intriguing*."

"I'll give you that," he said. "It's not every day you find out your father isn't your father, and your real father is a millionaire."

"Billionaire," Julia corrected him. "Drew's inheritance won't be as much as that. There's money tied up in the family's corporation, and there are inheritance taxes, and a big chunk is going to charity …"

"But it's a shit ton," Mike finished for her.

"Yeah. It's a shit ton."

"Intriguing," he said.

Chapter Seventeen

Colin arrived back in Cambria ahead of the McCrays. Drew had to wrap up some things at home before making the trip, and Julia wanted to travel with her brother. That gave Colin a chance to have a family meeting prior to Drew's arrival.

He picked his car up at the San Jose airport, where he'd left it when he'd caught his flight to Montana, made the long drive down to Cambria, and got checked in at the lodge. He knew his family would grouse at him—again—for choosing the lodge over the family home, but he did it anyway.

Even he wasn't sure why he was so stubborn on that point. There was plenty of room at the ranch, God knew. And he loved his family—there wasn't a single one of them he wouldn't have taken a bullet for. But being under their roof always made him feel itchy in his own skin in a way he couldn't put his finger on.

He was one hundred percent Delaney, but he had never quite fit in.

Part of it was the asthma.

When he was a kid, he'd had asthma severe enough to land him in the hospital more than once. It was triggered by allergens, mostly—something a ranch, with the hay and the animals and the infinite species of plants and other living things—had plenty of. So, while his brothers and Breanna were out riding, or helping to tend the cattle, or doing one of the million other things Colin couldn't do because his parents were afraid it might kill him, Colin was back at the house, feeling *other* in a way that never quite wore off, even when the asthma receded from a major threat to a minor annoyance.

So, yeah. That was one part of it. The other part of it, he supposed, had to do with Harvard.

Colin had excelled in high school in a way that none of his siblings ever had. Ryan and Breanna both had gotten solid grades, but nothing extraordinary. Liam had barely scraped by, preferring to work the ranch and hang out with his friends instead of studying.

But Colin had taken to schoolwork as though he'd been born doing it. Straight As, academic awards, student government. He'd been a National Merit Scholar, and he'd gotten a near perfect score on his SATs. So when it came time to apply to colleges, he'd set the bar high.

Orin and Sandra had been dismayed by their youngest son's desire to attend an Ivy League school. Despite their wealth, they were deeply down-to-earth people, and the pretentious lifestyle Harvard represented to them felt so foreign that he might as well have been asking to go to school on Mars. He'd wanted it badly, though, so when he got accepted, they'd reluctantly relented and sent him.

At least some of their fears came true. Colin had come home from the East Coast with a Harvard Law degree and a fondness for designer suits, cocktail parties, and socializing with the children of aristocrats and business titans.

He'd never looked down on his own family, had never felt for a moment that he was in any way superior to them because of his educational experiences. But when he'd come back, he'd felt a distinct chill from Liam, who probably felt judged for his relative lack of achievement, and disdain from Sandra, who simply couldn't relate to this newly upper-crust sophisticate she'd given birth to.

He knew they thought he was judging them, but that was ironic; he was the one being judged and who had come up lacking, in their estimation. And why? Just because he wasn't the salt-of-the-earth man of the land that his father, his uncle, and his brothers were? Just because he was interested in things they weren't? Since when had that become a crime?

He'd reacted to all of it by keeping his distance—which had only confirmed their suspicions that he had somehow become too good for them. It was a vicious cycle, and he didn't know how to get out of it.

The simple fact was that his family's world was different than his own, and while that should have been okay with everyone involved, somehow it wasn't.

When Colin had moved to San Diego, his mother, in particular, had taken that as a personal affront, as though Colin had done it to hurt her, or because he didn't love her enough to stay in Cambria. Or, because small-town life wasn't good enough for him.

He'd told his family that he had to leave because he needed to work at a major firm in order to properly launch his career. What would he do in Cambria? Open a storefront law office to handle people's wills and their lawsuits over their petty disputes with their neighbors?

His mother had responded that there would be plenty of work for him handling the Delaney holdings. The family's real estate interests were so vast and far-reaching that managing their legal concerns could easily be a full-time job.

That was true, of course, but he'd gone anyway.

He'd spent a few years at a big firm, learning how to practice law in the real world and not just in theory, and then had quit to work full time for his family. But he still hadn't returned to Cambria.

He'd stayed away because he'd needed to figure out his place in the world. He knew who he wasn't; he'd needed to get some distance to figure out who he was.

But the longer he stayed away, the more his mother seemed to resent him for it. The more he felt that resentment, the more he needed to stay away.

So, it would be the lodge instead of the ranch; that way, he wouldn't have to feel the weight of his mother's disapproving gaze any longer than he absolutely had to.

Once he'd checked in, unpacked, and gotten himself settled, he braced himself and drove out to the ranch.

It had rained on the day of Redmond's funeral, and it had rained on Salt Spring Island. In Montana, he'd had to deal with the snow.

But now, in Cambria, the world was green and lush, and the sky was a clear blue that seemed almost impossibly brilliant. The rolling hills were covered in waist-high grass the color of emeralds, and the pines towered above him. As he drove north toward the ranch, the calm, blue ocean spread out to his left into eternity.

While it was true that he'd chosen to leave, the awe this place inspired in him had never stopped. He'd never stopped feeling the magic.

He turned right onto the road that led to the ranch, and prepared himself for all that was to come.

It had only been a week or so since Redmond's funeral, and Liam hadn't left Cambria yet because he'd wanted to be with the family while this business of the will was being cleared up. So, the full complement of Delaneys—minus his nephews, Michael and Lucas, who were watching a movie upstairs—was gathered in the family room of the ranch house when he arrived.

They didn't mob him for information all at once, because their mother had taught them better manners than that. Instead, they exchanged small talk and inquired about his trip, and Ryan brought him a beer in a bottle sweating with cold.

When that was done and they were all settled in on the same sofas and chairs that had been there since Colin was a child, they launched into it.

"He's coming here," Colin announced. "Drew McCray. He wants to meet everyone, talk this out. His sister is coming with him."

A muscle clenched in Orin's jaw. "When?"

"A day or two, probably. Drew had some things to wrap up at home before he could make the trip."

"I don't recall him being invited," Liam snapped.

"Oh, he doesn't need to be invited, and you know it," Sandra scolded him. "He's family, no matter how it happened."

"Doesn't mean I have to like it," Liam said.

Of course Liam was the hard one. He always had been, in so many ways, about so many things. But this time, Colin found it especially predictable.

Liam, of all of the Delaney children, had been the one closest to Redmond. Their uncle had never had any children—at least, none they'd known about—and he'd treated Liam like his son. A lesser man than Orin might have been threatened by that, but Orin was not a lesser man. And so Liam had been particularly hard-hit by Redmond's death.

Colin supposed that Drew, Redmond's actual, blood progeny, presented a threat to Liam in a way that none of them fully understood. Things might get sticky when it was time for the two of them to meet.

"What's he like?" Gen, Ryan's wife, wanted to know. Colin imagined that she was attempting to get the conversation on safer, more stable ground.

"He's shocked about the inheritance," Colin said. "He's angry that his mother lied to him all these years."

"Well, I guess he would be," Ryan said.

"There's going to be a certain … resistance," Colin said. "At first, he didn't want anything to do with any of us."

"Well, if that's how he feels, then he can just—"

"Liam. That's enough," Orin interrupted him. Orin was a quiet man, who'd mostly left the control of his children to his wife. So when he corrected Liam, when he asserted himself with authority in his voice, they all stopped and listened.

"Of course he's angry. Of course he's shocked and he doesn't know what to think," Orin went on. "You'd feel that way too, I expect," he said to Liam. "This young man is Redmond's son, and we're going to welcome him into our home. And if he's a little testy with us, well, we're all going to have a little patience, a little compassion. That includes you." He glared at his son.

"Yes, sir," Liam uttered, his face grim and as hard as stone.

"Well, that's that, then," Sandra announced. "I'll make up the spare bedroom here. Gen, you suppose one of them can stay with you and Ry?"

"Of course," Gen said. She and Ryan had a big, new house they'd built on the ranch property when they'd gotten married, and they'd included plenty of rooms for the children they might have one day.

The ranch had a nice little guest house down by the creek, but Gen, an art dealer, had been using it to host visiting artists.

At the moment, she had some guy in there who painted portraits of himself. That was all—just himself. Himself as a man, himself as a woman, himself as a dog, and an angel, and as Christ. Colin supposed that said something about the basic emotional makeup of artists, though he wasn't sure what.

"We can put Drew in Colin's room," Ryan observed dryly, "since he's not using it."

And there it was—the inevitable jab at him for not staying at the ranch.

"Just because he's coming here to meet us doesn't mean he has to stay here," Liam said, still determined to be pissy about the whole Drew situation.

"He might not want to," Colin observed. "Might be more comfortable at a B&B, given the circumstances."

"Well, I'm sure you'd understand that way of thinking better than I do," Sandra groused.

Colin was sure she was right.

When the family meeting was over, Liam caught up with Colin out on the porch while Colin was finishing his beer and looking out over the hills toward the ocean.

"So, the sister's coming, huh?" Liam was trying to make his voice sound casual, but he'd never had much luck with that particular skill.

Colin looked at him, already feeling defensive. "Yeah, she is. So?"

"So," Liam said, pointing his own beer bottle at Colin and dropping the casual act, which had been a farce to begin with, "that's a car wreck waiting to happen. And you know it."

"Ah, shut up, Liam, would you?" Colin turned his back on his brother and faced the glorious landscape instead.

Liam, unfazed by having been told to shut up, continued

undaunted. "You told me yourself you made a move on her, so don't pretend there's nothing going on there."

"Yeah, yeah. I made a move, and I crashed and burned. So you can stop worrying about it."

"She might not want to go there, but you do."

"Maybe. So what?"

"Colin." Liam waited until Colin turned to look at him, and then he fixed his brother with the same glare he probably used on errant ranch hands in Montana. The one that said you'd better get your shit together or you'd be on a Greyhound bus to go live in your mother's basement by sunset. "Do not do this. She is that guy's sister."

"You can stop calling him 'that guy' any time now," Colin observed mildly. "He does have a name."

"She's that guy's goddamned sister," Liam went on, "and so she's caught up in this. The last thing our family needs is for this whole thing to get even messier than it already is. If you sleep with her, Colin, I swear to God …"

"What? You swear what?" Colin was puffing up now, like some kind of pack animal trying to appear bigger to the alpha male to avoid getting attacked. Which, when he thought about it, was exactly what he was.

"I swear to God I'll kick your ass, is what." Liam's face had reddened slightly, his brows drawn together like he was Clint Eastwood asking Colin whether he felt lucky.

"Says the guy who hasn't been laid in, what, two years? Just because you're living like a damned monk doesn't mean I have to."

The remark could have set Liam off, could have pushed him over the edge from belligerent to outright hostile. But instead, it seemed to have the opposite effect, and Liam deflated slightly. He stepped up next to Colin at the porch railing and leaned his forearms on the wood.

"Jesus, it really has been a long time," he admitted.

Colin slapped him on the back, brotherly order restored. "That's your own fault, you know."

"Yeah. Yeah, I know it."

Liam had caught his girlfriend cheating on him with one of the ranch hands two years before, and it was as though all of the air had leaked out of his balloon. He'd always had a hot temper, but now Liam seemed angry most of the time. And he hadn't been willing to take a chance on women again—a situation that just increased his overall irritability.

"If Julia and I were to get together," Colin said, "it wouldn't be just about sex. I like her. I like her a lot."

Liam shook his head sadly. "You're a shithead, you know that?"

"I believe I've heard that before," Colin remarked.

Chapter Eighteen

Julia was nervous as she drove the rental car south from the San Jose airport toward Cambria. She wasn't sure why, since she wasn't one of the principal parties in this situation and was only coming along to give her brother moral support. Still, there was no denying that she felt an unpleasant ache in her belly at the thought of how all this might go. Drew, in the passenger seat, was silent, his face grim.

"We should be happy," Julia observed as they made their way down Highway 101 past Salinas, acres of farmland stretching out into the distance. "You're inheriting a fortune. I mean, everybody dreams about that happening, but it never does. Except this time, it did. It actually did. And look at us. We're acting like we're heading off to have surgery without anesthesia."

"You're rambling, Jules," Drew said.

"I know. I know it. But I'm nervous, and usually I'd deal with that by eating a bunch of junk food, but I'm driving, and I don't have any junk food."

Shut up, Julia, she chastised herself. *Just shut the hell up.*

If she were being honest with herself, she'd have to admit that she wasn't just nervous for Drew's sake. That was part of it, of course. But this situation was layered with multiple reasons to be nervous.

It didn't escape her notice, for example, that she would be meeting the family of a man she was intensely attracted to. Usually, that happened after you were dating the person for a while, probably after you'd slept together, sometimes after you had agreed to get married. But Julia and Colin had done none of those things. They hadn't slept together, they weren't dating, and they certainly weren't engaged. Added to that, they were almost related in a tangential, convoluted way.

Meeting his family was throwing off the natural order of things. It was crossing some sort of finish line before the race even began, putting the cart before the proverbial horse. She would feel pressure for them to like her, but how could they like her when she—through Drew—represented a threat to their family fortune? That was how they would see her, anyway, almost certainly. As a threat. And that didn't bode well for them accepting her as Colin's potential girlfriend or lover … or something.

Plus, what if they did accept her as one or more of those things, and then she decided she didn't want to be that? That she didn't even want to pursue this thing with Colin, whatever it turned out to be?

But if she hadn't decided to come, if she'd just left Drew on his own to deal with the complexities of his newly discovered family, then she might never see Colin again, and that wasn't an appealing thought.

It was all so complicated.

Those were the thoughts running through her head when Drew said, "We should have gotten a hotel. Staying at their house? With them?" He shook his head. "It's weird, Jules. It just … it feels weird."

"They were very insistent on the phone," she said. Julia had been the one to broker the terms of the visit, and when she'd spoken to Sandra Delaney, the matter of their accommodations had seemed non-negotiable. Also, there was the fact that Drew was broke. He hadn't received any part of his inheritance yet, and until he did, he couldn't afford a hotel, even one of the cheap, older motels situated away from the beach, on Cambria's Main Street.

"I don't give a damn what they were insistent about," Drew grumbled.

"I got the idea that it would hurt their feelings if we don't stay with them. And you don't want to start this whole thing with hurt feelings." She glanced sideways at him as she drove. "Besides yours, I mean."

He scowled. "My feelings are just fine."

"Sure," she said.

He was quiet after that for a long time.

Eventually, Julia maneuvered the rental car down through Paso Robles, onto Route 46 with its breathtaking vistas of green hills and majestic vineyards, and up Highway 1 past the town of Cambria.

"I think this is the turnoff," Drew said.

She drove along a winding road that went through the hills until they arrived at a big farmhouse that looked like it had been built in the 1950s. The rambling two-story house had white siding, a wrap-around porch, a roof that came to a sharp peak with dormer windows emerging on either side, and dark brown shutters framing the windows. The building was exactly what Julia had imagined, from the time of her childhood, whenever someone said the word *farmhouse.* Off in the distance, down a wide dirt road, stood a hulking red barn, and beyond that, countless acres of pasture.

"Well, I guess this is it," Drew said, in the same tone he might have used if he were bidding Julia goodbye on his way to a long prison stretch.

"They're your family," Julia said. "And they didn't reject you; they just didn't know about you. Try to remember that."

Inside, the house wasn't what Julia had expected. Knowing that the family was shockingly rich, she'd expected a certain … *grandeur.* Instead, she found old, worn furniture that had probably been purchased thirty years before; wood floors that were slightly uneven and bore the marks of innumerable feet; a large stone fireplace with a fire burning merrily within; and, when Sandra ushered them into the kitchen, old linoleum floors and countertops that were slightly cracked at the corners.

That kitchen was where Sandra had brought them shortly after opening the front door. "You must be Drew," she'd said, looking him over with her hands on her hips. "And you're Julia. I'm Sandra—Colin's my son. Well, one of them, anyway. Come on in and get something hot to drink." Then she'd turned and walked toward the kitchen without waiting to see whether they would follow.

Sandra Delaney wasn't what Julia had expected, either. She was short and trim, with a wiry build that spoke of years of hard work. She looked to be somewhere between fifty-five and sixty, with hair that had been brown but was now turning to gray. Her hair was in a ponytail, and she was wearing a San Francisco 49ers jersey and faded jeans. Her feet were encased in a pair of fuzzy, pink slippers.

"I've got some coffee on," Sandra said. "If you want tea, I guess I can make some, but you'll have to wait while the water boils."

Julia couldn't quite tell whether the woman was no-nonsense by nature, or if she was irritated by their presence. She decided there was no benefit in assuming the latter, so she went with the former.

Once they were settled in the kitchen, Sandra peered at Drew, who was standing awkwardly beside the big farm table at the center of the room, and shook her head slowly. "I can see it, right near the eyes. And around the chin, too. Well, I guess you really are Redmond's boy."

"I'm Andrew McCray's boy, ma'am." Drew's face looked pinched and angry, though his voice was amiable enough.

"By God, I guess you are," Sandra agreed. "Seems like Redmond didn't do a damned thing for you. Sent some checks that your mother was too proud or too scared to take. Like a boy gives two shits from a rat's ass about the money. A boy needs a father, not a damned check. It's a good thing Andrew McCray was there for you when Redmond wasn't." She nodded crisply, her speech concluded. "Enough of that business. What do you take in your coffee? Seems to me a real man takes it black, but there's no accounting for how you were raised."

Julia couldn't help being charmed by Sandra. The woman was blunt, hard, and in what appeared to be a perpetual ill humor. But beneath that was an honesty and an intelligence that Julia had to admire. She could see that Drew was being won over, too. He'd started out defensive and ready for a fight when he'd come into the room, but Julia could see him gradually relaxing, his shoulders coming down a little at a time from the tense, defensive posture they'd assumed somewhere up around his ears.

She talked a little about Redmond and about the ranch, and the way they lived here. In turn, Drew talked some about himself, his and Julia's childhoods, his parents.

He didn't touch on his financial difficulties—it probably seemed prudent not to—and Sandra didn't ask, though she'd almost certainly heard about some of it from Colin. It seemed to Julia that not asking about it was a kindness that came from some innate understanding of where Drew was emotionally at that moment. It made Julia love Sandra, just a little.

They'd been talking for about twenty minutes and were into a second cup of coffee when a large, thick man who looked to be in his early sixties came into the kitchen. The man had thinning gray hair that showed the pink scalp beneath, and he was wearing faded jeans and a plaid flannel shirt that probably had been through hundreds of wash cycles. His mouth was tight, and his brow showed a vertical line down the center that indicated either intense concentration or deep discomfort.

"Well, hello there," the man said, as though he were greeting the dentist who was about to perform his root canal.

"Get on in here, Orin. Don't just stand in the doorway," Sandra scolded him. Then, to Julia and Drew: "This here's my husband, Orin. He's Redmond's brother. And he ought to have more damned social skills." Sandra glared at her husband, who came into the room sheepishly.

"Pleased to meet you." He offered his hand first to Drew, and then to Julia, nodding as though some unnamed question had been answered.

Drew shook the man's hand but didn't say anything, so Julia stepped in, thinking that Orin wasn't the only one who lacked social skills.

"This all must be a shock to you," she said. "I know it has been for Drew."

"Well, that's fair to say." Orin scratched the back of his head with one meaty hand. "I'd have to say I was as close to Redmond as anybody in the world, and he never gave me any idea about any of this. Not any idea." Orin's eyes grew red and moist, and for the first time since they'd arrived, it occurred to

Julia that the events of the past several days weren't just about Drew. They were also about a family who had lost someone they loved, someone who was an irreplaceable part of their world.

"I'm sorry for your loss," Julia said. She should have said it earlier, as soon as they'd arrived, and she felt foolish now because she hadn't.

Drew had been silent since Orin had come into the room, but Julia could see him studying the older man, probably looking for a resemblance to his own face, his own stature, his own way of being in the world.

When he did finally say something, it wasn't a nicety or a *pro forma* politeness. It was a simple, blunt question.

"What kind of man doesn't claim his son?" he asked.

It was the kind of question that might have started a fight, might have ignited a spark that would burn this tender new relationship to the ground. Instead, Orin scratched at his head again, and when he spoke, his voice was gruff and thick.

"Well, I don't know, son. I don't rightly know."

Chapter Nineteen

Because Colin, Sandra, and Orin had been straightforward and kind, and because all of this seemed like an odd and implausible dream, Julia was beginning to get the sense that maybe this—all of this—would turn out to be okay.

Until she met Liam.

She and Drew heard him before they saw him. The two of them were still sitting in the kitchen with Sandra and Orin, the four of them taking the first, tentative steps of getting to know one another in the warm and homey room, when they heard a commotion outside the kitchen door, in the living room.

"Screw that," a voice was saying. The voice was angry, raised. It was the voice of someone trying to pick a fight. "You can make nice all goddamned day long if you want to, but what's the point of that? What's the fucking point? This guy comes here like he thinks he's entitled to what we have, what we've built. And you want me to be nice? That's bullshit, Ryan."

Another voice, this one quieter, murmured something they couldn't hear.

"Ah, blow me, Ryan. You always have thought you were my goddamned dad."

They heard the front door open, and then a third voice—Colin's—was added to the mix. The dynamic was clear: Ryan and Colin were attempting to calm Liam, with results that were less than successful.

"You gonna go out there and do something about your son?" Sandra asked Orin.

Orin ducked his head, as though maybe he could avoid that eventuality if he could somehow make himself smaller and avoid Sandra's notice. "Well, I guess," he said. He left the kitchen reluctantly.

"Now, don't you two worry yourselves about Liam," Sandra said, her wiry hands holding a coffee mug. "He's my hothead. But he's a good man. He always comes around."

If Liam was going to come around, it wasn't going to be today.

When the three Delaney sons came into the kitchen, Colin introduced Ryan to Drew and Julia, and she thought the man seemed amiable enough. They all shook hands, and Ryan's smile seemed warm and genuine.

Liam, however, stood in the doorway with his arms folded over his chest, his face hard and his eyes narrowed in anticipation of what? An argument? A fistfight? He hadn't seemed to notice Julia's presence at all; his steely gaze was fixed squarely on Drew, who returned Liam's contempt with more of his own.

Julia rolled her eyes at the unknowable thought processes of men.

"Liam, for God's sake," Sandra snapped at him. "Get in here and act like your mother raised you right. Because I know I did."

Liam was motionless for a few moments more as he seemed to weigh whether to back down or face his mother's scorn. He opted for a kind of compromise: He stepped into the room and offered his hand to Drew, but kept the look on his face that said he was ready to kick somebody's teeth in at the least provocation.

That much was okay, Julia thought—at least it was something—but then Drew escalated the situation by refusing the hand Liam had offered.

"Seems like I'm unwelcome here, as far as you're concerned," Drew said, looking Liam in the eye and ignoring the hand that still hung in the space between them.

Liam scowled. "All I know is that you showed up out of nowhere, and I'm supposed to believe you're family." He dropped the hand palm-down onto the table in front of Drew with a smack.

"You don't have to believe a goddamned thing," Drew said, standing. "I don't give a flying—"

"Hey, hey, hey." Colin put one hand on Liam's shoulder and put the other one up, palm out, to stop Drew from finishing his sentence—a sentence that, once completed, would certainly inflame tensions that were already high. "Let's just take a minute."

"Liam, for God's sake," Sandra said, glowering at her son. "Get out of here and go cool down."

"I don't need to cool down. I need—"

"Boy, when I tell you to go cool down, you damn well better do it." Sandra stood facing Liam with her hands on her narrow hips, her brows drawn together so tightly that they looked like two caterpillars that had collided.

Sandra was more than a foot shorter than Liam, and she had to be half his weight. But to Julia, it was clear who held the position of power here—and it wasn't Liam.

Liam's hands clenched into fists. "Yes, ma'am." He shot Drew another challenging look and then left the kitchen, letting the door close behind him with a smack.

The remaining Delaneys in the room—Sandra, Ryan, and Colin—displayed a variety of reactions to what had just happened. Sandra looked irritated, Ryan looked embarrassed, and Colin just looked uncomfortable.

"As far as friendly greetings go, a basket of muffins might've worked better," Ryan quipped.

"Oh, God," Julia muttered. She already felt like an invader here, and now, Liam's reaction confirmed that she and Drew were exactly that. "We don't have to stay here. Mrs. Delaney, thank you, but we can go. We can—"

"We're staying," Drew said mildly.

"What?" Julia turned to him, not sure she'd heard him correctly.

"If the invitation still stands," he went on.

"Well, I guess it does," Sandra said. "I don't suppose I'm going to let one of my boys tell me who I can have as a guest in my own house. The day I do that is the day they carry me out of here feet first." Sandra folded her arms over her chest and scowled, just as her middle son had done a few minutes before.

"Fine, then." Drew nodded. "Since we're still invited, we're staying." He glared at the closed kitchen door, where Liam had just been.

"Well, whatever happens, it's going to be interesting," Ryan observed.

Julia looked down at the coffee in her mug and wished it were something considerably stronger.

Once Liam had stormed out of the house, things quieted down some. Breanna came home from picking her boys up from school, and Julia and Drew met her and the two boisterous children. Colin showed Drew to the guest room at the main house, and then he and Ryan took Julia about a quarter mile down the road in her rental car to a white wood and red brick farmhouse with a big front porch and a flower garden in the front yard.

As Colin took Julia's luggage out of the trunk and carried it up onto the porch, a pretty woman in her early thirties with red hair in long, wild curls came out the front door and onto the porch.

"This is my wife, Gen," Ryan told Julia as they climbed the stairs toward the front door.

Julia's encounter with Liam had left her stressed and on edge, and she didn't know what to expect from this new Delaney. When Gen smiled warmly and pulled Julia into an impulsive hug, it was hard not to be disarmed.

"It's so good to meet you," Gen went on, before Julia could say anything. "This whole situation is so crazy, isn't it? I mean, who could have predicted something like this? Come on in, we'll get you settled. I'm supposed to be at work today, but I wanted to be here to greet you."

Gen ushered Julia into a bright, new house that was warm from the fire in the fireplace, and that smelled like vanilla and cinnamon. "What is that smell?" Julia said, stopping just inside the front door with the strap from one of her bags slung over her shoulder. "It's wonderful."

"Cinnamon streusel coffee cake," Gen said. "I love to bake."

Julia let out an involuntary laugh. "That's good, because I need to do some stress eating after what just happened with Liam."

"I've got you covered," Gen said, giving Julia's arm a squeeze. "You can eat while you tell me what Liam did." She rolled her eyes. "Though I think I can guess."

It occurred to Julia that with Drew at the main house and

her here at Ryan's place, she had very much gotten the better end of the deal. "Lead the way," she said.

Colin's level of family-induced stress was at a particular high as he left Julia at Ryan and Gen's house. He was not a stranger to family-induced stress, of course, and in fact, he considered himself something of an expert in the subject. But now, one thing was compounding on top of another to raise the level to a peak.

Not only did he want things with Drew to go well—he felt an urgent need, one he didn't fully understand, to restore Redmond's son to the family—but he also felt more and more that he wanted to protect and take care of Julia, wanted her to be happy here, with the family, with him.

Which was ridiculous. He wasn't dating her, wasn't even sleeping with her. Still, there was something about her that put his male instincts on high alert. If he were a caveman, he'd have gone out and clubbed a mastodon to death just so he could drag it home to her.

And if Colin had two goals working in tandem here—one regarding each of the McCray siblings—then Liam was threatening both of them.

"Don't you have work to do back in Montana?" Colin asked Liam irritably when he'd gotten Julia settled and had arrived back at the main house. Liam was in the kitchen, nosing around and filching small pieces of food from the cutting board as their mother cooked dinner. Michael and Lucas were settled in at the kitchen table working on homework as Breanna helped Sandra prepare the meal. Drew, thankfully, was nowhere to be seen.

"Don't *you* have work to do down there in San Diego?" Liam responded.

"I do, but it can wait," Colin said.

"Well, there you go," Liam answered. "Same here. I've got Desmond keeping an eye on things while I'm gone. He'll manage."

Colin scoffed. "Desmond."

"You've got a problem with Desmond?" Liam wanted to know.

Colin ran a hand through his hair. "Shit. No. I guess not." Desmond Byrne had been working for the Delaneys for more than thirty years, first at the Cambria ranch, now at the Montana property just outside of Billings. Colin had never cared for the man much—mainly because he was surly and always seemed to be competing with Orin and Redmond for supremacy—but there was no denying that he knew how to run a cattle ranch.

Liam grabbed a slice of carrot from Sandra's cutting board and popped it into his mouth. Sandra set down her knife and smacked Liam's hand.

"Where's Drew?" Colin asked.

Liam leaned his butt against the countertop, his legs crossed at the ankles, arms folded over his chest. "He's gone straight to hell, I hope," he remarked casually.

"You quit that crap before I have to knock some sense into you," Sandra snapped at Liam, waving her chef's knife in his general direction. "And you know I'll do it, boy, I don't care how grown up you are."

"All right, not hell, then," Liam said. "I'm not that lucky. He's upstairs getting settled into the spare room." Then, under his breath: "I hope he falls down the goddamned stairs."

"Oh, for God's sake, Liam, I swear…" Sandra started.

"I thought they seemed nice," Breanna said as she arranged some rolls in a basket. Her dark hair, the same shade and texture as Colin's, fell down to her shoulders. "Especially her. Don't make trouble," she told Liam.

"Too late," Colin commented. "Before you and the boys got home, Liam gave them the welcome you'd expect."

"Oh … crap." Breanna scowled and smacked Liam on the arm, hard.

"Hey!"

"Can't you make him behave?" Breanna demanded of Sandra.

"If I haven't managed it so far, girl, what makes you think I can do it now?" Sandra responded, not unreasonably.

Colin regarded Liam, feeling increasingly uneasy and maybe a little pissed off. His brother had always been surly and quick to anger; he had their mother's temperament. While that temperament had, over the years, mostly been a minor annoyance, now it posed a threat to everything Colin was trying to accomplish here. If Colin had been the kind of man who got into fights, he might have gotten into one now with Liam; it would be satisfying to punch his brother in the damned face. But since Colin wasn't that kind of man, he took another approach.

"Let's step outside for a minute," Colin told Liam.

"Are we gonna fight?" Liam asked in a conversational tone, as though he'd somehow read Colin's thoughts.

"Don't be an idiot. Just come outside."

When the two of them were out on the front porch—the place where many serious discussions in the Delaney family took place—Colin turned to Liam.

"You need to knock it off," he said, without preamble. "We've got a somewhat delicate situation here, and you and your attitude—"

"My *attitude*?" Liam shook his head and looked out toward the distant ocean. "I don't see why everybody doesn't have my attitude. Welcoming that guy into our house? We don't even know if he really is Redmond's son. It's bullshit, Colin."

"He really is Redmond's son," Colin said. "And you know it."

Liam shrugged, still avoiding Colin's eyes. "Maybe."

"What's this about?" Colin's voice was quieter now. He could see that Liam was genuinely troubled, was having an honest-to-God difficult time with everything that was happening. His distress was real; it wasn't bluster. "What's it really about?"

Liam made a scoffing noise and turned to Colin. "He's scamming us, Colin. And you're letting him. You're *helping* him do it. Like you even care what happens in this family. You got out of here the first minute you could, and now here you are, acting like you know everything, like you're going to tell us all what to do—"

Colin looked at his brother like the man had taken leave of his senses. "You think I don't *care*? Liam, for Christ's sake. You think—"

"Hey, look." Liam held up his hands in surrender. "All of this right here? The ranch, the cattle? It's not your thing, and I get that. That's fine, okay? You bolted down south at the first opportunity, and if that's what floats your boat, then who am I to judge? But given all of that, I just wonder whether you're the person to decide what's right for all of us." Liam tucked his hands into the safe haven of his armpits and shrugged.

Colin gripped the porch railing, because it gave him something to do with his hands other than throttling his brother. "You think I'm not a part of this family? A part of all this?" He gestured toward the land around them. "Who do you think makes all of this possible? You think the cattle ranch supports itself?" He scoffed. "It's the goddamned real estate investments that keep this place running. Investments I made for this family.

You want to know how much the family's net worth has increased since I started managing the portfolio? Because I can show you the numbers, Liam. I can—"

"Ah, shut up." Liam's words didn't have much heat to them, and in fact, he'd seemed to deflate a little. He leaned his forearms on the porch railing and looked out at the hills and the trees. He shook his head slowly. "It's just … I wonder if we even really knew him. Redmond. If we even knew who the hell he was."

Colin suspected that this was at the heart of it—the mystery of what had really been going on in Redmond's head all those years.

"We knew him," Colin said. "We might not have known everything about him, but we knew what kind of man he was."

"Yeah? Because now, I think maybe we didn't."

Though he didn't say it, Colin thought his brother made a damned good point.

Chapter Twenty

Colin had been away from his home base in San Diego for a couple of weeks now to deal with Redmond's death, the funeral, and then the McCrays. Issues were piling up that he needed to deal with, not only with the Palm Springs land deal, but also with their commercial tenants, their charitable foundation, and their investment portfolio.

In the family room of his parents' house, he settled himself into a comfortable chair in front of the big fireplace and fired up his laptop to see what crises were being thrown at him today.

Colin sorted through what seemed like hundreds of e-mails: some spam, some regarding Delaney business, some from people or organizations soliciting donations from the foundation. The seller of the Palm Springs property still hadn't signed the contract. There seemed to be an issue involving the property boundaries, which would require a call to the county tax assessor's office.

When Colin finally managed to extricate himself from work, he felt drained in a way he hadn't felt since he'd left his condo in San Diego the day of Redmond's death. He prepared himself mentally for the phone call to sort out the property lines, and then was relieved to realize that it was now past five p.m. and the Riverside County government offices were closed.

He felt unsettled and out of sorts, and spent a moment contemplating what he should do next. He could spend the next five or six hours wading through the various demands of his role as the family lawyer; he could relax a bit and then have dinner with his family; he could go back to the lodge and settle into his room with a pizza and some beer and catch up on the TV-watching he'd neglected since the beginning of his law career.

But he didn't want to do any of that.

What he really wanted was to hear Julia's voice.

Chances were that if he asked to spend some time with her alone, she'd tell him she needed to soothe Drew's emotional wounds, or get to know the Delaneys, or settle in at Ryan and Gen's house. But even if that were the case, he still just wanted to talk to her, if only for a few minutes.

He closed his laptop and sat back on the sofa, enjoying the heat from the fireplace, and called her.

"Colin," she said. Not *hello,* just his name. Was he imagining the warmth he heard in the word? Was he imagining it that she was happy to hear from him?

"I just wondered how things were going," he said. "How are Ryan and Gen treating you?"

And despite everything that was going on, despite how emotionally fraught the entire situation was with his family and hers, she simply gushed.

"Oh, Colin. The ranch is gorgeous. I always thought I lived in the most beautiful place in the world, but Cambria … God. Why in the world did you move away? I love Ryan and Gen's house. It's so cozy, so much a *home.* And Gen's great. I haven't had much time to talk to Ryan yet, but Gen is just the nicest person. I couldn't have asked for a better welcome. And I know Drew is going through a lot right now, I know he's angry and stressed, and I should be thinking of him right now, but I'm just really excited to meet everybody and to see everything."

When she finally stopped to take a breath, he found himself smiling. He was going to say *I'm glad you're having a good time,* or *That's great to hear,* or maybe, *Yeah, Gen's really a sweetheart.* But instead, he said something different.

"Have dinner with me."

"Dinner?" She said it as though it were a new concept, a word she hadn't yet mastered.

"Yeah. The meal that people customarily eat in the evening, often in a social context. Dinner."

"I'm supposed to go to the main house for dinner. Your mom invited me. Actually, it's more like she summoned me."

That sounded like his mom, all right.

"I'll explain it to her," he told her. "I can take care of my mom. Just ... let me take you out. I really want to." As he said it, he realized just how much he wanted to. So many things were pulling at him. His work, the family, his nagging sense of discomfort whenever he was surrounded by his parents and his siblings. If there was comfort to be had, it was with her. If there was something he could do to soothe himself and make himself feel okay, he knew it would be spending time in her presence.

"Please," he said.

"You're sure your mom won't be upset?" she asked.

He chuckled. "Oh, she'll be upset. But it'll be with me, not you. And believe me, I'm used to it."

She didn't say anything, so he moved in to close the deal. "I know a place you'll like. I'll pick you up in half an hour."

He hung up before she could argue.

Smoothing things over with his mother turned out to be much easier than expected. When he told her why neither he nor Julia would be having dinner at the family home that night, she'd barked, "You're telling me you've got a date with a woman who's a real person, and not some glossed-up Barbie doll? Well, I guess I'm not about to stand in the way of that! You take her someplace nice, boy—not to some hole in the wall for buffalo wings, by God."

It occurred to him to wonder how his mother—all the way up here, so far from his home in San Diego—even knew that he was in the habit of dating glossed-up Barbie dolls, but he didn't linger on it much. His mother knew everything.

When Sandra had said to take Julia "someplace nice," there was no question that meant Neptune. The big, brick seafood restaurant in a historic building on Main Street had the best food in town, and that was saying something, considering the array of restaurants that catered to the steady flow of tourists who came through Cambria.

The fact that one of Ryan's best friends, Jackson Graham, was the head chef there was an added factor. If Colin decided to take Julia anywhere else, he'd probably face a grilling from Ryan about why he hadn't taken her to Neptune. So, there was that.

When he picked up Julia at Ryan's place, she was decidedly un-Barbielike. She was wearing a pair of jeans and a cream-colored cotton sweater, a poofy down jacket, and a pair of low-heeled leather boots.

"Was I supposed to dress up?" she asked uncertainly as she climbed into his car. "I wasn't sure, but I only brought casual things, so …"

"You look great," he said, and meant it. There was a thing she had going on, a kind of glow, that had nothing to do with her clothes. When Julia smiled in a certain way, she could have been wearing a hazmat suit or a Santa costume and he would only have noticed the smile, the glow. He wondered if he'd ever glowed like that, and he thought he probably hadn't.

On the way to the restaurant, they chatted about her day, and how she was settling in, and about Drew.

"I thought maybe you wouldn't want to leave him on his own, at the mercy of my family," Colin said.

"Honestly, I need a break from his brooding. I mean, I get that he has issues to work through. Anybody would, in his place. And I want to help him get through it—that's why I came. But it's a lot of negativity, when you're around it every day."

"And it doesn't help when Liam picks fights with him," Colin added. "I wouldn't be surprised if those two come to blows at some point."

"God. I hope not." Julia looked at Colin. "Liam seems to think there's some kind of scam going on, to cheat the Delaneys out of their fortune. But Drew never asked for this. He never expected or wanted any of this."

"I know." Colin nodded grimly. "And Liam knows, too. This isn't about Drew. It's about grief. He and Redmond were close. Redmond's death has been hard on Liam. He's pissed off, and he can't be pissed off at Redmond, because he's gone. Drew probably seems like a handy substitute."

"Drew's having dinner with your family tonight, at the house. Liam will be there, I imagine." She shuddered a little.

"Don't worry. If they come at each other with steak knives, my mother will knock their heads together and send them to their rooms." He grinned, thinking about his mother.

"She probably would, too," Julia said.

"Oh, hell yes."

They drove up Main Street toward the restaurant, and Colin said, "I'm glad you're here. Not just coming to dinner with me tonight, but here in Cambria. I'm glad you came."

He felt that special Julia glow all the way over in the driver's seat as he found a parking space on the curb.

Chapter Twenty-One

Neptune was a fairly upscale restaurant, and because of that—also because of the friendship between Ryan and Jackson Graham—it tended to be the go-to choice for first dates in the Delaney family. Not that Colin was even sure this was a date. He hoped it was. He supposed Julia might interpret it as a host showing hospitality to a houseguest, but he was thinking *date,* and he wanted her to think that, too.

When the hostess showed them to a table at a window looking out onto Main Street, Colin pulled out Julia's chair for her, as his mother had taught him to do. They ordered wine, and when it came, they sipped the pricey Chardonnay amid the chatter of the other diners and the warmth of the room with its bustling activity.

Just sitting there with the wine and the Julia glow, Colin started to feel happy for the first time since Redmond's passing. There was no accounting for it. He'd lost a loved one, he was embroiled in family drama, his work was growing increasingly backed up, and here he was, feeling happy. It could only have been Julia, but how did that make sense, when he'd known her for such a short time?

"Tell me what you were like as a kid," she said, interrupting his thoughts. "I can't imagine what it was like to grow up here, as a Delaney."

Colin shifted gears mentally and regarded her question. He considered giving her the appropriate line—that it was a good, wholesome, old-fashioned childhood in which he milked cows and learned traditional family values—but instead, he went with the truth.

"It was good, in a lot of ways. A lot of ways. I think Ryan, Liam, and Breanna would tell you they had the best childhood any kid could dream of. But for me … well. It was different."

A little crease formed between her brows. "How?"

He shrugged, trying to affect a casual air. "Our place—the ranch—it's all about the cattle, and hard work in the outdoors. That's what they value. Getting your hands dirty, working up a good sweat, working your ass off in the dirt and the hay and the cow shit. And I didn't do any of that. I didn't do any of the things they valued."

"Why? You didn't like ranch work?"

"At first, I couldn't do it. And then, they wouldn't let me." He launched into the story of how he'd been hospitalized with a severe asthma attack at the age of three and had almost died. His doctor had said that allergens—including hay, pollen, and animal dander, all of which were abundant in the outdoor expanses of the ranch—had likely triggered the attack.

"So, while my brothers and my sister were out riding, working with the animals, and doing all of the other things ranch kids do, I was inside reading and playing with my Legos. It's not like my parents had any choice—I get that. They were just doing their best to keep me healthy."

"But?" Julia prompted him.

"But, I eventually outgrew the asthma, for the most part. I still had some minor issues, but no more severe attacks. And even though my health changed, nothing else did." He paused, lost in his memories, and sipped some wine. "By then, my parents saw me as the fragile one. The one who couldn't do the things the other kids could."

"The one who couldn't do the things they valued the most," Julia said quietly.

Colin nodded slowly. "Right. And any time I wanted to do those things—to ride or to help with the cattle—they shut me down. 'You know you can't do that, Colin. You'd better leave that for the others.' " He shook his head absently. "I was the only one who didn't have a horse. Ryan, Breanna, and Liam all had one. But my parents were afraid that if I had one, too, I'd want to be out there in the stables, with the hay and the dust and all of the things that might shut down my airways. I always wanted my own horse."

"What about Breanna? She doesn't do ranch work, does she?" Julia asked.

"She didn't much like that kind of thing, but she's a girl, so it's different."

"Ah. Gender expectations," Julia said knowingly.

"Sure. She could help my mom with the cooking or the housework, and that was fine, because that's what girls were supposed to do. But me ..."

"You weren't doing what men were supposed to do."

He felt gratified that she got it, that she understood. His basic sense of otherness within his family—his sense of being less of a man than his brothers—had never changed, probably never would change.

"But you handle your family's legal issues, right? The real estate, the investments ..."

"Right, and I've done well with that. Very well. But that's pencil-pushing, if you ask my dad. That's not a man's work."

"He said that?" She looked appalled.

"Oh, no. He'd never say that. Nobody ever said that. Well, except Liam." Colin grinned. Liam would say anything to get under his brothers' skin when necessary, regardless of whether it was true. Liam saying such a thing out loud held much less sting than the rest of his family merely thinking it.

"Colin." She reached out and put a hand over his on the table. He didn't need her comfort, but he wanted it anyway. The feel of her hand on his made a wave of warmth run through his body. He wondered if her touch would create the same effect applied to other areas on his person.

"It's okay," he told her. "I'm okay." He made no move to take his hand out from beneath hers. "It's just … being here, with them, is always kind of weird."

The waitress came and took their orders—a steak for him and seafood pasta for her—and Julia considered what he had told her. She knew what it was to be an outsider in her own family. Ever since Drew had discovered the truth about his parentage, he and their mother had guarded the secret from Julia as though it were a matter of national security. Drew was trying to protect her, she knew that—protect the image Julia had of her mother. And of course, Isabelle was trying to hide her own infidelity, her own shame.

But regardless of their reasons, the result was that Julia felt excluded, as though they hadn't loved her enough, trusted her enough, to tell her the truth.

She'd been placed outside of the circle, and so had Colin. The circumstances were different, but emotionally, it was probably much the same.

"I think I get it," she told him. "Feeling like everyone in your family is in one place, and you're in another? Not just geographically, but emotionally? This thing with Drew and my mom

. . . It hurt. It still does."

His hand, the one she had been holding, had been palm-down on the table. But now he turned it upward and closed it around hers. The thrill of that touch rushed through her, and she wondered what this was that she was feeling. Lust? Certainly. But it was more than that. Something deeper than that.

"Colin," she said. Her eyes pleaded with him for something, some connection.

He leaned toward her, drawing closer, and paused with his mouth just inches from hers. "I want to kiss you," he murmured. "Is that all right?"

Instead of answering, she closed the gap and touched her lips to his gently, tentatively.

When they pulled apart, she saw movement out of the corner of her eye. She looked up, and they both saw Liam standing outside the window on Main Street, watching them, his face red with fury.

"Oh, shit," Colin said.

Before Julia knew what was happening or what to do, Colin got up from the table and headed toward the front door of the restaurant. He didn't make it that far, though. Before Colin could get fifteen feet, Liam intercepted him.

"What the fuck do you think you're doing?" Liam demanded, puffing up his chest and getting in Colin's face. Diners at nearby tables stopped eating to watch.

"Why are you here?" Colin asked. "You're supposed to be having dinner at the ranch."

"I had a change of plans. Don't change the goddamned subject. What the fuck—"

"Liam, just calm down. Let's—"

"You're going out with her? You're *kissing* her? After I told you how I felt about it?" Liam gestured toward Julia, who was on alert, standing next to the table.

"If you're tempted to talk shit about Julia, you'd better watch yourself," Colin told his brother. Between the two of them, Liam was the one you'd expect to get into a fight in the middle of a restaurant. But the look on Colin's face, the low intensity of his voice, made Julia wonder whether he might be the one to bet on if a brawl did break out.

"Goddamn it, Colin, she's his sister," Liam went on. "The sister of the guy who's trying to bilk us out of millions of dollars of Redmond's money. Where's your goddamned loyalty?"

The manager, a tall, thick guy with a name badge that said NEIL GOODWIN, approached the brothers. Julia supposed that everyone in a town this small must know each other, because Neil needed no introductions before he said, "Colin, Liam. Let's settle down, now. Is there something I can help you boys with?" He wisely stood back a couple of feet from the two Delaneys.

"You can tell Liam to get his head out of his ass," Colin said, his expression fierce.

"Yeah? Well, you can tell my brother to stop thinking with his dick," Liam snapped.

"You two are going to need to take this outside," Neil said. Liam took one threatening step toward Colin, and Neil—whose substantial stature couldn't be ignored—stepped between them. "*Outside,*" he said again.

The fight was between Colin and Liam, so Julia wondered if maybe she should stay inside and avoid getting involved. On the other hand, the fight was about her, so she was already involved. As the two brothers stormed out of the restaurant with Neil on their heels—presumably, to make sure they really went—Julia scurried after them, adrenaline making her heart pound.

When they were all on the sidewalk in the evening chill, Colin faced Liam and raised his hands in a gesture of calm and reconciliation. "Now, let's calm down for a second, Liam. You can't just—"

"You are *not* getting involved with her," Liam said, pointing at Julia.

Colin glared at him, his eyes cold. "First of all, I'll get involved with whomever I please, and you'll have no say in it," he said. "And second, I think you owe Julia an apology and some damned respect."

"Fuck off," Liam said.

Colin smirked. "That's about the level of intellectual discourse I'd expect from you. 'Fuck off.' Brilliant, as always."

Julia was new to the Delaney family dynamics, but she could see what was going on between them as clearly as if she'd watched them grow up together. Colin was the family outsider because he used his Ivy League intellect instead of doing hard physical work like the rest of the Delaneys. And Liam was sensitive about the fact that he thought he wasn't as smart as Colin. Liam didn't have to say it; his reaction said it for him.

Colin knew Liam's sore spot, and he'd hit it with brutal accuracy. Liam reared back and sent his fist sailing into Colin's face, and Colin rocked backward as he absorbed the blow.

Colin heard Julia cry out in horror—or maybe that was just his own ears ringing. He managed to stay on his feet, but goddamn it, Liam could hit hard.

"Whoa, whoa, whoa!" Neil, the manager, grabbed Liam by the arm and pulled him back, away from Colin. By now, a few other people had joined the crowd, including a handful of male diners and Jackson Graham, Ryan's friend and the restaurant's head chef.

"Hold it, hold it, Jesus." Jackson, a tall, auburn-haired man still in his white chef's coat, emerged from the restaurant and inserted himself between Colin and Liam, just in case Liam broke away from Neil's hold on him. "What are you guys doing? You can't fight at my restaurant. Assholes." They both knew Jackson fairly well, and they both knew better than to challenge him. While they were forbidden to fight at Jackson's restaurant, Jackson himself had done it more than once—and he usually won.

Liam was attempting to pull his arm out of Neil's grasp, probably so he could clock Colin again. He yanked himself free, and then Jackson grabbed both of his arms and hauled him away from Colin. "Hey. Hey. Stop it right goddamn now. Or you want to take this up with me?" Jackson said.

Liam looked like he was considering it, but then he put his hands up in surrender. "Nope. I'm done."

"You?" Jackson turned to Colin in question.

Liam scoffed. "Him? He's too good to fight. Wouldn't want to hurt his manicure."

Colin moved toward Liam, but somebody in the crowd held him back—he didn't see who it was. His head was foggy and his jaw hurt like he'd been hit by a truck.

"Liam? Go home. I mean it, or I'll put you on the ground, I swear to God," Jackson told him. Liam didn't seem to doubt it. He shot Colin one more heated look and then turned and walked toward his truck, which was parked at the curb on Main Street.

"Colin, come inside and I'll get you some ice," Neil offered.

"I don't need any ice." In fact, he could already feel his jaw swelling, but pride prevented him from admitting it.

"Fine, then go on home."

Colin tested his jaw with his fingertips. Nothing seemed to be broken. "I haven't paid the check."

"Forget it. It's on me. Just get out of here," Neil said.

Colin nodded. The crowd began to dissipate, and Colin

stood there on the sidewalk, gathering himself.

Julia approached him tentatively and put a hand on his arm.

"I should take you back," he said.

He wouldn't have blamed her if she'd wanted to go back, not to Gen and Ryan's, but all the way back to Montana, never to see or think about the Delaneys again.

"I don't want to go back. Not yet," she said. "Not unless you need to be alone."

He looked at her. His mouth quirked up in a half grin, but even that hurt.

"You've got to admit I'm not a boring date," he said.

Chapter Twenty-Two

Neither of them was much in the mood for a restaurant after that, but they still had to eat, and there was no way Colin was going back to the ranch—where he might run into Liam—except to drop Julia off and then get the hell out of there. They went back to the Cambria Pines Lodge, where Colin was staying, and ordered burgers and fries from room service. They sat on top of the comforter on the king size bed, their backs propped up against the headboard, the room service tray between them. Both of them had taken off their shoes to avoid getting the comforter dirty, and their socks poked up side by side companionably.

The room had walls the color of butter and a gas fireplace that offered a comforting glow. A big window faced out on the darkness of the evening, but in the morning it would have a view of the greenery beyond.

"I'm sorry," Colin told her as he toyed with a french fry, swirling it in a puddle of ketchup. "About what happened, and also about how Liam is treating you."

"It's all right."

"No. It really isn't." He tossed the fry back onto his plate. "It's mean, and it's wrong."

"Well. It is, but it's not you doing it, so you have nothing to be sorry for."

Colin shrugged. She couldn't tell whether the shrug indicated agreement or argument with her point.

"I'm more worried about Drew," Julia said after a while. "If Liam has that much anger toward me …"

"I can handle Liam."

"Really." It wasn't a question.

Colin shot her a sideways look and grinned. "Yeah, you're right. That's crap. I can't handle him."

"So, what are you going to do?"

"I'm going to do what I've always done since I was a kid." He let out a short laugh. "I'm going to tell Mom and Dad on him."

They ate their burgers and fries and drank a couple of beers in sweating longneck bottles, and then Colin gathered up the plates and the tray and put them out into the hallway for housekeeping to find.

It was only then, with dinner over and the tension of what had happened earlier starting to ebb away, that Julia started to be intensely aware of the fact that they were alone together in a hotel room. What would happen from this point? Would he simply take her back to Ryan and Gen's house, say goodbye, and wish fervently that this evening had never happened? And was that what she wanted?

He must have been wondering the same thing, pondering those same questions, because he stood awkwardly near the door of the room, his hands in the pockets of his slacks, his gaze fixed on some detail of the carpeting.

"I can take you back now," he said.

Okay, there it was. Julia felt a raw sense of disappointment in her core that told her what she hadn't been able to articulate to herself: She didn't want to leave him. She didn't want to go back. Not now. Maybe not ever.

"That is, if you want me to," he said. He was still looking down at the carpet, but he shot her a quick look that was impossibly shy and sweet.

She got up from the bed, walked over to him, and rested one hand lightly on his bicep. "I'm not in a hurry," she said.

She was so close to him she could smell the light, spicy scent of soap, aftershave, and his own warm skin. He brought his gaze to hers, and she felt a tremor of anticipation.

"Kiss me again," she said, on a whisper. She gave him a tentative grin. "I don't think Liam can see us."

He brought his hand up to touch her cheek. "I'd kiss you again even if he could."

He touched his lips to hers gently at first, as though he were searching for the answer to a question. He caressed her cheek with his thumb.

She had an idea that this wasn't smart, that getting involved with a man who represented so much drama for her family—and who lived a third of the way across the country from her—was reckless at best. But right now, she didn't care. All she knew was that she didn't want to go back to the ranch. She didn't want to leave this room. She didn't want to go anywhere, if it wasn't with him.

He deepened the kiss, and she melted into him.

She'd felt lust before, of course. She had enjoyed men, and they had enjoyed her. But she couldn't recall ever feeling exactly this, this warm, liquid feeling of being transported out of the moment and into an infinitely better place.

She could no more have pushed him away at that moment than she could have decided to stop breathing.

"Julia," he murmured into her ear. "I don't know where this is going, if it can go anywhere. I'm not—"

"*Shh.*" She quieted him, then tangled her fingers in his hair and kissed him with her lips, her tongue, everything she was, everything she had.

It didn't matter where this was or was not going. What mattered was that they were here, together, now.

She unbuttoned his shirt slowly, taking her time. Then she slid it off of his shoulders and let it fall to the floor. She ran her hands over the firm territory of his arms, his chest.

"Are you sure this is what you want?" His voice was rough, a little unsteady.

In answer, she put her hands on the back of his neck and pulled him to her, bringing his mouth to hers.

For Colin, sex was mostly just fun. It was the likely conclusion of Date Four, usually, after dinner at an expensive restaurant with one of the "glossed-up Barbies" his mother had so accurately referred to. So much was about appearance. Her appearance, always perfect and well-planned. His appearance, built around an image of affluence.

There was a script to be followed, a set of procedures in place. He did this, and then she said that, and it all came to a predictable and mostly satisfying conclusion.

But tonight, there was no script. Colin felt raw and hurt and vulnerable after what had happened with Liam, and somehow, Julia was making all of that go away. She was a cure, a soothing balm. Touching her, he felt whole in a way he hadn't in so long.

And because she was so different from most of the women in his life, so *real,* being with her and seeing the way she looked at him felt fresh, as though this thing they were doing was an entirely different species of act from any he'd performed before.

He kissed her, and his jaw ached from where Liam had hit him.

He didn't care.

He needed to feel her skin against his, so he took the hemline of her sweater in his hands and lifted it over her head. The sweater dropped to the floor beside his shirt. Under it, she was wearing a white tank top that hugged her curves, and he could see the straps of her bra peeking out from beneath it. He slid a hand beneath the shirt and cupped her breast in his palm, over the silky fabric of her bra.

She drew in a breath as he rubbed the pad of his thumb across her erect nipple.

Something about that—the sound of her soft gasp—made him lose whatever sense of calm patience he'd had. He guided her to the bed and lowered her onto it, his body covering hers.

Somehow, the fact that they were both in this thing together—this tangle of family secrets and obligations—made him feel close to her, as though they had things they could teach each other, comforts they could give one another. Whatever he was feeling, she could feel it, too. He knew it.

He wanted to bury himself in her, surround himself with her, and forget everything else. He lifted the tank top to bare her smooth midriff, pulled down one of the cups of her bra, and closed his mouth over the rounded peak.

Was there some part of him that wanted to defy Liam? That despite Liam's bullying, wouldn't be told what to do? Maybe. But that aspect of him was deep beneath another part, one that simply wanted to be loved.

Colin was beautiful, with his brooding eyes and his lean, athletic body. But it wasn't his beauty that Julia's body was responding to. Instead, it was some unnameable thing, some voice in her head that said, *This is the one.* She knew she shouldn't feel that way, shouldn't even be entertaining the idea. And yet, that gut feeling of rightness, of being exactly where she belonged, was impossible to deny or ignore.

And then the feeling of his mouth on her breast pushed all other thoughts away as she felt a pulse of pleasure rushing through her body.

He reached down and unsnapped her jeans, then eased the zipper down. One hand slipped into her panties, and his fingers slid into her. She threw her head back and closed her eyes, focusing on the delicious sensations he was giving to her.

She moved her hands over his body, memorizing the ridges and planes of his chest.

He brought his mouth to the base of her throat and caressed it with his lips and tongue. His fingers glided smoothly inside her, his thumb circling her engorged nub.

All thoughts of whether this was wise, or where things might go between them, or what their union might do to either of their families left her. She couldn't think, she could only feel. Her body was rising on a tide of pure pleasure, and the wave was about to crash with devastating force.

When her body exploded with bliss, she clenched against him and whimpered from somewhere deep in her throat. He kept touching her, caressing her, kissing her, until her spasms subsided.

He pulled her into his arms, but she was barely aware of it, or of the room, or of anything other than this feeling of satiety.

"Oh," she murmured. "Oh."

His hands caressed her arms, her smooth belly, as she slowly came back to her senses.

"You've done that before," she commented. It wasn't a question.

"I've done some other things before, too, that I'd really like to show you," he murmured against the hot skin of her neck.

She laughed, a low, throaty sound. "Yes, please."

Julia hadn't done this in a while—any of this. It wasn't that she hadn't wanted to; no emotional wound or trauma had driven her away from men. She'd just been experiencing a dry spell, and Colin, for her, was a long, cool rain.

She drank him in, kissing, touching, tasting everywhere. They both discarded the rest of their clothes and clung to each other, reveling in the delicious feel of skin on skin. She wrapped her hand around him and he sucked in a breath.

"Please tell me you have a condom," she said.

He got up off of the bed, rummaged around in his suitcase, and emerged with a square foil packet.

"Thank God," she said.

She helped him to put it on, and then he lay back and she straddled him, drawing him deeply into her. She would have thought that she couldn't become aroused again so soon after her shattering orgasm. But they began slowly, and he coaxed her with his fingers, caressed her with his hands, and she felt herself rising again, first gradually, and then with more intensity. Just the way he was looking at her, his eyes on her, his face showing his pleasure, was nearly enough to tip her over the edge.

He grasped her in his arms, rolled her onto her back, and thrust into her deeper, harder, and she gasped for breath. Her body shuddered again as she spasmed in pleasure. Her breath came fast, and she wrapped her legs around him and pulled him in close as he stilled and shook with his own release.

They stayed there, limp, their breathing ragged, until he rolled to the side and brought her along with him, cradling her in his embrace.

"Wow," she said.

He kissed her temple, which was damp with sweat.

They lay that way until they started to get cold despite the warmth of the fireplace. Then they got under the covers and held each other beneath the comforter.

"This date wasn't so bad after all," he said.

"Usually, when someone gets punched, it doesn't bode well," she said.

"Go figure."

She felt his hand roaming up and down her back in a way that felt protective, comforting.

"Colin?" She wasn't sure what she was about to say. Something about the mess they were in with his family and hers, about her home so far from his, her life, so different than his.

"*Shh.* We can talk about it later." His voice was a gentle rumble.

And so she let herself drift off to sleep in his soothing embrace.

Later—she didn't know how much later—she woke up to find that he was deeply asleep. She thought about what to do. She didn't want to wake him, but she also didn't want to stay here all night. It would raise too many questions if she didn't come back to the ranch until morning. Surely Liam would notice, and then what would happen between him and Colin? And Liam might not be the only Delaney who would raise an objection.

She got up, found her clothes on the floor, and got dressed. Then she hunted around in the dark for her purse and her coat, and slipped out of the room and into the hallway, closing the door behind her with a gentle click.

In the lobby of the lodge, she checked her phone and saw that it was past two a.m. The place was deserted. Cambria wasn't exactly a town where you could step outside and grab a cab in the dead of night.

She thought about who would be the least mortifying witness to her walk of shame, pulled up Drew in her contacts, and called him.

Chapter Twenty-Three

If Julia had thought that Drew would be less angry and judgmental than Liam or some other Delaney, then she'd miscalculated. As they made the drive back to the ranch in their rental car through the empty streets of Cambria, Drew's face was pinched with tension in the glow from the dashboard.

"What?" she said, after several minutes of silence. "Just say it, Drew."

He started to say something, stopped, and then said something else instead. "Why isn't *he* driving you back?" He sounded pissed, as though he was barely restraining himself from yelling. "The guy just abandons you at the lodge? Who the hell—"

"He didn't abandon me. He's asleep. I didn't want to wake him, so I snuck out."

"Still, he should have—"

"He'd have driven me back, Drew. Jeez. If he were conscious, I'm sure he'd be absolutely delighted to drive me back. So can we let that go now?"

She knew that her transportation needs were not the primary concern on Drew's mind. She waited for him to get around to what was really bothering him.

He did.

"What are you doing sleeping with that guy?" He smacked

the steering wheel with his hand. "Colin Delaney? Jesus, Julia."

"You're not my father, Drew."

"Yeah, well, Dad's not here, and maybe somebody needs to do the job. Somebody needs to set you straight. Because you're not thinking clearly, Julia. You just … God."

Julia was silent for a moment as she gathered her thoughts. When she spoke, her voice was calm but firm. "Drew, what's happening between me and Colin has nothing to do with you. Your issues are just that—*your* issues. They're not mine. Don't try to make them mine."

In the dim light of the car, she could see his tight, angry expression.

"There's such a thing as loyalty," he said.

The comment almost exactly mirrored what Liam had said earlier that night.

The question of why Julia should have to be loyal to Drew against a family that was responsible for him becoming a multimillionaire remained unclear to her.

"The Delaneys aren't your enemies, Drew," she said. "Except maybe Liam."

He grunted. "Yeah, well."

"How did your dinner with them go?"

"You're trying to change the subject from you and Colin Delaney."

She had been doing exactly that, and she was dismayed that he'd called her on it so quickly. "Maybe," she admitted. "But I still want to know how dinner went."

He shrugged. "It went fine, I guess. If you like tension so thick you can cut it like the damned pot roast."

"At least Liam wasn't there."

He glanced at her. "How do you know he wasn't there?"

She sighed. "It's a long story."

"It's still ten minutes to the ranch."

She thought about telling him everything that had happened, but how would that help the situation? If Drew knew that Liam had attacked Colin because of her, it was likely to make a volatile situation even more explosive.

"We saw him, that's all," she said. "When Colin and I were out to dinner. We saw him at the restaurant. He was walking by on Main Street." She wasn't lying to Drew; all of that was true. He didn't need to know the rest.

"And?" he prompted her.

"And what?"

"And what else? That's not a long story; it's a short one. So, what's the rest?"

Why had she said it was a long story? What had she been thinking? She was silent, pondering what to say. Then she realized that it didn't matter what she did or didn't tell him. The incident was witnessed by at least twenty people, if you included everyone on Main Street at the time and everyone who'd watched through the windows at Neptune. This was a small town, and Julia knew how small towns could be. If she didn't tell Drew what happened, he'd find out anyway, and then he'd be mad at her for lying to him.

"Jules?"

"Okay." She prepared herself, then let it all out in one long, rambling stream. "Colin and I were having dinner at Neptune and Colin kissed me, and Liam was walking by and saw us through the window, so he came in and started yelling at Colin, and then the manager made them go outside, and they yelled at each other some more, and then Liam hit Colin, and we all got asked to leave, so we did. And I didn't want to tell you, because I thought it would make things worse. Which it will."

Drew was silent, his eyes fixed on the road as he drove.

"Drew? Say something," Julia pleaded.

He still didn't speak as he turned off on the road that led to the ranch.

"Drew, come on."

"You're not going to keep seeing him."

At first, she wasn't sure she'd heard him correctly. She'd expected Drew to go off on an angry rant about Liam, so this wasn't what she'd been primed to hear.

"What?" She stared at him in surprise.

"You heard me."

"I must not have," she said. "Because I thought I heard you telling me what to do like it's your decision, and it is not your decision."

He pulled the rental car up in front of Ryan and Gen's house, turned off the ignition, and turned in his seat to face her. "You are not going to keep seeing him. That guy. Colin. You're going to break it off—whatever it is you two have going on."

She tried to answer him, but she found herself sputtering instead. "That's … You … That's just …"

He looked at her with hot anger in his eyes. "These people. These Delaneys. They didn't want me when I was born"—he swallowed hard—"and they don't want me in their lives now. I'm only here because I need answers. I need …" His voice cracked with emotion, and he looked out into the night for a moment before continuing. "I needed to see them for myself. So I'm doing that, and I'm going to stay here and keep doing that until I feel like I've got what I need. But you." He looked at her again, his face hard. "I thought you were here to support me. I thought you were here to *help*."

"I am. Drew …"

"You're not here for me, you're here for him." He wasn't asking; he seemed to have already decided it was true. And she had to admit to herself that on some level, it was. She was here for Colin. She was here for both of them.

"What do you even think is going to happen?" he went on, looking at her with contempt. "You think he's going to fall in love with you? Whisk you off to his goddamned penthouse? He's a fucking *billionaire,* Julia. What's a guy like that going to want with someone like you? He's playing you, don't you get that?"

She was struck speechless by his words, partly because of their cruelty, but partly because she wondered if they were true.

"We're here. Go inside," he said.

"Drew, this isn't—"

"Go, Julia."

He might not have been her father, but he certainly sounded like him now.

"We'll talk about this tomorrow," she said. She gathered her purse and got out of the car. "Thanks for the ride." She would have slammed the car door and stomped her way up the porch steps if she weren't trying to sneak in without being heard. Instead, she closed the door softly and walked as quietly as she could, taking care not to make the porch floor squeak.

Drew waited until she'd let herself in with the key Gen had given her, and then he drove, too fast, down the dirt road and back to the main house.

Colin woke up at about seven the next morning, feeling surprisingly good despite the dull throb in his jaw. His first thoughts were of Julia, and before he'd even opened his eyes, he reached over to her side of the bed to touch her.

And found nothing but cold sheets.

At first he assumed she was in the bathroom, but when he glanced over, he saw that the bathroom door was open and the light was out. Which either meant that Julia had left the room to get some breakfast—or that she'd simply left.

He grabbed his cell phone from the bedside table and sent her a text:

Where did you go?

He didn't get a response right away, so he puttered around the room doing the usual morning things: He used the bathroom, made coffee with the little pot that was provided in the room, and checked his e-mails, finding several that needed his attention, even though the business day hadn't yet started.

While he was brooding over one particular e-mail dealing with the land boundary issue at the Palm Springs lot, he heard the *bing* of an incoming text message:

Went back to Ryan's last night. I thought there'd be too much talk if I stayed out with you all night.

He might have thought that was a good point, except for the fact that after what happened at Neptune, everyone would be talking about them anyway. He wrote back:

How did you get back to the ranch without a car?

Moments later, she responded:

I called Drew and he picked me up.

Damn it. Now Drew probably thought that Colin was the kind of guy who would sleep with someone's sister and then be too inconsiderate to drive her home. Colin wasn't that guy; he hated that guy. Anybody would.

You should have woken me up, he texted her.

And he really wished she had. Partly because he didn't want to be that guy, but also—more importantly—because he'd expected to see her when he awakened, and when he didn't, he'd felt a kind of emptiness. He didn't like the emptiness.

When can I see you again? he wrote.

◆◆◆

Julia pondered his question, still under the thick down comforter in Ryan and Gen's guest bedroom. She wanted to ask, *How soon can you get here?* But there were feelings at stake, and not just hers and Colin's. If she and Colin were to pursue a relationship, it would cause a rift between Colin and Liam that might never heal. And what about herself and Drew? If she kept seeing Colin, Drew would see it as a betrayal. He already felt that their mother had turned against him. If he felt the same way about Julia, how would that affect him?

And was Drew right? Was it impossible that a man like Colin could get serious about a woman like her? She wasn't in his league; surely they both knew that. If she fell for him—which she was starting to think was pretty much a done deal—he could hurt her more deeply than any other man ever had. If she got out of this now, it would hurt like hell, but it wouldn't destroy her. Let it go a little longer, and it might.

He was still waiting for an answer to his question.

I don't know, she responded. *I'm not sure this is a good idea.*

She felt a little bit sick just typing the text, and worse when she actually sent it. After what had happened between them last night, the thought of never seeing him again—at least, not in that way—seemed impossible. But she had to consider the bigger picture. She had to think things through.

She expected a return text, but instead, her phone rang. Colin's name came up on the screen. She wanted to answer it, but she knew she wouldn't be able to think if she heard his low, sexy voice murmuring into her ear.

And she really had to think.

Julia hit the DECLINE button on her iPhone, cursed softly to herself, and then shoved the phone under her pillow so she wouldn't have to think about it.

Colin Delaney. She should never have gone there, but now

that she had, all she wanted was to go there again, as soon as possible. But that had the potential to go horribly wrong. It had the potential to hurt people, including herself.

God, Julia, get a grip.

Chapter Twenty-Four

She didn't take his call. Goddamn it, why didn't she take his call?

Colin stared at the phone. Never in his life had a woman refused to take his calls after a night of great sex, though he guessed there was a first time for everything. He thought of the chick flicks Breanna liked, full of women sobbing to their friends about men who used them for their bodies and then didn't call.

Was Colin the scorned woman from a chick flick?

He could text her again; after all, she had answered his texts. But that would injure his pride in a way he wasn't quite prepared to accept. If she didn't want to talk to him, there wasn't much he could do about it. But that didn't mean he had to like it.

That didn't mean he understood it, either. What had gone wrong, apart from the incident with Liam? What had changed between the time they'd been together, and now?

And then it hit him: She'd gotten a ride back to the ranch from her brother.

Colin groaned softly and ran a hand through his hair.

Drew.

Nothing like a little scolding from a brother, a little guilt-inducing, angry rant, to change a person's mind about a budding relationship.

Colin tossed his phone on the bed and thought about it while he took a hot, steamy shower. What was he supposed to do here? What was the best way forward?

One thing was certain: If Julia didn't want to be with him for her own reasons, then that was fine. He could be a man about it and walk away. But if she didn't want to be with him because of Drew or Liam—because those two hot-tempered fools couldn't accept the fact that Colin and Julia had something developing between them—then he'd have something to say about it.

He'd have a lot to say about it, as a matter of fact.

Julia got showered and dressed and went downstairs at Ryan and Gen's place, and the news about the fight between Colin and Liam had already spread. Ryan was gone; Gen said he usually left the house at the crack of dawn. But Gen was bustling around in the kitchen, pulling freshly baked muffins out of the oven and putting them on a rack to cool. Over the scent of the muffins, Julia smelled strong coffee.

"Good morning," Gen greeted her. Gen had a white cotton apron on over a pair of jeans and a T-shirt. Her red curls were piled on top of her head.

"That smells wonderful," Julia said. "I thought you'd be at work already."

"The gallery doesn't open until ten, and I wanted to make sure you got a good breakfast," she said. Gen was an absurdly good and happy host; when Julia had come into the kitchen, Gen was actually *humming*.

Gen shot Julia a look out of the corner of her eye. "I heard there was a thing between Colin and Liam last night. Punches were thrown. Jackson Graham had to break it up." Gen's voice was calm and conversational, as though this sort of thing happened every day around here. Who knew? Maybe it did.

"You heard about that already?" Julia paused, coffee mug in her hand, and looked at Gen.

"Sure. Ryan was out in the barn after dinner tending to a sick calf, and Liam came in, all pissed off and brooding. He told Ryan, and Ryan told me." Gen's face was serene as she puttered around the kitchen. Such a lack of response over her brothers-in-law coming to blows could only mean it wasn't a rare occurrence—or it wasn't unexpected.

"Is Liam always such a"—she searched for an apt description—"a seething ball of fury?"

Gen turned toward Julia, put one hand on her hip, and considered the question. "Always? No. But it doesn't take much."

"Well, God." Julia poured herself a cup of coffee and added milk and sugar.

"I'll tell you what, though. He's a good guy. I mean, he's a really good guy. He might occasionally punch his brother, but he'd throw himself in front of a train for any one of us."

"Well." Julia plunked down onto one of the kitchen chairs at the big table in the center of the room. "I couldn't imagine him throwing himself in front of a train for Colin last night. Throwing me in front of it, maybe."

Gen put a muffin on a plate, added some cut fruit beside it, and placed the plate in front of Julia with a napkin and a fork.

"This looks amazing," Julia said.

"This? This is nothing." Gen sat across from Julia at the table. "So. I heard you come in last night. Almost three a.m." She wiggled her eyebrows meaningfully.

Julia froze. She'd hoped that she'd managed to sneak in on the sly, but apparently Gen had the superhuman hearing of a dolphin, or maybe a bat. Julia opened her mouth to say something, but didn't know what to say, and so she shoved her muffin in there instead.

"Oh, come on," Gen said. "You're not going to give me a little dirt on you and Colin? I know we just met, but you can tell me. I'm an in-law. I don't have any emotional baggage! At least, not about this."

Gen did seem like she'd be easy to talk to, and Julia really wanted to talk to someone. She chewed her bite of the exceptional muffin, swallowed, and was just about to launch into the story of her date with Colin, when the kitchen door burst open and Breanna rushed in. Breanna most resembled Ryan, with her thick, dark hair and deep brown eyes. Her cheeks were pink from the chilly morning air, and she whisked off her jacket and scarf as she came into the kitchen.

"Okay, Julia. The kids are at school. I've got time on my hands, and I heard you slept with my brother last night. So, dish." She grabbed a muffin from the cooling rack, sat down at the table next to Julia, and focused on her.

News really did spread fast around here.

Julia shifted uncomfortably in her seat and said to Breanna, "You don't really want to hear about your brother's sex life, do you?"

Breanna winced a little. "Ideally, no. But I'll do it, because it's been so long since I've had a sex life of my own, I have to live vicariously through someone. Ooh, coffee." She got up, took a mug from the cupboard above the coffee pot, and poured herself a cup.

Julia shook her head a little to clear her confusion. "But, wait. I thought the Delaneys hated the idea of Colin and me together."

"Just because we're a family doesn't mean we share the same brain," Breanna said.

"Right. Okay," Julia said.

Despite the discomfort of being put on the spot like this, she was beginning to think she liked both Gen and Breanna, despite whatever the Delaney family politics might be. She'd never been good at making female friends—in school, she'd found the things girls talked about to be silly and frivolous. But right now, in Gen's warm kitchen, it felt good to be talking to women—it felt good to think that these women might become her friends.

"All right. Colin took me to dinner at Neptune, and Liam saw us in the window, and—"

"We know that part," Gen said.

"Okay, right. So, then there was the fight, and—"

"We know that part, too," Breanna reminded her.

"Oh. So what you want to know is …"

"How was it? How was my brother-in-law in bed? And are you going to keep seeing him? Are you in love? Is he?" Gen leaned forward, her elbows on the table, her chin propped in her hands. She batted her eyelashes at Julia.

Julia couldn't help but laugh. That was, until she remembered how she'd left things between herself and Colin. Her heart sank, and her face fell. She swallowed hard. "I told him we shouldn't see each other anymore."

"Oh, no. Was it that bad?" Breanna asked.

"What? No! It wasn't that bad. I mean, it wasn't bad at all. It was … well, kind of spectacular, actually. It was amazing. It was—"

"Then why did you dump him?" Gen looked genuinely puzzled.

"Did you miss the part about Liam?" Julia said, flustered.

"What about him?" Breanna demanded.

"What do you mean, 'What about him?' He hit Colin! He punched him right there on Main Street, in front of everybody!

Because of me! I don't want to come between two brothers! I don't want to be that woman who tears a family apart!"

Breanna waved dismissively with one hand. "One: I don't think this family could be torn apart with a bulldozer and a chainsaw. Two: People can't choose who to fall for based on how other people feel about it. And three: Liam didn't hit Colin because of you. He hit Colin because of Redmond. He just doesn't realize that yet."

Gen nodded her agreement. "Liam and Redmond were close, and now Liam's grieving and he's hurting, and all of that hurt has to go somewhere. So he's pointing it at you and Drew. But he'll work all of that out and get past it. And if he doesn't, Sandra will smack some sense into him."

"If she hasn't done it already," Breanna added.

As if on cue, Sandra came into the kitchen. Didn't anyone knock around here?

Sandra was wearing faded jeans and a football jersey, this one for the Oakland Raiders. Her graying hair was in a ponytail, and she wore blue and white Nikes on her feet, in place of the fuzzy slippers Julia had seen her wearing before.

"Good, you're here." Sandra nodded at Julia.

"Um … I …" Julia started.

"I'm here to tell you not to pay any attention to my dim-wit son. Liam, I mean, if you didn't know which one I was talking about. It's inexcusable the way he acted last night—yes, I heard all about it—and I won't have it. He can take his butt back to Montana if he can't respect someone who's a guest in our home. And I guess that's all I have to say about it." She nodded to herself, apparently satisfied with her speech.

Julia looked at Sandra in surprise. "Sandra, I appreciate that, but—"

"There's no *but* about it," she snapped. "Bad manners are

bad manners, and that's that. The boy's lost his mind, you ask me, and there's nothing more to be said about it. I raised him better than this, by God. What kind of muffins are those? Blueberry?"

"Lemon poppy seed," Gen said.

"Well, I suppose that'll do." Sandra grabbed a plate from the cupboard, put a muffin on it, and then put it on the kitchen table and got herself a mug of coffee. She plopped down into a chair as though she belonged there. Which, from the look of things, she did.

"We were just talking about Julia and Colin," Breanna said. "And their date. She was going to tell us how Colin was in b—"

Julia kicked Breanna, hard, under the table.

"Ouch! That's going to bruise." Breanna glared at her.

"All I can say is that he'd damned well better call you today, after the thing you kicked Breanna to keep her from saying. A man who doesn't call a woman after being with her the night before is just a—"

"Julia dumped him," Gen broke in.

"I didn't—"

"Oh, come on. You did," Gen said.

"Well, what the hell?" Sandra demanded. "What'd he do to bring that on?"

"He didn't ... It's just ..." The conversation was moving too fast, and in too many directions, for Julia to keep up with it.

"It's because of Liam," Breanna put in. "She doesn't want to cause trouble."

Sandra fixed Julia with a glare that probably had served her well as the mother of four children. "Liam decks somebody who's just trying to eat his damned dinner, and *you're* the one causing trouble? For God's sake."

When Sandra put it that way, it did seem kind of stupid.

Julia was just pondering whether the older woman had a point, and whether she should try talking things out with Colin, when the kitchen door opened and Colin himself came in. Julia began to wonder whether Gen's kitchen had some kind of gravitational pull that dragged everyone within a certain radius into it.

"Colin," Julia said. She could feel herself blushing.

"Oh, good. You're here," he said, repeating his mother's words from earlier almost exactly. "We need to talk."

"You're goddamned right you two need to talk," Sandra groused. "This one over here thinks she shouldn't see you anymore because Liam doesn't like it." She snorted and shook her head. "*Liam.*"

"I just wanted—"

"I heard there's muffins in here," Orin said, coming into the kitchen with a sheepish look on his face. "That is, if you've got enough, Gen."

"I've got plenty," Gen said. "Have a seat."

"Well, I thought I'd just take one to go, if you don't mind. Ryan needs me in the barn." He stuffed his hands into the pockets of his work pants and rocked back and forth on his feet.

"How about if I pack some up and you can take some to Ryan, too?" Gen said.

"Well, that's fine, Gen. Appreciate it."

Gen started to pack some muffins into a paper bag, and Colin tried again to get Julia's attention amid the bustle of a room that was teeming with people.

"Julia," Colin said, more firmly. "Could we maybe step outside?"

Julia looked around her for some kind of help, and her gaze fell on Breanna.

"You used him for sex and now you're not even going to talk to him?" Breanna said in a low voice, so only Julia could hear her amid the chaos of the bustling room. She raised her eyebrows and fixed Julia with a look full of meaning. "Because we all find that so attractive when guys do it to us."

Breanna was right. Julia was acting like one of those guys, even if her motives were more true. She steeled herself, got up, and followed Colin out of the room and onto the front porch.

Chapter Twenty-Five

"What do you mean, you don't think this is a good idea?" Colin was leaning his butt against the porch railing, his arms crossed over his chest. He looked impeccably groomed, if slightly overdressed, as he always did; his khaki pants sported knife-sharp creases, and his shoes gleamed with polish.

"Colin. Last night was wonderful. It really was. But—"

"Don't give me the standard kiss-off line. 'Last night was great, it's not you, it's me.' I know that line, I've sure as hell used it enough times. Don't do that." He narrowed his eyes at her, and she could imagine him using the same look when he was trying to intimidate someone in a business negotiation.

"Colin …"

"This isn't about what happened with Liam, is it? It's about Drew."

It was, partly, but she hadn't wanted to say that. She didn't want to give anyone any more reason to dislike her brother.

She didn't answer.

"What did he say to you last night?" Colin demanded.

"He's going through a lot right now," she said. It wasn't an answer—not really—but it likely told him all he needed to know.

"We all are. We lost an uncle, and we gained a cousin we

didn't know about, who apparently can't stand the sight of us. We're all going through a lot."

"I just … I think my loyalty has to be to Drew right now," she said.

He pressed his lips together tightly and nodded. "Loyalty."

It had been a key word over the last twenty-four hours. Liam had accused Colin of disloyalty, and Drew had accused Julia of the same thing. How far did family loyalty have to go? Did her loyalty to her brother matter more than what she was beginning to feel for Colin? She didn't know, but she suspected that, given more time, she might choose Colin. She had to stop this before it came to that.

And she couldn't stop thinking about what Drew had said—that Colin could never really be serious about her. She didn't want to believe she was that insecure.

"I came here for him," she said. "To help him."

"And there's not some part of you that came here for me? Not even a little?" His voice was low and intimate, and he took a step toward her and reached out to gently touch her face.

"That's not …"

"What did he say to you?" he asked again.

She couldn't think, not with Colin's hand caressing her face. And she needed to think. She shook her head and stepped backward, away from his touch. "It doesn't matter what he said. What matters is that he's right. There's just too much drama right now, too much conflict. Too many people could get hurt."

He leaned against the railing again and shoved his hands into his pants pockets. He nodded slightly, as though answering a question that she couldn't hear.

"So, it doesn't matter if I'm one of the people who gets hurt?"

◆◆◆

He regretted the words the moment he'd said them. He didn't want her to see him again because he was manipulating her into it, because she felt guilty about hurting him. He needed her to see him again because she wanted to, because she was beginning to feel the same things for him that he was feeling for her.

But what was he feeling for her? Was it love? Not yet; it was too soon for that. At least, that's what he told himself. The thought that he might be falling for her already was ridiculous. But he couldn't deny that being with her last night had given him a glimmer of hope, a feeling of rightness, that he hadn't gotten any other way for as long as he could remember. When he was with her he felt light and at peace, and when he wasn't with her, he felt like some part of him was dark and empty.

Was that love? It sure as hell was something.

He looked at her and remembered her touch, her scent, her skin, the way she'd looked lying sleepy and satisfied in his bed. His chest hurt at the thought that she might not want him, or at least not enough to overcome the obstacles. But he wasn't going to beg her; he wasn't going to manipulate her; and he wasn't going to whine about it, either. She had to want it, too.

Since there was nothing more to say, he walked down the porch steps, got into his car, and slammed the door. He started the ignition, turned the car around, and then drove down the road that led to the main house. He'd heard Julia call after him, but he hadn't acknowledged her.

Colin was a man with things to do. He had to talk to Drew and force some sense into the man's damned head. But before that, he had something else to attend to. He already felt like hell, so this was as good a time as any to talk to Liam.

It took some time to track Liam down on the big ranch.

Colin couldn't get him on his cell phone, either because he didn't have it with him or because he was screening his calls and didn't want to hear whatever Colin might have to say. He wasn't in the house, but the old Ford F-150 he used when he was in town was parked in front.

Colin figured that Liam was probably out working on the ranch, with the cattle. He was most comfortable that way, and he couldn't understand why anyone would choose to work behind a desk, the way Colin did. It was just one of many things that separated them.

Liam might not have been responding to phone calls, but Ryan was. Liam had crossed paths with him out in the southeast pasture earlier in the morning, Ryan said, and then he'd gone to the barn to check on a calf they'd culled from the herd so the vet could check her over. He was probably still there.

Colin considered driving from the main house to the big, state-of-the-art barn, but he decided to walk instead, because it gave him a chance to clear his head. So much was going on in there: Julia, Liam, Redmond, Drew. And on top of all that, he'd learned just this morning that one of their biggest commercial tenants was pulling out of the family's Los Angeles property when the lease was up. He'd need to get someone else in there as soon as possible, but it wouldn't be easy given that the place had been extensively customized for the former tenant. He pushed that out of his mind for the moment, because he couldn't focus on it. He couldn't seem to focus on anything since his talk with Julia.

The morning was cool, and the ground was dark and rich from a recent rain. The hills that stretched out over the ranch were carpeted in tall, green grass, and the sky was a clear, pale blue. The day's chill made him wish he were wearing a heavier jacket. The tree branches whispered and swayed in the breeze.

When he got to the barn, he noticed an unfamiliar pickup truck parked outside the front doors. Inside, at the far end of the cavernous structure, he found a young, pretty woman inspecting the calf as Liam looked on. The woman had long brown hair pulled back into a ponytail, and she wore tortoiseshell glasses that made her look studious. She was wearing a pair of faded jeans, work boots, and a thick flannel shirt, and she was on one knee examining the calf, which was lying on its side in the stall. She raised one of the calf's eyelids and checked its eye, then pinched the skin on its side with her fingers.

Colin had never met this particular vet before, and the first thing he thought when he saw her was, *good.* With a pretty woman in the room—especially one who was a stranger to them—it was less likely that Liam would have another angry tantrum at Colin.

The second thing he thought was, *hmm.* Liam was paying so much attention to the vet that he hadn't even noticed Colin coming into the barn. Maybe if Liam had a woman in his life for a change, he might focus on his own love life and forget about Colin's.

"She's dehydrated," the vet was saying as Colin reached the stall where the calf was being kept. "You've tried oral fluid therapy?"

"She wouldn't take it," Liam told her.

"No suckle reflex," she said. "I'm going to have to put her on an IV."

"All right, then," Liam said.

When he noticed Colin, his face changed so slightly that a casual observer would not have noticed it. A slight narrowing of the eyes, an almost imperceptible flex of the chin. But Colin noticed it; he'd had a lifetime of experience with Liam's moods.

"You got a minute?" Colin asked.

"Not really," Liam replied.

"It's fine if you need to step away," the vet said agreeably, looking up at them from where she knelt beside the calf. "I can manage here."

They walked out the door of the barn and stood under an oak tree a few yards away.

"Since when do you need professional help to deal with a dehydrated calf?" Colin asked, side-eyeing his brother.

"Since never," Liam said.

Colin nodded. "Sounds about right." They stood there companionably enough, given all that had happened between them. "This new vet's an attractive woman," Colin observed.

"Yes, she is," Liam agreed.

They thought about that for a minute.

"If that calf hadn't had a problem, something tells me you'd have invented one," Colin said.

Liam grinned, and Colin did, too. He couldn't help it.

"Look. About the thing at Neptune ..." Liam looked intensely uncomfortable as he rocked back and forth on his feet and scratched at the stubble on his chin.

"You don't have to apologize," Colin said, feeling generous.

"Well, hell, I wasn't going to," Liam said. "I was going to say, you take a punch pretty well for a guy who works in an office all day."

"Thanks, I guess."

Liam scratched the stubble some more. "You didn't hit me back. I guess it would have been fair enough if you had."

Colin shrugged and accepted it for what he knew it was—the closest thing to an apology he was going to get.

"I like her, Liam. A lot. And I'm not going to stop seeing her, unless she decides that's what she wants." He didn't feel the need to mention that she already had decided that very thing.

"Well, shit." Liam stuffed his hands into his pockets. "I can't say I'm comfortable with that."

"You don't have to be. It's not your life, and you're not the one who's going to be seeing her." Colin kept his tone light, casual. He didn't think it would gain him much to escalate the situation, not when Liam's temper seemed to have run its course. "Seems like you have something in common with Drew, though. Other than DNA."

Liam grunted. "Like what?"

"Like going ballistic over me seeing Julia."

Liam's eyebrows shot up. "What's his problem with you seeing his sister? He thinks you're not good enough for her? He's got a lot of fuckin' nerve. For God's sake …"

Colin couldn't help but grin affectionately at his brother, despite having been hit by the very same man about fourteen hours earlier. It was just like when they were kids. If Liam wanted to pick on Colin, that was business as usual. But if anyone else tried to bully him or hurt him in any way—at school or anywhere else—he'd have to answer to Liam.

Some things didn't change.

"You're not gonna hit him, too, are you?" Colin asked.

"I'm leaving my options open."

"Liam …"

"Relax. He's safe, at least for now. He's with Ryan somewhere out on the ranch. And Ryan's never hit anybody, far as I know."

That was true. Ryan was a gentle soul, so much so that he'd become a vegetarian because he couldn't stand eating the same animals he'd raised from birth. The thought of him hitting anyone was absurd.

They stood there together in the awkward silence common to men who loved each other but didn't consider it manly to say so. Liam rocked back and forth on his feet again, peeked in the barn door to see how the pretty vet was doing, and then looked at Colin uncomfortably.

"So, are we good?"

"Yeah, I guess. As long as you agree to play nice with the McCrays."

"Mom already told me. And told me," Liam said ruefully.

"Well, good, because I don't have time for any more drama," Colin told him. He gave Liam a friendly slap on the shoulder. "You'd better get back inside, find out if that vet is married."

"She's not," he said.

Liam turned and started to walk back into the barn, where the vet and the sick calf were waiting for him. In the doorway of the barn, he turned and pointed one finger at Colin.

"I still think you're making a mistake. You and Julia McCray."

Then he went back into the barn without another word.

Chapter Twenty-Six

For a woman who'd just announced that she didn't want to pursue a relationship with a man, Julia certainly was thinking a lot about the man in question.

As she went about her day—visiting Gen's gallery to see where she worked, strolling up and down Main Street to browse the charming shops, walking at Moonstone Beach to take in the breathtaking views—she couldn't seem to keep Colin, or what had happened between them the night before, out of her head.

Of course she was thinking about him after the intimacy they'd shared. It was only natural. But there was thinking about someone, and then there was *longing* for someone. If pressed, she would have to admit that what she was doing was veering out of the first category and dangerously deep into the second.

Looking out at the pounding surf from the Moonstone Beach boardwalk, she found herself reliving the things he'd done to her. On Main Street, she thought she saw him, just for a second, and her heart raced. It turned out to be a tourist carrying a bag of souvenirs from Caren's Corner. Good thing she hadn't impulsively run up to him and leaped into his arms, the way she'd wanted to do. That would have been embarrassing, especially because the guy was with his wife.

She told herself she was being ridiculous. One night of great sex shouldn't be turning her upside down this way. Even if it had been *really* great sex.

The day was clear and warm, so she settled in on a bench at a lovely little park at the foot of Bridge Street, not far from the shops and restaurants.

She listened to the breeze in the trees and the gentle whoosh of the nearby creek, which was swollen with rain. Then she pulled out her cell phone and dialed Mike.

"What can I do for you, Julia?" he asked when he answered the phone. His tone was world-weary and cautious, as though he knew this conversation was going to meander off into places he'd rather not go. Which it surely would, and without delay.

"I need to do girl talk, but I don't have a girl here I can talk to. Well, I do—a couple of them, actually, but they're mostly Colin's family, and that won't work, so …"

"Fine. As long as it doesn't have anything to do with hair or makeup. Or sex."

"Well …"

"No," he said. "Forget it. Call me when you need advice on building a deck."

"Mike, come on."

"I'm hanging up now."

"No! Wait!" She thought, desperate. "Okay—a deck. I need to talk to you about building a deck."

"A deck," he said, sounding skeptical.

"Yes." She took a deep breath and thought about her metaphor. "Colin and I … last night … we …"

"Built a deck," he supplied.

"Right. And it was a really good deck. This was the best deck I've ever … stood on. Redwood planks, plenty of space, a view …"

"Okay. So, what's the problem? Did it collapse while you

were on it?"

"No!" She thought about what that analogy might mean in terms of sex, and decided it wasn't very flattering to Colin. "No. The deck … held up. Really well. It was a very durable deck."

"Well, good for you. You can have a lot of parties on that deck. Barbecues and whatnot."

"No, we can't. Because I told him I don't want to … use the deck anymore."

"Why not? You said it was a great deck."

"It is! It is. It's so great. So great. But … Drew doesn't want me to build any more decks with Colin. Ever. And neither does Colin's brother Liam. Nobody wants me on that deck, Mike, and I don't want to cause trouble. I don't! I don't want to hurt people or cause fights or … I don't want to trash the *house* that the deck is attached to."

"Ah. Got it. Well, what does this Colin guy think?"

"I think if he had his way, he and I would be building decks all over town."

Mike sighed, and she could picture him in his living room, in sweatpants and socks, shaking his head with weary annoyance.

"I think you should build any damned deck you want with any damned … *carpenter* you want, and to hell with what anybody else thinks."

"I want to, Mike." She closed her eyes and imagined the deck-building of the previous night. "I want to so much. I want to sand and varnish and … pound nails. Oh, God, I want to pound nails."

"This conversation is making my head hurt," Mike said.

"I'm sorry. It's just … what should I do?"

"I think you should build whatever deck you want to build. And if the house falls down, it wasn't a very strong house."

◆◆◆

When Julia got back to Ryan's house, Drew was there waiting for her. He'd spent the morning on the ranch with Ryan, and he looked a little tousled and dusty after hours atop a horse. They both knew how to ride—they'd grown up in Montana, after all—but she suspected it had been a while for Drew. He moved like his ass hurt.

She could hear Ryan moving around upstairs—doing what, she didn't know. Gen was at work at her gallery, and that left Julia and Drew alone in the big living room.

The awkward silence between them was heavy, until Julia broke it with small talk. "I hear you got to see the ranch this morning."

"Yeah." He stuffed his hands into his jeans pockets. "It's huge. And beautiful." He shook his head in wonder at the situation he'd found himself in. "Ryan thought that since I'm going to own part of it, I ought to see it."

"You and Ryan. How did that go?" She wanted to ask if he'd picked a fight with all of the Delaney brothers and made it a perfect trifecta, but she kept that last part to herself.

Drew shrugged. "He's all right, I guess. Kind of a hard guy to be pissed at."

"Though you tried, I'm sure," Julia said.

Drew shrugged again. It seemed like his default mode of communication today.

"Look, Julia." He was fidgeting a little, and he couldn't seem to look straight at her. "Colin wants to meet with me this afternoon. To go over the specifics of the will." He cleared his throat. "I'm freaking out a little here. I wondered if you could come with me."

The nervous way he stood there, with an uneasy mix of fear and defiance, made Julia see him for a moment not as the man he was today, but as the child he'd been when they were growing up together. He was still her little brother, and it was still her job to protect him.

"Of course I will."

"But then, after that"—he looked at her with a stubborn challenge in his eyes—"I think you should go home."

Her mouth fell open slightly. "What?"

"I think … Look. I need you for this, okay? For this meeting. Because I don't think I can handle all of this alone. But after that, I'm going to drive you to the airport, and I want you to go back to Montana."

"But … why?"

He glared at her coldly. "You know why."

"Because of Colin?"

His silence was his answer.

She could have told him that she'd already broken things off with Colin. That would have appeased him, surely. She could have told him that she'd chosen him—she'd chosen her family over a man. But instead, she found herself reacting with anger over the fact that he thought he could tell her what to do, how to live.

She crossed her arms over her chest and tipped her chin up in defiance. "Like hell. I'm not going anywhere."

"Julia—"

"No, Drew. You do what you want, but I'll go when I'm ready."

"These people. They aren't—"

"They aren't *what,* Drew? Because I've got to tell you, the victim act is getting a little old. Liam's been acting like an asshole, I'll give you that, but everyone else is doing their best to welcome you. To welcome *us.* And all you can do is … is be *pissed* about it!" She threw her hands into the air. "You got a raw deal when Mom lied to you and kept you away from your biological father. Fine. We all agree on that. But now you're getting *millions of dollars*! You'd think you could pull yourself together and … cope!"

"I never asked for their money. I never—"

"Fine. You never asked. But you're getting it anyway." Warming up to her topic, Julia was rolling now, with a head of steam that was just getting hotter the further she went with it. "You're getting the money, and you could have a new *family* if you would just try! If you would just … just *try* to *assume* that maybe everyone you meet is not out to *screw you*!"

It was true; Drew had the opportunity to be part of something here—part of this big, messy family with all of the good and bad that implied. But what did Julia have? Her relationship with her brother was rough at best, and she wasn't sure things between herself and her mother would ever be fully repaired. And now, Drew was playing the brother card to take away any chance she might have had to build something with Colin.

Suddenly, everything seemed so overwhelming. She'd been right to tell Colin that she wouldn't continue seeing him. Any potential relationship simply faced too many obstacles. From Drew, from Liam—from her own feelings that she could never really fit into Colin's world.

"You know what?" Drew looked at her with contempt. "I think I'll just go to that meeting alone after all."

"Yeah? Well, you know what? I think you were right. I should go home. I'll be out of here today. Don't bother driving me to the airport; I'll take the rental car. You can get another one."

She stalked upstairs to the guest room, tears stinging her eyes and blurring her vision. She slammed the door behind her, used her phone to check flight times, and started to pack her things.

Chapter Twenty-Seven

Orin, as the senior Delaney, was sitting in on the meeting with Drew. Colin and his father sat on an old, plaid sofa in Orin's upstairs study, and Drew sat in a threadbare wing chair across the coffee table from them. The room was done in dark paneling, with shag carpeting on the floor that had been there since it had been fashionable back in the '70s. One side of the room was lined in bookcases filled with a variety of volumes, including veterinary reference books, old almanacs, and the crime paperbacks Orin favored.

"I thought Julia was going to be here," Colin commented. Drew had told him earlier that he wanted his sister to join them, and now, Colin asked after her as though he were merely inquiring about a simple change of plans. He hoped it didn't show how disappointed he was not to see her here.

"She had other things to do." Drew glared at Colin as he said it, and Colin wondered whether there was some sort of hidden message he was supposed to divine from the man's tone.

"Well, that's fine." It wasn't—not as far as Colin was concerned—but he thought it best not to say that.

Colin had a file folder on the table in front of him.

"I guess we should get started, then," he began. He turned the file folder around and pushed it across the table toward

Drew. "This folder contains a list of the assets Redmond bequeathed to you in his will. I'm prepared to go over each item, line by line. You should understand that coming up with exact dollar amounts of the value of each asset is problematic, given the fluctuating stock and real estate markets."

He sounded like a lawyer, and that was by design. The man had made it clear that he didn't like Colin; it was best to keep this professional.

Drew looked at the folder on the table but didn't pick it up. He looked at Colin, then Orin. "Is this the part where you ask me to take a DNA test?"

Orin rubbed his chin, looking uncomfortable. "Well, we weren't planning on it. Redmond named you as his son; I guess that's good enough for me."

"Legally, it doesn't matter if you're his biological son," Colin said. "He listed you as his beneficiary by name, with no mention of it being contingent on a DNA test." He spread his hands. "Even if you took a test and it turned out that you and Redmond aren't related, you'd still be his heir."

Drew shifted in his seat. "Still … I think I'd kind of like to know for sure."

Colin nodded. "I can arrange that, if it's what you want. I have to tell you, though—if it turned out you weren't his son, certain members of the family … Well. I can't guarantee …"

"You're saying Liam might challenge the will."

"Yes. That's what I'm saying."

"Well, wouldn't you? I sure as shit would," Drew said. It was the first thing he'd ever said to indicate he might have some common ground with Liam. "Let's do it anyway," he said. "The test. I want to know."

"I'll set it up," Colin said.

Colin figured Ryan had probably told Drew the family's

background during the time they'd spent together earlier in the day. If he hadn't, Drew had undoubtedly Googled the Delaneys and read it for himself. Still, it seemed important to go through it. If the man was going to own a hefty chunk of the Delaney fortune, he ought to know where it came from in the first place.

He told Drew about how Kenneth Delaney, an ancestor from seven generations ago, had immigrated from Ireland and received a huge parcel of acreage as part of a Mexican land grant in 1846. Colin's grandfather, a man with a keen sense of business, had sold off a lot of the land and had put the profits into commercial properties all up and down the state, as well as the family's ranch in Montana. The result was a portfolio that regularly landed the Delaneys on various lists of California's most wealthy families.

"Most of Redmond's wealth was in the form of shares in the family's corporation," Colin continued. He explained that Redmond and Orin, who had been their parents' only heirs, had each held fifty percent of the corporation, until Orin had given ten percent shares to each of his children, keeping ten percent for himself.

"That meant that Redmond, who retained fifty percent, had by far the largest voting share," Colin went on. "According to Clayton Drummond, the lawyer who prepared the will, Redmond thought it wouldn't be fair to all of us if you got a larger voting share than any of the Delaneys. He thought it would cause a certain amount of discord." And that was understating it significantly. "So, he split his shares equally among his niece and nephews, and you."

"There's four of you and one of me," Drew said.

"Which means we each inherit a ten percent voting share," Colin went on.

"With what the boys and Breanna already have, that means

they'll each have twenty percent of the corporation, and you'll have ten," Orin said. He shrugged apologetically. "Puts you on equal footing with me, I guess."

"Voting shares," Drew said, looking stunned. "But I don't know anything about … about what you all do."

"I can help you with that," Colin said. "I can teach you what you need to know, if you're willing to learn."

Drew nodded mutely.

"Now, that brings us to Redmond's personal assets, everything that was not a part of the corporation. Real estate, stock portfolio, cash accounts." Colin leaned forward with his elbows on his knees, his hands laced together loosely. He focused on Drew. "It's all itemized here." He pushed the folder a little closer to Drew. "You get everything."

If Orin was feeling emotional about what was happening, the only sign was in the way he cleared his throat rubbed his chin with his thick, callused fingers. Drew's emotions were a little more evident; his hand shook as he reached out to pick up the folder.

As Drew opened the folder and looked wordlessly at the contents, Colin went on, "It'll take some time for Redmond's assets to be transferred over to you. It has to go through probate, and that can take as long as a year."

"A year," Drew repeated, his eyes still on the paper in front of him.

"But the shares in the corporation pay dividends quarterly, and that'll transfer to you immediately. The next disbursement is next month."

"Next month." Drew seemed to be repeating whatever Colin had to say. Colin figured that was because the man's brain had shut down, unable to absorb the enormity of what was happening to him. Drew began to say something else, and it came out as a breathy squeak. He tried again. "I … uh … I have a lot of debt …"

Colin knew what he was asking. "I don't know yet exactly how much that check will be, but it's going to be roughly in line with last quarter, and I can tell you what a ten percent share came to then." He told Drew the number.

The man's face seemed to pale, and he was starting to sweat.

Orin, who'd been mostly quiet all this time, spoke up. "Son, there are things we'll need to talk about. Money like this—it makes you a target for all kinds of people. The cockroaches are gonna come out of the woodwork, all right. If you're not prepared …" He left the thought of the cockroaches—and what they might do to Drew once they got hold of him—hanging there.

"I can help you with that, too," Colin said. "But right now, I figure you need some time to absorb everything."

Drew looked like he was going to faint or throw up. Colin thought it would have been good if Julia had come to the meeting; Drew really did need some support, and he seemed to see most of the Delaneys as the enemy. Colin hoped that would change, but for now, it was just how things were.

Drew's hands were still shaking as he leafed through the papers in the folder.

"Maybe I'd better call Julia," Colin said. "You look like you could stand to see a friendly face."

"She … uh …" Drew cleared his throat and looked up at Colin, seeming to notice him there for the first time since the figure had been named. "I'm not sure if she's still here."

Colin assumed he meant that Julia had gone into town, or maybe for a sightseeing excursion up to Hearst Castle.

"When do you expect her back?"

"I ... We had a fight." He looked at Colin, and his expression hardened. Colin could guess what the fight was about. "I told her to go home, and ... I think she went."

Colin gaped at him. "She *left*?"

When he didn't get any answer from Drew, he got up, left the room, and pulled his cell phone out of his pocket. In the relative privacy of the upstairs hallway, he dialed her number. The call went straight to voice mail. Then he called Ryan and Gen's place. No one was home; it was midafternoon, and both Ryan and Gen would still be working.

He muttered a string of expletives and headed out of the house, taking the stairs two at a time. He hurried out to his car and drove to Ryan and Gen's place. The rental car Drew and Julia had been sharing wasn't parked in front of the main house, and Colin hoped like hell he'd see it at Ryan's place.

It wasn't there.

Ryan and Gen weren't in the habit of locking up their house during the day, so Colin went right in the front door, as all of the Delaneys often did. "Ryan? Gen?" he called from the entryway, but he got no answer. "Julia, are you here?" He didn't expect a response to that one, but he'd hoped he might get one anyway.

"Shit," he muttered. "Shit, shit, shit."

Again taking the stairs two at a time, he went to the guest room where Julia had been staying. He found the closet and dresser empty and the bed neatly made, with a note propped up against the pillow. He snatched up the note and quickly read it.

Dear Gen and Ryan,

Thank you so much for your wonderful hospitality. I'm sorry I couldn't thank you in person, but I was called away to deal with an urgent matter at home. Please tell Colin I said goodbye.

—Julia

That was it? That was all he got? *Tell Colin I said goodbye?* When she'd dumped him, he'd thought he would have a chance to change her mind. He'd thought he would at least be able to try. Now this. She hadn't even bothered to tell him she was leaving.

Everything in him told him to *do something*. By the time she got to the airport in San Jose, it would be early evening. She might not be able to get a flight out tonight. She'd probably be in San Jose overnight—he could drive up there and try to catch her before she left. He could buy a ticket so that he could get through security and stake out the gate.

The options running through his head for what he could do narrowed as he started to apply logic. What if she'd decided to fly out of a different airport? What if she'd decided to drive? He could get all the way up to San Jose and never find her.

And what if he did find her? She'd made it clear she didn't want to continue seeing him. Would he track her down in some grand romantic gesture only to have her cut him off at the knees again?

Drew said they'd had a fight. Colin had no doubt the fight was about him and his involvement with Julia. Did Colin even have a right to try to change her mind about being with him? She'd told him about the tense and dysfunctional state her family was in, and how much that hurt her. Did he have a right to pursue her, knowing it would throw her family into even greater disarray?

He crumpled up the note and threw it onto the bed.

Fuck.

He wasn't in love with Julia, he told himself. He couldn't be. They hadn't known each other long enough for love. But whatever he felt for her—whatever this was—it hurt like a bitch. It hurt like there was a goddamned truck parked on his chest.

He stood there in the guest room a while longer, staring at the wall, trying to process.

Then he walked downstairs and out of the house, and went to tell his mother there'd be one less guest for dinner.

Chapter Twenty-Eight

"I did the right thing, Mike. Why does it hurt so much?" Julia was crying on Mike's sofa, still in the puffy jacket and knit hat she'd worn to protect her from the Montana cold. She had come straight here from the Bozeman airport because she'd needed someone to talk to. The idea of returning to her empty house to wallow in self-pity was not an option.

Much better to wallow in self-pity here.

As Colin had predicted, she'd had to stay overnight in San Jose and had taken a flight out that morning. She'd had a two-hour layover in Salt Lake City, most of which she'd spent mired in misery, fueled by airport junk food and the bad coffee she drank on the plane.

Now that she was home, she was seriously reconsidering her decision to flee California. What had Colin thought when he'd realized she was gone? Had she handled things all wrong? Should she have stayed? And, most importantly: What if Colin Delaney could have been the love of her life, and she'd thrown all of that away?

"Here." Mike handed her a roll of paper towels he'd retrieved from the kitchen. "I don't have any Kleenex, so this'll have to do."

She took the paper towels gratefully, tore one off of the roll, then wiped her eyes and blew her nose. She was being stupid, and that's exactly how Mike was looking at her: as though she were seriously lacking in any kind of common sense.

"I know it's dumb," she said, holding the wadded-up paper towel in her fist. "I know. I'm the one who decided to leave. It was my decision. I should just … *suck it up*. Because I did the right thing!"

"Did you, now?" Mike was looking at her with his head cocked, using the expression he most often put into use when one of the guys on his crew had screwed up and Mike wanted to make him squirm under the pressure of his scrutiny.

"Yes!" Julia threw her hands up in exasperation. "Yes! The thing between me and Colin was causing problems for everybody! Colin actually got into a fistfight with his brother! And Drew was so angry, Mike. So angry. I just got him back, and things are so fragile between us. I can't lose him again."

Mike cocked his head and peered at her. Everything in his expression said he thought that what she'd said was utter bullshit. "Since when do you let your brother tell you who to sleep with?"

"Since … since I started sleeping with my brother's cousin! That's when!" She waved her hands around for emphasis.

"It's not the usual scenario, I'll give you that," Mike said thoughtfully.

"I know!"

She sniffled a little, tore another sheet off of the paper towel roll, and dabbed at her eyes. Evening was darkening the sky outside Mike's window, shutting down the gloom of the day.

"I did the right thing," she said, her voice small.

"Uh huh," Mike said. "If you're so sure about that, then why are you crying?"

She didn't look at him. She focused instead on the wadded paper towels in her hands.

"Because I'm an idiot. That's why." She sniffled again.

"You'll get no argument from me."

She let out a harsh laugh, then shook her head at the folly of getting involved with someone like Colin Delaney. "It wouldn't have worked anyway," she said. "He's a billionaire, for God's sake. And I'm just … me. I'm just this … this mess!" She gestured toward herself, toward the epic disaster that she'd become.

"Well, now you really are being an idiot," he said.

"Hey!"

"Take off your coat," he said as he got up and headed toward the kitchen. "I've got beer and Doritos."

Colin left Cambria the day after Julia did. He'd claimed that he had to get back to Southern California to work on the Palm Springs land deal. And that was true, but it was only part of the story. He'd also left because he was afraid he'd punch Drew McCray in the face if he didn't.

Colin knew it had been Julia's decision to leave, and he knew that she was an adult who was responsible for her own choices. But he doubted she'd have made this particular choice if her brother hadn't given her such a ration of shit.

Drew was at least part of the reason Colin felt the way he did—a substantial part—and it was hard to look him in the eye without wanting to throttle him. And since physically attacking Drew would be counterproductive to his own goals of restoring the man to his rightful family, Colin thought it best to pack his things and go.

"You could always call her. Or, if that doesn't work, go out there and talk to her," Sandra had said when Colin announced his intention to return south. She'd stood there with her hands on her hips, fuzzy slippers on her feet, that challenging look in her eyes.

"I'm not leaving because Julia went home," Colin told her. "I have work I've been neglecting while I've been up here."

"Boy, you might think I'm stupid, but from where I'm standing, I'm not the one who doesn't have any God-given sense," she'd groused at him. She'd narrowed her eyes. "Unless what you two had together was just sex."

"Mom!" If there was one thing that could make this situation worse for Colin, it was talking to his mother about his sex life.

"Well, was it?" she demanded.

"No. No, it wasn't. At least, it wasn't for me." And there it was … this conversation was officially more awkward.

"I didn't think so. I guess I know you well enough to read the signs. Well, if you've got real feelings for the woman, you're a fool if you don't go out there. And I didn't raise any fools. Except maybe Liam." She'd abruptly turned and scuffed off into the kitchen, leaving him to wonder exactly what kind of fool he was going to be: the kind who walked away from a woman he had real feelings for, or the kind who ran partway across the country for a woman who didn't want him.

He'd decided to be the first kind of fool, because although it was painful, it was a hell of a lot less humiliating.

He'd left Cambria the morning after Julia's departure, and he'd arrived at his condo on the waterfront in the Gaslamp Quarter just before dinnertime. He let himself in the front door, flipped on a light, and dropped his luggage onto the floor with a thump.

The contrast between his parents' house and his condo was

stark. Where the ranch house was warm, a little run-down, and decidedly lived-in, the condo was all cool, clean lines and modern décor. His decorator had done the place up in black and gray, chrome and glass. A large-screen TV dominated one wall, and another was floor-to-ceiling glass looking out over San Diego Bay and the bridge to Coronado Island.

It looked like the cleaning lady had been here while he was gone; the tabletops were gleaming, and there were fresh vacuum lines in the carpeting.

Too bad she hadn't brought groceries. Colin crossed to the stainless steel refrigerator, peeked inside, and saw a jar of olives, a carton of milk that had gone bad, and a bottle of Dijon mustard. And a single bottle of local craft beer.

He twisted open the beer, took it to his sofa, and plopped down with a sigh.

It was fucking lonely here.

And by *here,* he meant the condo, the neighborhood, the city of San Diego, and the whole of Southern California. Maybe even the state, the country, the world.

He didn't have friends here; not really. He had people he knew who he sometimes drank with, or went sailing with, or sat with to watch some game or another that he didn't really care about. He had hangers-on, people who kept themselves within his orbit because they thought his wealth might somehow rub off on them. He had women he dated—the glossed-up Barbies. But he didn't have family here. He didn't have real friends. He didn't have people he genuinely cared about, and who genuinely cared about him.

Sure, he'd come here initially to escape his family, so that part was on him. But his intention had been to create a home for himself somewhere that was outside the Delaney field of gravity. He'd learned two things: This was a residence, but it wasn't really a home. And the Delaney field of gravity was so all-consuming he wouldn't be free of it even if he were on the moon.

He carried his beer into the bathroom, then stripped off his clothes and took a long, hot shower without bothering to unpack. Afterward, he dressed in sweatpants and a T-shirt and ordered some food for delivery. While he was waiting for it to come, he composed a text message for Julia. Then he deleted it. Then he wrote another version. Then he deleted that.

God, he was a fool. He felt like he had in high school when he'd asked Karen Stewart to the junior prom, and she'd waited until the day before the dance to tell him she was going with Eric Romero instead. He felt gutted, as though his insides had been scooped out and replaced by nothing but self-loathing and regret.

The worst part—the part that made the least sense—was that he'd only known Julia for a couple of weeks, and they hadn't even really been dating. They'd slept together once. Once! And yet she had a hold on him that had turned him back into that awkward, crushed seventeen-year-old who hadn't had a date for the prom.

He tried calling her again—he'd tried several times since he'd gotten the news that she'd left—and it went straight to voice mail, as it had each time before. He decided to leave a message this time.

"Julia? Ah … I just … I wanted to make sure you got home safely. Call me."

He sounded pathetic, even to himself.

Love—if that was what this was—sucked.

Chapter Twenty-Nine

Julia should have known that her mother would nag her for the details of everything that had happened in Cambria. And who could blame her, really? If Julia had borne the illegitimate child of some California billionaire, and then that child had grown up and gone out there to meet the family he'd never known, she'd sure as hell want to get the blow-by-blow dish on how that had gone.

Still, Julia wasn't up for talking to her mother right now. She felt so emotionally raw after her experience on the West Coast that she didn't feel ready to rehash it with Isabelle. And part of her worried that her mother would immediately sense that Julia had fallen for a Delaney. After all, who better to recognize the signs than someone who'd been through it herself?

Isabelle had always been able to read Julia's emotions on her face. If Julia talked to her now, she'd be too exposed. She wanted to keep this heartache safe, where her mother couldn't poke at it and reopen the wound.

On her first full day back in Bozeman, Julia ignored three phone calls from her mother and answered four texts with the minimal amount of information she could get away with. Yes, she was home. Yes, things had gone fine. No, she didn't know if Drew had returned home from Cambria yet. No, she couldn't talk; she had too much work to do.

That last part was a line of crap. While it was accurate that Julia had work she should have been doing to prepare for the hotel job that was coming up, she wasn't doing it. She was mostly wallowing in her heartbreak. She stayed in her pajamas until noon and ate a pint of Ben & Jerry's for breakfast, and that helped somewhat. She listened to Colin's voice mail message no fewer than ten times, and that didn't help at all.

She managed to put Isabelle off for a couple days, which was a better result than Julia had expected. When her mother showed up on her doorstep on a gloomy Wednesday afternoon, Julia was past the pajamas and ice cream phase and had moved on into a mostly manageable sadness.

Apparently, she didn't have a lock on sadness; when she opened her front door and found Isabelle standing there with pink cheeks from the cold and the slushy remains of snow on her boots, Julia could clearly see that Isabelle had been feeling some of it herself. The older woman's face was lined with worry, and her eyes were rimmed with red, as though she'd been crying.

"Mom." All at once, Julia started to feel guilty about the way she'd brushed her mother aside when she'd gotten home from California. Julia hadn't wanted to deal with her mother's neuroses, but she'd forgotten that all of the events involving Drew and the Delaneys had been difficult for Isabelle, too.

She stepped aside to let Isabelle into the overheated house. Isabelle came in and removed the snowy boots and her other winter gear. She put the boots on a mat by the door and hung her other things on the coat rack. Only then, when she was standing in her thick socks in Julia's living room, did she give Julia the reproachful look that she probably deserved.

"I'm sorry I didn't return your calls," Julia said lamely. "It's just, I had a lot to do when I got home, and …"

"You were avoiding me," Isabelle stated, her mouth tensed in a way that emphasized the fine lines in her skin as they feathered away from her mouth.

"Well ..." Julia's shoulders fell. "Yeah. Maybe."

"But why?"

"It's just ... It's all been a lot to deal with, that's all."

Her mother glared at her. "Well, Julia, it has been for me, too." Then Isabelle's face softened. "Honey? Are you okay?"

Was it that obvious that she wasn't? She knew her mother could read her, but she hadn't expected her to manage it quite so fast.

"Come on into the kitchen," Julia said. "I'll make coffee." This was likely to be a long conversation, and Julia didn't think she could manage it without caffeine.

"Well ... why did Liam think that any of this was Drew's fault? Drew was as blindsided by all of this as anyone."

Isabelle was seated at Julia's kitchen table with a mug of coffee in her hands. She looked both stunned and pained by Julia's recounting of the events that had taken place in Cambria—a recounting that had strategically omitted her own involvement with Colin Delaney.

"I don't think he really blamed Drew," Julia said. "I think Liam is grieving over his uncle, and he didn't know how else to express it. He's not exactly the kind of guy who's comfortable talking about his feelings."

"Neither was Redmond," Isabelle said. She seemed like she was somewhere far away, wrapped up in her memories. A faint smile played on her lips. "He was such a man's man. Stoic. Strong. I know it must have hurt him when we stopped seeing each other, but he never said it." Her eyes became shiny, and she blinked a few times.

"Mom?" Julia's voice was soft. "Why did you do it? Why did you ..."

"Why did I cheat on your father?" Isabelle filled in the words Julia couldn't seem to say.

"Well, yeah."

Isabelle was quiet for a while, thinking about how to respond. Maybe she didn't know the answer herself, or maybe she was just figuring out how best to frame it so Julia could understand.

Finally, she looked at Julia with tired, sad eyes.

"Redmond Delaney was the love of my life."

The simple truth of it took Julia's breath away.

"He wasn't like anyone I'd ever met," Isabelle went on. "It was like we'd known each other forever. I knew what we were doing to Andrew was wrong, but ... Oh, honey. I couldn't have done anything else."

Listening to her mother, Julia realized that she hadn't been considering Isabelle's point of view before now—not really. She'd seen her mother's actions as scandalous, careless, a betrayal. And while she wasn't ready to accept the idea that Isabelle had been anything but wrong to cheat on her husband, Julia began to wonder if the situation might be more multidimensional than she'd thought.

"You loved him," Julia said, absorbing what her mother had told her. "And Redmond ... Do you think he loved you?"

"I know he did. He would have married me. He wanted me to leave Andrew."

Julia thought of the life she would have had as part of the Delaney family—insanely wealthy, but separated from her father. She couldn't imagine what that would have been like—living without her father's reassuring, steadfast presence every day.

"Why didn't you?" Julia's voice broke at the thought. "If

you loved him, then why?"

"Andrew was my husband," she said. "I made a vow. And he was a good man. I wasn't in love with your father, not like I should have been. But I did care for him, and he didn't deserve what I did. He didn't deserve to be left." Isabelle looked up from the tabletop and focused on Julia. "And then there was you. You were so little, and you adored your daddy so much. I couldn't do that to you."

Julia wanted to ask her mother so many questions: How had she and Redmond met? What was he like? How did she keep the affair a secret from Julia's father? How had she felt when she'd heard about Redmond's death?

She couldn't ask the questions, though, because she could barely absorb what she'd been told. The information made Julia reevaluate everything she'd thought she'd known about her childhood and her family. Julia sat mutely at the table, staring at her mug of coffee that had now grown cold.

"How is Drew?" Isabelle asked when the silence became too much for either of them.

As far as Julia was concerned, this change of topic didn't help matters.

"I don't know," she said. "I don't even know if he's still in Cambria. He … We had a fight. It didn't end well."

"What kind of fight? About what?" Isabelle's voice began to rise.

Julia considered lying to her mother—she could make up some story, something that wouldn't result in a difficult conversation she didn't want to have. But Isabelle could read her too easily. And anyway, there had already been too many lies.

"About me. And Colin Delaney." She couldn't meet her mother's gaze, and so she got up from the table and made a big production of rinsing her coffee mug in the sink.

"What about you and Colin Delaney?" Isabelle asked. She'd taken the insistent, somewhat accusing tone of a mother who knows her child has misbehaved in some highly predictable and yet infuriating way.

Julia set the mug down on the countertop and turned to face her mother. "I went out with him. We … were dating." Julia wondered if her mother would understand that *dating* was code for getting naked and having mind-blowing sex. Given Isabelle's own history with a Delaney man, she probably did.

"You're dating one of the Delaneys," Isabelle repeated, as though the information were so improbable she thought she had to carefully confirm it.

"Was. I *was* dating him. But that's over now. So over." Just saying the words caused a new pain to jab Julia's heart.

"What happened? Why did it end?"

Julia considered how much she should say. On one hand, telling her mother about her love life was awkward. They'd never had the kind of relationship some mothers and daughters had; she'd never come to her mother with her hopes and fears regarding the men in her life. But she needed to talk to someone about it, and Isabelle was here.

"Liam went nuts when he saw us kissing, and he attacked Colin. And then Drew found out about it, and that was almost as bad. He didn't hit anybody, but I think he wanted to." The memory of that caused tears to spring to her eyes.

Isabelle leaned back in her chair and regarded Julia with a frown. "I still don't see what that has to do with you and Colin."

"Of course it has to do with me and Colin! Of course it does! If we'd kept seeing each other, it would have torn both of our families apart!"

Isabelle narrowed her eyes at Julia. "That's a little dramatic, honey. It's not like you two are Romeo and Juliet."

"But Drew said I betrayed him!" She remembered the look on Drew's face, the hurt she saw there, and pushed the image away.

"Honey. Just because he *felt* like you betrayed him doesn't mean you actually did. Who you date is your business. Drew's feelings about it are his own issue." Rarely had she heard her mother make quite this much sense. It was unsettling.

"But …"

"But nothing. Since when do you let your little brother tell you what to do, Julia?"

"Well, I don't, but …"

"Listen, honey. What I did to your brother was wrong. I shouldn't have kept that kind of secret from him. I thought I was doing the right thing at the time, but I didn't consider what it would do to him if he found out the truth on his own someday. It hurt him, and I'm deeply sorry for that."

Julia started to say something, but Isabelle interrupted her.

"But he's going to have to find a way to get past it, to move forward." She shook her head. "He's got so much anger inside him, and it's just not good for him. It's not good for anybody. All of that anger is hurting him, but you can't let it hurt you, too."

Julia understood what her mother was saying, and she saw the wisdom in it. But at the same time, it would always be her instinct to protect her little brother, to shield him from anything she thought might be a threat to him. She'd done it when they were kids, and she was still doing it now. How could she just … stop?

"I see what you're saying, Mom. I really do. But you didn't see his face. You weren't there." If Isabelle had seen Drew's eyes when he'd found out about her and Colin—if she'd seen the hurt in them, the judgment—then surely she'd feel differently.

"I think I'm familiar with your brother's moods," Isabelle say wryly. "I think I ought to be, after I raised him."

Julia came back to the table and sat in the chair across from Isabelle. She slumped down in defeat. "It's not just that. It's not just Drew."

"Well, what else, then?" Isabelle was looking at her with such love and concern, it made Julia feel sorry for the distance that had formed between them over the past few years. She'd convinced herself that she didn't need her mother, but in fact, she did.

"It's just … Colin is obscenely rich. And … and he's so …" She gestured vaguely with her hands to indicate the entire, profound scope of male beauty. "Have you *seen* him?"

Isabelle chuckled lightly. "Honey, I've seen him."

"Well, then you know what I'm trying to say!"

"I'm afraid I don't." Isabelle crossed her arms on the tabletop and peered at Julia with interest.

"What would a man like that want with me?" She gestured at herself, indicating with a sweep of her arm her old hoodie, her faded jeans, her messy ponytail. "He wears Ferragamo shoes, for God's sake. He's the tenth most eligible bachelor in business!"

"He's … Honey, he's *what?*"

"According to *Fortune* magazine," Julia clarified. "Liam is fifteenth. I'm thinking *that* must have been awkward around the dinner table."

"Sweetheart … Are you saying you think you're not *good* enough for him? Because that's just—"

"No! Yes. Maybe. Or … maybe it's just that we're from entirely different worlds, you know? He's from a world where people dress up in designer clothes and eat meals with way too many utensils. Well, the rest of his family doesn't do those things, but he does. He went to Harvard Law!"

It just all felt so hopeless.

"You stopped seeing a good-looking man you really like because he went to Harvard Law? I've got to tell you, honey, I wouldn't have considered that a deal-breaker."

Julia looked at her mother and saw a hint of a smile on her face.

"You're making fun of me."

"Just a little, sweetie." Isabelle reached across the table and took Julia's hand. "Do you like him?"

Julia felt tears welling up in her eyes. "I like him so much it's making me irrational."

There was that whisper of a smile again. "Well, Julia, I can't really argue with that."

This was what it had come to: Julia's mother, who wasn't exactly known these days for making wise decisions when it came to love, was ridiculing her for her relationship choices. That had to be some kind of rock bottom.

As though reading her mind, Isabelle said, "Look. I know I don't have all that much credibility on this subject right now. But I've learned a few things the hard way. Redmond was my soul mate. And I let him go."

Julia gaped at her. "Are you saying you wish you'd left Dad?"

Isabelle squeezed her hand. "I'm not saying that. I'm just saying … I never stopped loving Redmond. And it never stopped hurting."

Chapter Thirty

Over the next couple of weeks, Colin went about his business. He closed escrow on the Palm Springs property, and he began plans to develop the land as a retail space. He disbursed the dividends from the family corporation to all of the relevant parties, which meant Drew McCray—who'd long since returned to Salt Spring Island—was now a wealthy man.

He talked to Drew a few times about getting him the support he needed now that he had enough money for it to start being an issue. The man needed a financial planner, a tax attorney. He needed advice on how not to fall prey to the many various people and organizations that might consider him to be an easy mark. But Colin hadn't gotten very far with that; Drew insisted he didn't need anybody's help. He was going to find out he was wrong, and he was probably going to have to learn it the hard way.

Colin wondered if this was how it felt to have a teenager who wouldn't listen to a goddamned thing his parents said. The thought of Drew and parents made Colin wonder whether Isabelle might be able to get through to him. It was an interesting idea. According to Julia, the two had been estranged for a while, but your mother was always your mother.

He made a mental note to get in touch with Isabelle and see what she thought.

In the meantime, he had a date coming up that he really didn't want to go through with. He'd bought tickets to a literacy foundation black-tie fundraiser months ago, and he'd asked Shelby Ross, a San Diego socialite and a fellow Harvard alum, to go with him. This was back when he was still interested in Shelby, before Julia had eviscerated him by joining him in his bed and then summarily dumping him.

Given all that had happened, he had about as much interest in Shelby these days as he had in advanced knitting techniques. Which was to say, less than none. But he'd asked her, and now he could hardly back out without looking like an ass. Worse than that, an ass who didn't care about literacy.

So, he got his tux cleaned and got a fresh haircut, and on a Friday evening in April, he drove to Shelby's home in La Jolla, picked her up in his Mercedes, and took her to the benefit.

As they walked into the ballroom at the Fairmont Grand Del Mar, Shelby on Colin's arm, he looked at her and thought that this was the kind of woman he should be seeing. She was beautiful, with her silky, golden hair falling like a flawless curtain down her back; her deep blue eyes; her impeccable sense of fashion; and, of course, her body, which looked like she spent two hours a day pounding away on the stair climber at the gym. She was accomplished in her career as an aide to a state senator. And she was smart. If he were looking for someone to be a partner to him as he advanced his name as an attorney and a businessman, then he likely couldn't do much better.

But somehow, every time he thought about one of Shelby's attributes, his mind kept going back to Julia, as though she were some kind of irresistible force field drawing his attention. He couldn't admire the sway of Shelby's hips without remembering what it had felt like to touch Julia's. Couldn't enjoy the sight of Shelby's hair without thinking of Julia's thick auburn waves.

He knew it was wrong to compare women; it was unproductive, and, hell, it was probably disrespectful. But he couldn't look at Shelby without thinking that Julia was somehow more intriguing, more appealing—more everything. Did Shelby ever laugh in a way that wasn't calculated to show off her smile? Did she ever spend a day in a T-shirt and gym shorts? Did she ever leave home without makeup? Did she ever really eat? The look of her size two figure suggested the answer to that last question was negative, unless you counted kale salad without dressing—which Colin decidedly did not.

The thing about Julia was that every aspect of her offered comfort, from her careless beauty to her easy laughter. If Shelby was a night out on the town, Julia was *home*. Going out was nice on occasion, but you certainly didn't want to spend your life that way.

"Colin? Is there something wrong?"

Shelby's question brought him out of his reverie. She was holding onto the crook of his arm, looking at him attentively. God, she was lovely. Fine features, and perfect, smooth skin.

He knew he was being a heel. Shelby deserved his full attention, and she didn't deserve to be unfavorably compared to a woman she'd never met—a woman who had declared her intention to be finished with Colin.

Julia didn't want him, but Shelby did. Why couldn't he just stop pining over a relationship he didn't have, and start focusing on one that was within his grasp? What was wrong with him?

"I'm sorry." He gave her a rueful grin. "I'm just a little distracted."

"Of course you are." She squeezed his arm. "You're still grieving over your uncle." She shook her head and pursed her lips prettily. "It must be miserable coming to events like this when you've got so much else on your mind."

She wasn't wrong that he was grieving; not a day went by when he didn't think about Redmond. But his uncle wasn't the main loss he was feeling right now. He and Julia had spent such a short time together. How could be this broken up about losing her? How could he be this pitiful?

"Listen, Shelby—"

"Photo, Mr. Delaney?" A guy Colin recognized as the literacy foundation's official event photographer stood poised with his camera. Colin dutifully put his arm around Shelby, and they both smiled for the photo.

He'd been planning to say, what? That he was sorry for fantasizing about another woman while he was out with Shelby? That he regretted acting like a lovesick teenager? That he just wanted to go home?

He was just considering the possibility of pleading some kind of sudden illness when the emcee for the evening took the microphone and encouraged everyone to find their seats. The round banquet tables were covered in white tablecloths and done up in flowers and candlelight.

Colin decided that he might as well stick it out for the sake of literacy. But he looked forward to taking Shelby home and going back to his place where he could pout in private.

Only about four hours to go. There was always the possibility of earthquake or tsunami. He took his seat and rooted for the quake.

"If you could stop moping around and focus on what you're doing, that would be great," Mike said wryly as he and Julia were looking over her plans for the Bozeman hotel job.

"What are you talking about? I'm working. I'm focused."

Mike scoffed. "I guess you could call this working, but you're sure as hell not focused. You've got the damned reflecting pond in the parking lot."

"What are you . . . I do not." Oh, shit. She did.

These weren't any kind of final plans, thank God—they were just sketches, ideas that she was running past Mike before drawing them up more formally to show them to the client. And she really did have the goddamned reflecting pond in the parking lot.

"I'll fix it." She tried to act like putting the reflecting pond in the parking lot was something she did every day.

"You'll fix this, sure," Mike said. "But what about next time, when you tell me to build a gazebo in the middle of the tennis courts?"

He was making fun of her. Why was he making fun of her for one simple mistake?

"Just call him," Mike said. "For Chrissake."

"Call who?" Julia looked at him with exasperation. "The client isn't expecting to hear from me until next week, so—"

"Not him," Mike grumbled. "You know exactly who I'm talking about, so don't give me the whole wide-eyed, clueless bit."

"If you're talking about Colin—"

"Of course I'm talking about Mr. Billionaire Prince Charming. Who else? Jesus."

They were at Julia's house, sitting at her kitchen table with the sketches and a topographical map of the property for reference. She gathered her papers and stood up. "That's over. That was over *weeks* ago."

Mike did that sucking thing with his front teeth again. "Yeah, well. Based on how ditsy you are these days, I'm thinking it's not as over as you'd like people to think."

Part of her was angry about the insult. Part of her was indignant and defensive. And another part of her was surprised that she was that transparent. What good was it having secret feelings of torment when they weren't even secret?

"I'll tell you what. Why don't I fix these and we'll look at them again in a couple of days?" She kept her voice bright to indicate the sheer magnitude of her indifference toward Colin Delaney.

"That's your way of saying shut the hell up. I get it," Mike said. He made no move to get up from the table.

"I didn't say that. I appreciate your concern. But . . ."

"But shut the hell up," he finished for her.

"Well, yes."

He regarded her for a minute more before he got up from the table and headed toward the coat rack by the front door to retrieve his parka. With her following behind, he went to the rack, picked up his coat, and turned back toward her.

"Look. Call him or don't call him. It's no skin off my ass. But let me leave you with this thought: Emma, the only woman I'll ever love, is married to another guy." He shrugged, raised his eyebrows meaningfully, and put on his coat.

Julia tilted her head, looking at him quizzically. "And?"

"And your guy is the tenth most eligible whatsis. How long you think he's going to be on the market? He likes you, you like him. But he's not going to be single forever. And that's the *last* girl talk I'm doing." He shook his head sadly. "I gotta get out of here before I get the urge to shave my legs."

When Mike was gone, Julia found herself still standing there, looking at the space where he'd been. Was he right? Was Colin going to meet someone else?

Then she chided herself. Of course he was. He was the tenth most eligible whatsis. He probably had women calling him more often than telemarketers. And they were probably rich women who got whole-body waxes and monthly facials. Julia had never gotten a facial, and she shuddered to think about hot wax on her most sensitive places.

The idea of him ending up with some supermodel-gorgeous woman in size six Jimmy Choos made her feel grumpy and more than a little hopeless. How could she possibly compete with that? And then she reminded herself that she didn't want to compete with that. She didn't want to be with Colin. Well, she did, but she knew the family turmoil it would cause on both sides would be too much. The cost would be too high.

Chapter Thirty-One

By the time Sandra's sixtieth birthday rolled around at the end of April, Colin should have been over Julia. He hadn't seen her for weeks, after all. He'd dated other women; he'd gone places, done things. He'd gotten on with his life. He should have been over her, but he wasn't, and he wondered what was taking so long.

The first clue the rest of the Delaneys had that something wasn't right with Colin was that when he came to Cambria for Sandra's party, he agreed to stay at the ranch instead of booking a room at the lodge. The fact was, he was feeling lonely, and the loneliness was, for the moment, greater than his sense of discomfort around his family.

"Well, I suppose there's no point in getting your room ready," Sandra had groused when she'd called him to invite him to the get-together she was planning.

"Actually, I think I will stay with you," he'd said. "If that's all right." Of course he knew it would be all right, but he also knew it would be a surprise that would spark questions and a certain amount of prying.

"You will?" Sandra had said. "What the hell's going on with you, boy?"

There was no way he could tell her what was really wrong—

that the brief glimpse he'd had of what was possible, of something more than what he'd always known, had left him feeling bereft in its absence. And now it was somehow not enough to be in a room at the lodge, alone with his laptop and his stubborn independence.

So, instead, he'd offered a lame excuse. "It's the drive." He'd felt transparent even as he said it. "It's too inconvenient to have to go back and forth from the house to town."

Sandra was silent for a moment, and he'd wondered if they lost their phone connection.

"Well, hell," she'd said after a moment, in surprise rather than irritation.

The second clue they had that he wasn't himself was that, once he arrived at the ranch for the birthday celebration, he was lukewarm on Sandra's cooking. Colin might have had a number of issues with his family, but his mother's culinary ability wasn't one of them. He usually dug into her pot roast and pies with as much enthusiasm as anyone, but now he was mostly shoving things around on his plate like a picky toddler.

He hadn't been picky even when he *was* a toddler.

"Now, you go ahead and tell me what's wrong with my fried chicken," Sandra demanded a day or so after Colin's arrival, as the whole family was sitting at the dinner table—minus Gen, who was working late at the gallery. Liam had come from Montana for the party, which was to be held the following day.

"Hmm?" Colin had been distracted, as he was so much of the time these days, and he hadn't heard what his mother had said.

"You're poking that poor bird with your fork like you think it's going to fly away," Sandra barked at him. "What the hell's wrong with it? It's the same recipe I've been using since you were in kindergarten, and I don't recall you having any complaints about it then."

"Oh." He looked at the chicken as though seeing it for the first time. "It's not that. It's just … I'm a little tired, is all."

And that part was true. He hadn't been sleeping well. He tried to tell himself that it had nothing to do with Julia or with his juvenile heartbreak, but the fact was that he couldn't sleep because his bed seemed empty without her in it.

You'd think he'd never been dumped by a woman before. He had plenty of experience with that—all of the Delaney boys did—so it made no sense that he was such an amateur at dealing with it.

"Oh, just call her, for God's sake," Breanna said. She was looking at Colin with scorn.

"Who is Uncle Colin going to call?" asked Michael, Breanna's nine-year-old son.

"He knows," Breanna said.

"But I want to know, too," said Lucas, who was seven.

"Nobody, that's who," Colin told him. "I'm not going to call anybody."

"Well, that makes Uncle Colin an idiot," Breanna said mildly.

"You always tell me not to use that word," Michael said sternly.

"You're right, honey. I do." Breanna ruffled his hair.

Colin didn't like the direction this conversation was going. He squirmed a little under the scrutiny.

Finally, he dropped his fork onto his plate with a clank. "I have called her. Okay? Several times. She doesn't take my calls." He shot a look at Liam, who at least had the good sense to look guilty.

"Because of Liam?" Sandra scoffed. "I gave the girl credit for having more sense than that."

"Yes, because of Liam," Colin said. He threw back the last of what was in his wineglass. "But not just him. Because of her brother, too. She thought it was all too *complicated*." He said the word *complicated* as though it were surrounded by air quotes.

"Oh, Colin. I'm really sorry," Breanna said. She reached out over Lucas's head and rubbed Colin's arm. He should have found the gesture irritating or condescending, he supposed, but instead, he found it comforting. At the moment, he wouldn't have minded much if his big sister had wanted to pat his head and sing him a lullaby. Not that he ever would have admitted it.

"If you're that hung up on her, you should try again," Ryan offered mildly. "Liam will get over it."

Liam, who was the subject of a good bit of the conversation, didn't speak. Instead, he shoveled chicken into his mouth so he wouldn't be expected to defend himself.

"Liam's been seeing that good-looking vet," Sandra said. "Having some kind of long-distance relationship, I guess. You'd think he'd want his own brother to make some kind of progress in his love life, too." She kicked Liam under the table.

"Ow," Liam muttered, through a mouthful of chicken.

"Can somebody pass me the rolls?" Orin said, apparently oblivious to the family drama going on around him.

Colin hadn't wanted to talk about this with his family, but now that the topic was out there, he found himself wanting to unload on them, and once he started, he didn't want to stop.

"I can handle Liam, all right?" he said, as though Liam himself weren't right there. "I'm not going to run my life based on what Liam might punch me in the face for. If I did, I'd never get anything done."

Breanna smirked.

"But," Colin went on, "it's not just about that. She said she didn't want to see me anymore. She screens my calls. She doesn't answer my texts. And I know that's about Drew, about how she doesn't want to lose him any more than she already has. But if she really wanted to be with me …" He paused, because emotion was starting to well up in his chest, and he needed to tamp it down. "… then she would be with me. Right? She'd say to hell with her brother, and she'd be with me."

"I don't know." Breanna looked doubtful. "Love is one thing, but brothers"—she looked around the table at hers. "I'd do just about anything for you guys. I really would."

They all paused so Colin, Ryan, and Liam could deal with their embarrassment.

"Except give you the last roll," Breanna put in. "Liam, you've had, what, five? Give me that."

Liam grudgingly handed Breanna the roll he'd grabbed from the basket in the middle of the table.

"Look," Liam grumbled, finally adding something to the conversation. "I was just upset about Uncle Redmond. And about that Drew guy's attitude. If you want to go out with Julia again …" He shrugged, leaving the thought incomplete.

"It doesn't matter what I want." Colin shoved his plate aside. "She doesn't want me."

"Hmm," Sandra said. "We'll see."

Colin had the uneasy feeling that he might not want to find out what she meant by that.

Julia may or may not have been stalking Colin on social media. She didn't think of it that way—she merely thought of it as keeping in the loop on her brother's new family. But if someone else had called it stalking, well, she might not have put up a very good argument in her own defense.

He didn't seem to have personal Facebook or Twitter accounts—and how weird was that in this day and age—but when she searched for him on Facebook, she got a few hits for him on other people's timelines and pages.

She'd been Facebook friends with both Gen and Breanna since shortly after she'd met them, and they both had posted photos from Sandra Delaney's sixtieth birthday party. Colin appeared in a few of the photos, mostly group shots of Delaneys and various Cambrians posing for the camera. It looked like a fairly large get-together at the ranch. Liam had come all the way from Montana for the event, and she saw a photo of him with his arm around a very attractive woman with long brown hair and tortoiseshell glasses. The way they were standing together, it didn't look like the two of them were just being friendly. Apparently, Liam had a girlfriend.

I'll bet Colin didn't punch you for it, either, she thought with some bitterness.

She hunted around a little more and saw that Colin was also named in a photo on the page for a San Diego literacy foundation that had just had a big gala fundraiser. She clicked on the photo—and felt the earth drop out from underneath her.

Colin, looking incredible in a tux, was standing with his arm around the most beautiful blond woman Julia had ever seen. The woman, dressed in a royal blue satin evening gown, had a tiny, perfect figure, elegant features, and skin that looked like it had been touched up in Photoshop. Colin was smiling at the camera, but the woman wasn't facing forward—she was gazing adoringly up at him.

Mike had warned her about this, and here it was, happening: Colin had moved on. He was seeing someone else. And not just someone else, but someone Julia couldn't hope to compete with, even on her best day.

Shit. Shit, shit, shit.

Julia reminded herself that she was the one who'd decided

she didn't want to pursue things with Colin. But none of that seemed to matter right now, while she was struggling not to hyperventilate.

She needed to gather more information. Who was this bimbo? Except, she didn't look like a bimbo. She looked like someone who'd gone to a top private school, someone raised with the help of a nanny who spoke French.

Julia hovered her cursor over the bimbo's face and saw that her name was Shelby Reed. So she Googled Shelby Reed and got a lot of hits, but none of them did a goddamned thing to ease her mind.

Shelby Reed had, indeed, gone to a top private school, where she'd been valedictorian. She'd graduated from Harvard with honors. She did volunteer work with children, for God's sake. And now, she worked as an aide to some politician or another.

Shelby and Colin weren't just together, they were a power couple! How could Julia possibly match up? How could she convince Colin to dump Shelby and be with Julia instead?

And then she remembered the very valid reasons she'd decided not to continue seeing him. Nothing had changed. Liam still would want to punch Colin in the face for dating Julia, she assumed. And Drew would still consider it an unforgivable betrayal.

Not that it mattered what Julia thought or wanted. She'd be powerless in any competition with Shelby Reed. Shelby Reed was every gorgeous, popular girl who'd ever looked down her nose at Julia in high school. Shelby Reed was every prom queen whom Julia's own date couldn't take his eyes off of. And Shelby Reed was more than that; she was the symbol for every inadequacy Julia had ever had, every insecurity she'd ever felt, every loss she'd ever suffered because someone prettier, smarter, or better had taken the win instead.

Screw Shelby Reed.

She closed her laptop, got up, went into the kitchen, and looked for a snack—something she could stress-eat to avoid thinking about Shelby Reed. She stood at the open freezer door and devoured the remains of a carton of ice cream, then threw the empty container in the trash and regarded herself with disgust.

She was pathetic, and she was certainly no Shelby Reed.

Julia told herself to forget it, to just get on with all of the things she had to do and put Shelby Reed out of her mind. She folded a load of laundry, and when that was done, she scrubbed her bathroom sink.

When she ran out of domestic chores, she went to where her cell phone was sitting on the kitchen table and paced in front of it a few times. Then she snatched it up and called Gen.

"Julia," Gen said warmly as she answered the phone. "It's great to hear from you. I was just thinking about you. How—"

"Who is Shelby Reed?" she demanded. It was possible that she sounded a little bit crazed.

"I . . . What? Who?"

"Shelby Reed!" Julia said. "A blond bimbo Colin is seeing. Except she's not a bimbo. Damn it, she's not a bimbo!"

"Julia? I'm going to need you to slow down," Gen said.

Eventually, amid an assortment of expletives and monologues about her own inferiority, Julia got out the part about Shelby Reed and the literacy benefit, and the Facebook photo in which Shelby looked both stunning and deeply infatuated.

"Damn it, he's moved on!" Julia wailed.

"Julia," Gen said in the kind of voice one might use to talk someone off of the railing of a bridge. "Calm down and listen to me. He has not moved on."

"He … What?"

"I don't know who Shelby Reed is—I've never heard of her. But Colin's here for Sandra's birthday, and I am telling you, he has not moved on." Gen enunciated each word as though she were talking to someone who didn't know much English.

Julia sputtered. "Well … but …"

"Look. You broke his heart," Gen said, and the words made Julia feel a clutch of pain in her chest. "He's been moping around here, all sad and pathetic. He looks terrible. He'll barely even eat."

Julia struggled to comprehend what Gen was telling her. She'd hurt him? Could that be? "I never … I didn't mean …"

"Whether you meant to or not, you crushed him," Gen said. "And I've got to tell you, I'm a little pissed at you for it. He's my family, and I care about him. And he didn't do anything wrong here. He deserves someone who's going to stand by him, not someone who's going to take off as soon as Liam has a mood."

Julia felt tears spring to her eyes.

"It wasn't just Liam. It was …"

"Drew. I know. And I get that he's got some legitimate feelings going on, feelings that must hurt like hell. But finding a way through that is his own responsibility, Julia. You shouldn't have to be miserable just because your brother is. And Colin sure shouldn't have to be miserable along with the two of you."

Julia was silent as the tears that had threatened to come spilled over. She wiped her eyes with her fingers and took a deep breath. "You've been wanting to say that for a while."

"Yes, I have," Gen said. "But for what it's worth, even though I'm pissed at you, I'm still rooting for you and Colin."

"You are? But why?" Julia was astonished that Gen could still be on her side, given all of the things she'd just said.

"Because Colin's in love with you, you jerk. And I think you're in love with him. And I'm a fool for romance, even when at least one of the people involved is being an ass."

After a pause, Gen said, "Listen, I've got to go. I've got a client in the gallery. But we'll talk more. I'll e-mail you."

She hung up the phone before Julia could respond.

Was she right? Was Julia being an ass?

Shelby Reed probably would never be called an ass by the sister-in-law of the man in her life.

And was Colin the man in Julia's life?

There was more than one man in her life, Julia thought. And she had to gather her courage and talk to one of the others.

Chapter Thirty-Two

Drew had left Cambria shortly after Julia had, and he was continuing to be stubborn in regard to the Delaneys. But at least things between him and Julia had improved somewhat. At least now, he usually took her calls.

This time, he probably wished he hadn't.

"You need to forgive them," she said the moment the call was connected, and before he even spoke.

"No, I actually don't," he said. He didn't question who she was talking about; Julia supposed it was obvious.

"Damn it, Drew, it wasn't their fault that Mom lied to you! It wasn't their fault that she cheated on Dad! And it wasn't their fault that Redmond didn't come forward to claim you! They didn't even know about you! Be mad at Mom if you want to—though I personally think you should reconsider that, too—but the Delaneys are not the ones you should be blaming here!"

He was silent, and she could imagine the angry, brooding look on his face. "Are you finished?" he said.

"I guess so. Are *you* finished holding your precious grudge?"

"So, what prompted this call, anyway?"

She was sure he already knew the answer, and she was equally sure that if she said it, her response would only make things worse. She didn't answer him.

"This is about him, isn't it?" Drew sounded like he was clenching his teeth hard enough to crack a walnut.

"Yes. It's about him. Please, Drew. I like him so much. I even think … Oh, God, I think he could be *the one* if I could just give it a chance, but I turned him down because of you! Because I didn't want to hurt you! And now I can't stop thinking about him, and I'm miserable as hell because I have to choose between the man I've been waiting my whole life for and my brother!" She paused, breathless, waiting to hear what he would say—whether he would put aside the anger he'd been carrying to let his sister be happy.

"If you really cared about my feelings as much as you say you do, then this wouldn't even be an issue," he said, his voice tight and angry. "You could choose any other guy in the world—any other guy—but it's got to be him? That's bullshit, Julia. You're doing this to hurt me, and you goddamned well know it."

"Drew—"

"I don't know why you think you need my approval, but you don't have it." And he hung up on her. She couldn't believe that he'd just hung up on her, but she didn't know why it should be hard to accept. He'd been shutting her out, accusing her, and turning his anger on her for three years now. Why did she think he would stop now?

For the first time, she began to see the intensely self-involved nature of Drew's misery. He couldn't see that she'd been standing by him, reaching out to him, all this time. He couldn't see that the Delaneys—with the exception of Liam—were blameless, and had done their best to be accommodating. He couldn't see that their mother had made a mistake and was sorry for what she'd done, and was eager to make amends. He couldn't see that Redmond had done what he did to try to keep Drew's family life intact. He couldn't see anything beyond his own pain, his own determination to wallow in the fact that he'd been wronged.

Julia had stuck by her brother even when he'd all but cut her off. She'd gone with him to Cambria so he wouldn't have to face the Delaneys alone. She'd even given up the man she was more and more certain was intended to be her one true love—all for Drew. And what was he willing to give back to her? Nothing. How much did he care about her feelings, her pain? Not at all, apparently.

She'd given up Colin to avoid losing Drew, but she didn't have Drew—not really.

But she could hardly make things right with Colin now, after she'd rejected him, and after so much time had passed.

Drew wasn't the only one slogging around in misery—Julia was doing a pretty good job of it herself.

When Gen e-mailed her later that day, as promised, to continue their discussion of everything that had happened between Julia and Colin, Julia had needed to unload. She had needed to unburden herself to someone who might understand.

She wrote to Gen:

I think I'm in love with Colin. And I think walking away from him was the biggest mistake of my life.

It felt good to get it out there—even if there was nothing she could do now to correct her terrible error.

"Don't take my word for it. You can read it yourself," Gen told Colin as they sat together at the kitchen table in the main house at the ranch. It was two days after Sandra's party, and somehow, Colin found himself still here. Typically, he'd have headed out first thing the morning after the party, but the loneliness of his San Diego condo just seemed like more than he could handle right now.

Gen turned her laptop around and showed Colin the e-mail on her screen.

An e-mail from Julia.

I think I'm in love with Colin, it said. *And I think walking away from him was the biggest mistake of my life.*

He froze as he looked at the words on the screen. His heart was beating faster, and his fingers and toes had gone numb. Could this be real? Could Julia really have written this? He checked the sender address to be sure.

"I …" He was speechless. He swiped his hand over his face. He cleared his throat, and tried to regain some coherence. "I don't think you were supposed to show me this," he said.

"Desperate situation, desperate measures," Gen said. "I had to do something. You're a mess!"

She was right; he was. He was still managing to do his job; he was still managing to take a shower every day and get dressed and do the things a reasonable man was expected to do. But he didn't feel like himself. He wasn't the happy, optimistic guy he wanted to be. He figured he'd left that guy with Julia.

He looked at Gen helplessly. "Well … what am I supposed to do with this?" He gestured toward the computer screen and the e-mail still displayed there.

"Go out there! Talk to her! Woo her!" Gen said it as though it should have been obvious. But she wasn't taking into account the fact that he'd been dumped.

"She told me she wasn't interested." Just remembering that made him feel a little sick.

"Well, she obviously is," Gen insisted. "She was just worried about her brother."

"And that situation hasn't changed," he reminded her.

"She said giving you the brush-off was the biggest mistake of her life!" Gen exclaimed.

Sandra had been puttering around the kitchen while the two were talking. She'd been cleaning out the refrigerator in the wake of the party, and she'd had her head shoved into the freezer section during the last part of the exchange. Now, she withdrew from the freezer, turned around, and put her rubber-gloved hands on her narrow hips.

"If you two could give it a rest for a minute, I've got something I want to talk to Colin about," she announced.

"What's that?" Colin asked. He was glad to be off the subject of his love life, though he felt a prickle of dread about what his mother might want.

"Well, since we're talking about pain-in-the-butt brothers, there's something you can do for yours."

Given the description, there was no question she was talking about Liam.

He raised his eyebrows in question.

"Well, you know he's crazy about that vet," she said, a scowl on her face that, in anyone else, would have meant that she didn't much care for Liam's girlfriend. But in Sandra's case, it was just her usual expression.

"Yeah. And?" Colin prompted her.

"And, they're trying to do some kind of long-distance relationship, one or the other of them always flying here or there. It's a waste of money, you ask me. Plus, that kind of thing never works. A recipe for some kind of ugly breakup, and before you know it, Liam's going to be moping around even worse than you are."

"They seem to be managing it," Colin said. "They—"

"Are you going to listen to what I have to say, or are you going to talk just to hear the sound of your own damned voice?" Sandra groused at him.

Colin couldn't help grinning. "Sorry. Go on."

"Well …" She peeled the rubber gloves off her hands and threw them onto the counter. "I figure it's time for Liam to move back home. He's been asking about it."

"He has?" This was the first Colin had heard of it.

"Of course he has. You think I'd lie to you?" She glowered at him. "I told him he should come on back. But that means we've got nobody out in Montana to keep an eye on the place. Desmond's good with the cattle—he knows how to run a ranch—but he's not a Delaney."

Colin could feel the beginnings of a headache, and he rubbed his forehead with weary forbearance.

"You want me to move out there. To where Julia is. And that's, what, just a coincidence? I'm not supposed to realize this is a matchmaking scheme?"

"Well, I guess it doesn't matter what you do or don't realize," she snapped at him. "I still need somebody out there in Montana. And once you're there, if you're too big a fool to make a play for your woman, well, there's not much I can do about that."

She snapped the gloves up off the counter, put them back on her hands, and went back to scrubbing the inside of the freezer.

"Send Ryan," Colin suggested.

"Don't be an ass," Gen told him.

"I'm not moving to Montana," he said.

Colin got up from the table, went upstairs to his room, and settled in with his laptop to get some long overdue work done. He had to check in with the property managers he had working for him all up and down the state. He had to deal with a frivolous lawsuit that had been filed against the family by a tenant who was just looking to reach into the Delaneys' deep pockets. And he had to try again to get through to Drew.

The DNA test had been completed, and Drew was, indeed, Redmond's son. So, that was taken care of. But the man had refused to take Colin's advice about getting a financial adviser, and he'd also resisted Colin's efforts to educate him on the Delaney holdings—and his own new holdings, in particular. He did generally accept Colin's phone calls, but the conversations were brief and ended with Drew shutting him down.

Colin understood that Drew was having a rough time adjusting to everything that was happening to him, but McCray wouldn't have the luxury of brooding for much longer without some serious consequences. Now that his new status as a man of wealth was becoming public, the vultures would start circling. If Drew wasn't prepared, he'd get eaten alive.

Colin had compiled a list of very good advisers who could help Drew, if he'd let them. Which he probably wouldn't. He e-mailed the list to Drew along with a plea—one of many—that he get his head out of his ass and start taking the responsibility of his inheritance seriously.

Then, he found himself staring blankly at the wall and thinking about Montana.

Would it be such a bad idea to move out there? He'd been growing increasingly tired of San Diego. More and more these days, he felt like the city and the people he knew there didn't have much to offer him. His condo was top of the line, but it wasn't a home. It was beginning to feel like a beautifully furnished prison.

He'd been out to the Montana ranch many times, and if there was anywhere on this earth as beautiful as Cambria, it was there. A man could have space to think in a place like that. He'd have room to consider what he really wanted. To reevaluate.

And if things happened to start up again with Julia, well, that could only be an item in the plus column.

After a day or two of thinking it over, he announced to his parents that he would go to Montana after all. At first, he decided to make the move on a trial basis. He'd keep his condo in San Diego just in case things didn't work out. And by *things,* he meant Julia. If she shot him down again, he'd have a place he could slink away to—somewhere he could feel sorry for himself and lick his wounds, as far away from her as possible.

But the more he thought about it, the more it seemed stupid to think that he needed an escape plan. If he did this thing half-assed, it was like begging to fail. Since when had he taken the safe route? Since when had he ever been afraid to commit?

He didn't even like the San Diego condo. Why would he even want to escape there, in any event?

He got back to San Diego after his mother's birthday thinking that there was only one course of action for him. He had to plunge headlong into this thing, and if Julia didn't want him, then he'd man up and find someone who did. And he'd do it in Montana, on his family's ranch. Not in some sterile penthouse in a city with too goddamned many surfers.

He had some loose ends to tie up in Southern California, and so he tied them over the next few weeks. Then he packed the things he wanted to take with him to Montana, and arranged for movers to put everything else in storage.

When it came down to choosing which of his possessions he liked enough to haul them 1,300 miles, he was surprised at how little made the cut. Two suitcases, a few boxes.

On the day he put the boxes and the luggage into his Mercedes and headed north on Interstate 15, he expected to feel the loss of all that he was leaving behind. But he didn't.

He felt free.

Chapter Thirty-Three

By late May, Julia's professional life was gaining momentum again; the warmer weather had thawed the ground, and she could begin to work in earnest on the projects she'd sketched out and thought about through the cold of winter.

Her final designs had been approved for the Bozeman hotel job, and the necessary permits were in hand. Mike and his crew were set to begin construction on the structures and the hardscape, and Julia and her team of gardeners were ready to begin the plantings.

She couldn't wait to get her hands into the soil. She was pretty sure hard outdoor work was the only thing that would get her mind off of Colin, and that was something she needed even more than she needed the money from the job. Thinking about him had put her off her game, and that wasn't okay, especially now, when she had entire crews of workers dependent on her for their incomes. The crews were counting on her, and the client was counting on her, so being distracted and incompetent was not an option.

And aside from her various obligations, she simply loved the work. Throwing herself into her job was the only thing that might make her feel like herself again. It was the only thing that might make her feel whole.

Late one Thursday afternoon when she got home from the job site, she was feeling so relatively okay for a change that she almost forgot to stalk Colin on the Internet.

Almost.

She showered, put on clean sweatpants and a T-shirt, poured herself a glass of wine, and began to think about what she should have for dinner. But the thought of dinner made her think about how much it sucked to eat alone. Which made her think about dinner dates, which made her think about Colin.

Which made her think about how horribly, pathetically lonely she was without him.

You're hopeless, Julia. Absolutely frigging hopeless.

And that was how she found herself in front of her laptop, calling up whichever Delaneys she could find on Facebook.

It would have been so much easier to stalk Colin if he'd had his own Facebook profile, but because he didn't, she had to stalk him through Gen and Breanna. She perused Breanna's timeline, fairly convinced that she wouldn't find anything useful there, but giving it a try nonetheless.

What she saw made her gasp as though she were drowning and had just come up for air.

On Breanna's timeline was a picture of her with Liam, each of them with an arm thrown over the other's shoulder, both smiling at the camera. In her post, she commented about how happy she was to have Liam home for good.

In the comments below, someone inquired about how that had come about. And Breanna answered that Colin had taken Liam's place at the ranch in Montana.

Julia felt dizzy, and she realized she'd stopped breathing.

Oh, my God. Colin's here.

How long had he been here? Was he staying permanently?

And, more importantly, had he come here for her?

Oh, God. Oh, God.

Julia's mind was all over the place. What if he really had come all the way out here for her? What did it mean? What should she do? Why hadn't anyone told her?

And then, another thought struck her: What if the reason no one had told her was that his move here had nothing to do with her? What if it was just Delaney business? What if she hadn't entered into his decision at all? What if she called him, and he didn't want to hear from her?

"Oh, crap," she said, looking at her computer screen. "Crap. Crap."

The biggest part of her wanted to feel joy, hope, jubilation at the thought that he'd come here to try again with her, to reclaim what they'd had so briefly and turn it into more. But another part of her was afraid to hope it was true. What if she was misinterpreting his move? It was one thing to walk away from a man she'd been falling in love with for the sake of her brother. But it was something else entirely to have hopes and feelings, only to have the rug pulled out from beneath her.

Kind of like the way I pulled the rug out from under Colin when I chose Drew over him.

She felt the sting of guilt at the memory. She'd told herself at the time that she wasn't really hurting him, because they'd known each other so briefly. But the truth was, she knew that was a lie. A brief time or not, there had been something between them, some kind of chemistry, some kind of magic. That didn't happen every day. In fact, in some fifteen years of dating, it had never happened to Julia before.

And she'd run like hell from it.

That wasn't just about Drew, and she knew it. She was scared then, and she was scared now. What if he really had just chased her more than a thousand miles?

Right now, she wanted nothing more than to let him catch her.

Colin was disgusted with himself. He'd uprooted himself, coming 1,300 miles just to try to get back together with Julia. And he hadn't been able to drum up the courage to even talk to her yet.

The problem, he told himself, was that he hadn't come up with a good strategy. Should he call her? Show up at her house? Text? E-mail? Have flowers delivered?

And when he did one of those things, what would he say?

I know you said you didn't want to have anything to do with me, but I moved out here to be near you, so how about it? What part of that didn't sound like stalking?

Should he throw himself at her feet and beg her to be with him? Or arrange to casually run into her one day? Should he ask Breanna or Gen to mention in an offhand way to Julia that he was here, and then see if she made a move?

This was stupid. He was being stupid.

He could make this kind of move in the hopes of winning a woman's heart, but he couldn't even bring himself to talk to her.

"Man up," he told himself. "For God's sake."

The day he finally decided to make his move, the weather was sunny and clear, and the sky was so starkly blue it almost didn't seem real. It seemed like some optimistic child's painting of a sky; he almost expected to see a big smiley face on the sun.

Colin set out in his Mercedes in midafternoon, thinking to complete the two-hour drive just as Julia was getting home from work. If she wasn't home yet when he got there, then by God, he'd wait for her. If he didn't see her today, there was no telling when he'd muster up the courage to try again.

He spent the lengthy drive grumbling and brooding. The closer he got to her house, the more he was prepared for her to kick him out on his ass. And the more he thought about that very real possibility, the angrier it made him.

He was Colin goddamned Delaney. He was one of the wealthiest men in the state of California. He'd graduated from fucking Harvard Law. He was smart and accomplished, and women had been known to think he was attractive. If she couldn't or wouldn't accept what he had to give, then it was her mistake; it would be her damned loss.

Just when he'd worked up a good head of steam, he'd lose it again thinking of how much he wanted her. He wanted her more than he wanted anything, more than he wanted to keep standing upright and keep breathing in and out. And that was the truth of it, not some false confidence he was trying to make himself feel.

By the time he parked the Mercedes in front of her house, he had worked himself up into such a state that there was a good chance he might throw up on his shoes the moment she opened the door.

He steadied himself and went up the front walk anyway. Her car was in the driveway, and a light shone from inside the house. He stood on her front porch, took a deep breath, closed his eyes, and exhaled slowly. Then he rang the bell.

The curtain beside the front door moved slightly, and he saw her face, saw her eyes widen. Then the door was opening and she was standing there in front of him, like a vision from his dreams.

Sweatpants, tank top, bare feet. Her hair was pulled back into a ponytail, loose tendrils trailing down into her face. She wasn't wearing makeup. Of course she wouldn't be; she'd probably been working in the dirt all day, in the sun and the dust, planting things, making things grow.

She had never looked more beautiful to him than she did right now. He opened his mouth to say something—some rational thing about relationships and families and brothers—but instead, he took one step forward and pulled her into his arms so suddenly that she gasped in surprise. Then he kissed her with everything he had, everything he'd been feeling. He claimed her mouth with his own, and he felt her go limp and weak in his arms.

She felt like promise and hope. She felt like his future.

After a moment, and with some difficulty, he let go of her and pushed her gently away from him. She brought a hand to her mouth, her fingertips touching her lips. The taste of those lips was still on Colin's tongue.

"I'm living here now. In Billings," he said.

She nodded.

"You didn't want me before. But I hope you will now." He took a deep breath, cleared his throat, and nodded at her. "Ball's in your court."

Then he walked back to his car, got in, and drove back to Billings.

Chapter Thirty-Four

The kiss left Julia so stunned and speechless that she didn't move, didn't go inside, didn't even close the door for several minutes after Colin was gone. Her heart was pounding, her knees were weak, and she seemed to have lost the power of coherent thought. Parts of her body that had been sorely neglected lately felt like they were about to burst into flames.

The ball's in your court.

When she finally went inside and closed the door, she sat on the edge of her sofa in a daze and thought about what, exactly, it meant for the ball to be in her court. The last time the ball had been in her court, she'd dropped it. She'd rejected him even though he'd done nothing to deserve it, even though he was nothing short of her dream man. What was wrong with her? What had she been thinking?

She had blown what was perhaps the greatest opportunity of her life for the sake of a brother who insisted on sabotaging his own life, who couldn't see beyond his own determination to be wronged, joyless, inconsolable.

And now, Colin was giving her that opportunity again. He was handsome, not to mention filthy rich; he could have had any woman in the world. And yet he wanted her so much that he'd moved halfway across the country for her. What had she done to deserve that? What had she done, other than hurt him?

This time, she decided she was going to smash that ball back over the net, or die trying.

She gave Colin enough time to get back to the ranch, and then texted him.

We need to talk. There are some important things I have to say to you.

He didn't answer for a long time. When he did, the response was businesslike, and not quite what she'd expected.

I have some time next Friday. I'll be out of town all day. Should be home around six. Drive out, and we'll talk.

Next Friday? Julia blinked, feeling stung. After he'd come all the way out here, after that kiss, he couldn't spare time for her until next Friday? And he wanted her to come to Billings, two hours away. What did that mean? Was he testing her? Was he creating hoops for her to jump through to find out whether she was serious?

Well, if she had to jump through hoops to get Colin, she'd do it.

She'd do it even if the damned things were on fire.

Julia spent some time thinking and formulating a plan. Then she called Breanna to run an idea past her.

By the end of the day, she had a tentative scheme in place. But she couldn't pull it off alone; she needed help.

She called Mike and explained what she had in mind.

"Couldn't you just buy him some flowers and a damned box of candy?" he grumbled.

"Does that mean you won't help?" she asked.

"I'll help," he said grudgingly. "If only to get you to shut up about your love life."

Colin hadn't put Julia off until next Friday to make her

jump through hoops, or to test her, or anything as premeditated as that. He'd done it because the wording of her text—*We need to talk*—was universal woman-speak for *I'm about to crush your heart, and if you kiss me again I'll seriously consider a restraining order.*

If that was the way she felt, then he'd have to hear it sooner or later. But he wasn't ready to hear it yet, so he'd given himself until next Friday to get ready to take the hit. He wasn't quite ready to give up hope. Not that it would be any easier next Friday, but at least he'd have some time to mentally prepare.

And as for why he'd told her to come to the ranch, rather than him coming to her? If he had to drive two hours just to get his ass handed to him, it would add insult to injury.

She'd said in her e-mail to Gen that letting him go had been the biggest mistake of her life. But from where Colin was standing, it looked like it was a mistake she didn't intend to correct.

He spent the week leading up to Friday acting moody as hell, which pissed Desmond off to no end.

"Why'd you even bother to come out here if you're gonna act like it's some damned prison sentence?" Desmond, a stout, weathered man in his midfifties, complained one day when Colin went out to the little two-bedroom house on the property where Desmond had been living with his wife for the past two decades.

Colin had been meeting with Desmond semiregularly since his move so he could learn a little about how the place ran. That irked Desmond, who felt that it was one thing to put up with Liam—an experienced cattleman—but quite another to have to tolerate a lawyer who didn't know a damned thing about ranch work, even if his last name did happen to be Delaney.

For the most part, Colin had been handling Desmond's disdain with calm professionalism. But since he'd set the date to meet with Julia, he'd grown increasingly intolerant of the man's surly behavior.

Colin was getting more short-tempered and irritable the closer Friday came, until finally, the Tuesday before the big day, the two of them had it out.

"I don't have to justify to you why I'm here," Colin said in response to Desmond's taunt. "If having me on my own property is too big an inconvenience for you, Desmond, you can always find yourself another job."

Desmond scoffed. "Who do you think would run this place without me here? You might mess up your nice manicure if you had to come within ten feet of the herd."

"What in the world?" said Mona, Desmond's wife, when she overheard the two men arguing. She'd been working in the back bedroom—which she'd turned into a sewing room—while the men had been talking at the kitchen table. Now, she stood in the kitchen doorway, wringing her hands with worry. "Desmond, for goodness sake, Colin's got more of a right to be here than we do."

Desmond made a *hmmph* noise and continued glaring at Colin.

Mona, a soft, gray-haired woman of his mother's generation whom Colin had known for many years, walked up behind him and put a hand on his shoulder.

"Colin, dear, what's wrong? You're not yourself."

"I'm fine, Mona," he lied.

"Nonsense," she shot back. "I can see with my own eyes that's not true. I told your mother I'd look out for you, and I'd never hear the end of it if I don't find out what's got you so wound up."

Colin blew out some air, glared at Desmond, and then looked up to where Mona was standing over him.

"There's this woman …" he began.

"Ah, Christ. There's always a woman," Desmond broke in.

"You be quiet," Mona told her husband. Then, to Colin: "Go on."

Mona was so caring and maternal that Colin found himself opening up to her, telling her the whole story of all that had transpired with Julia.

"Oh, honey," Mona said when he was finished. "She's a fool if she can't see what kind of man you are."

"I'd guess she does see," Desmond said. "That's the problem."

"Hush!" Mona swatted her husband's shoulder with her hand.

When she spoke again to Colin, her voice was soothing and affectionate. "Don't you worry," she said, giving him an encouraging smile. "I have a feeling all of this is going to work out for the best."

She said it as though she knew something that he didn't.

Given the vast variety of things Colin felt like he didn't know at the moment, he thought that was pretty damned likely.

Chapter Thirty-Five

On the Friday that Julia was expected to arrive, the weather was perfect, without a cloud in the great expanse of the sky. The temperature was in the high sixties. The Bighorn Mountains, still topped with snow, rose into the southeastern sky, and the sandstone Rimrocks stood sentry over Billings and its inhabitants.

Colin had needed to make a quick trip to Southern California two days earlier to deal with some issues regarding the commercial development of the Palm Springs land, and he'd caught a flight back to Billings Logan International Airport that afternoon. Now, he was back in his car and heading out toward the ranch with a sick feeling in his gut.

The idea that he was on his way to be rejected by Julia—again—made him as nervous as he'd been when he'd taken the bar exam. And that time, he'd thrown up twice. This didn't feel a whole hell of a lot better.

On the drive back to the ranch, he briefly considered turning around and not going, but then he told himself to show up and act like a man. If the woman didn't want him, it was better to know.

He drove up the narrow road that led to the ranch through stands of Ponderosa pine and aspen trees, following the route of a creek that was swollen with May rains. The sun was still well above the western horizon, and its gentle light filtered through the trees.

Nothing looked unusual when he pulled his car up to the house, a big, rambling single-story that had been built back in the '70s and that was sorely in need of a remodel. Maybe he'd do that, if he was going to stay here any length of time. And maybe after today, he'd be ready to go back to California and never look at this place again.

Desmond would like that.

He pulled his Mercedes into the driveway and found that Julia's car was already there. His heartbeat sped up, and his palms started to sweat. Stupid. It was just stupid to let a woman make him feel this way.

Colin got out of the car and wondered where Julia could be. She wasn't on the porch, and she wasn't in her car. Maybe she was taking a walk by the creek. It was a good day for it.

He stepped up onto the porch and let himself into the house. He was a meticulously tidy man by nature, but before his trip, he'd left the place looking a little ragged. He hadn't felt much like keeping house lately.

In the kitchen, he opened the refrigerator and pulled out a beer in a longneck bottle. Just as he was about to open it, something caught his eye out the window over the sink.

What the hell?

He set the beer on the counter and went out the back door and into the yard behind the house.

On the long expanse of new spring grass, Julia stood beneath a cottonwood tree like some kind of mirage, wearing a white, floaty dress that made her look like an angel.

Beside her was a white-linen-covered table with two chairs. There were place settings, serving dishes, and candles waiting to be lit. She'd strung lights in the branches of the trees.

And right in front of him, its reins looped around the porch railing, was a gorgeous chestnut mare, its coat gleaming in the early evening sunlight.

"What … what is all this?" Colin asked, feeling dazed as he approached her.

She started talking fast—he could see that she was nervous. "My friend Mike—I think I told you about him—likes to ride, and he has a horse trailer. He helped me find her for you, and he brought her out here for me." She gestured toward the mare. "And there's dinner, too. I didn't cook it myself, I had a caterer … I talked to Breanna about it and asked what she thought, and she called the Byrnes and cleared it."

"But …" He was speechless. He just stood there, unable to form a coherent thought.

She must have taken his hesitation as a sign that he was displeased, because a worry line formed between her eyebrows.

"I'm sorry, Colin. For letting you go. For choosing Drew over you. For … for being too scared, and thinking you couldn't want me." Tears began to shine in her eyes. "But if I'm too late, if it's too late for us …"

"You brought me a horse," he said. He walked over to the mare and stroked her neck. The mare let out a huff of air in greeting. "I can't believe you brought me a horse."

"You never had one of your own," she said. "You said you always wanted—"

She didn't finish her sentence, because while she was speaking, he closed the distance between them, took her into his arms, and silenced her with a kiss. His heart pounded and his body felt liquid and weak as he held her, as he devoured her with a kiss that held all of his heartbreak and all of his hopes.

When their lips parted after what felt like a lifetime, he

tangled his fingers into her hair and leaned his forehead against hers. He could feel her warm breath on his skin, and she smelled sweet, like jasmine.

"You brought dinner," he murmured.

"Umm … yes." Her eyes were closed, her voice dreamy.

"You think we could warm it up a little later?"

Her eyes opened, just a little, and she gave him a slow smile. "I'm sure that'll work."

So he scooped her into his arms and carried her up onto the back porch, into the house, and into his bedroom.

Julia had been so scared about what he would say, what he would do. Yes, he'd come to her house and kissed her. But then he'd put her off when she'd asked to see him. She'd been so frightened that he'd changed his mind about her, that he'd decided she wasn't worth the trouble she'd put him through.

When he'd kissed her under the cottonwood tree, she'd felt her body hum with happiness. And now, here in his bedroom, she couldn't wait to show him everything she'd been feeling for him, feelings that she should have been true to from the beginning.

"Colin." She breathed his name as he kissed her jawline, her neck, her shoulder where it met the gauzy fabric of her dress.

She wanted to touch him everywhere, all at once. She ran her hands over his chest, his face, his arms, but there was too much between them—far too many clothes getting in the way.

She pulled his shirt from where it was tucked into his pants and unbuttoned it as he ran his lips and his tongue over her hot skin.

This time, she didn't want to take—she wanted to give. She wanted to show him all of the things she was feeling, and make up for the hurt she'd made him feel. So she reached down and unbuckled his belt, slowly lowered his zipper, and then freed him from the confines of his clothing.

Julia looked into his half-closed eyes, and then lowered herself to kneel in front of him. When she took him into her mouth, he let his head fall back, and he let out a ragged gasp, his hands in her hair.

There was a feeling of power in what she was doing to him, in how she was making him feel. Anyone could take pleasure, but giving it, at this moment, was so much richer. So much *more*.

She caressed him and stroked him with her mouth until she could feel his body tense, and he took her by the shoulders, easing her back up to him. "Not yet," he said. He put a hand on her face. "Let's take our time."

He pulled her dress over her head, and his eyes widened in pleasure when he saw the silky, lacy, tiny things she was wearing beneath it.

Julia pulled off his shirt and let it fall to the floor. She ran her hands over his strong, warm body, feeling the tension of her own need growing. He undressed her completely, and she him. Then she stepped into his arms and felt her entire body sigh at the feel of his skin against hers.

"Julia, are you sure?" His voice was a low rumble.

She understood what he was asking. He wasn't asking about this moment, this act between them. He was asking about more. About the two of them, together, and the limitless future they might have. He didn't want to get hurt again. He was asking if he could trust her with his heart.

"I'm sure." She took him by the hand and led him to the bed.

Later, when they both were feeling sated and exhausted, they got the mare settled in the stables, then reheated the dinner

Julia had arranged and ate it by candlelight in the twilight of early evening. The air was cool, but she'd planned for that—a portable heater warmed them as dark descended.

Colin wanted to be completely happy, to set aside his fears and vulnerabilities, but there were things he had to know. Questions he needed her to answer.

"What about Drew?" He toyed with his wineglass, turning the stem in his fingers. He felt the flitter of nerves in his chest. "What if he pressures you again?"

"Drew has a lot of feelings, but I can't fix that for him." She reached out her hand for his. He set down his glass and held her small hand on top of the table. "I'm sorry about what my mother and Redmond did, and I'm sorry it hurt him. But none of that was my fault. Or yours. And it's not my fault that I fell in love with you."

Then she smiled, and he was lost.

"You're in love with me?" He caressed the back of her hand with his thumb.

"Of course I am. Would I have done all of this"—she gestured around them—"if I weren't?"

"Probably not," he conceded. He released her hand and picked up his wineglass, savoring the crisp Chardonnay she'd brought. A California wine, he noted.

"I can't promise nothing will ever go wrong between us," she said. "But I can tell you that I'm in. Completely, one hundred percent. Whatever happens, I'm here. I'm in."

Looking at her in the candlelight, with her sun-kissed skin and her white dress, her glorious hair resting on her shoulders, he thought that he'd never seen a more beautiful woman. He looked at her, and his heart said, *yes*.

No matter the risks, no matter where things might go, no matter whether she changed her mind about him. The only answer he could give her, the only word in his heart, was *yes*.

"You know, Bozeman's quite a distance from here," he mused.

"It is."

"Stay with me," he said. "No more running off in the middle of the night. Just ... stay with me." He was asking about tonight, but he meant forever. There would be time to talk about that, time to plan.

"Yes," she said.

He stood up and took her hand, and they blew out the candles. They went back into his house and into his bedroom, and for the first time since he could remember, Colin Delaney felt fully at ease.

He was exactly where he was supposed to be.

Finally, after all this time, he'd found what he was looking for. It had nothing to do with geography; it was about this woman.

Colin Delaney was home.

Epilogue

A few months after he and Julia left Cambria, Drew McCray began to think that his sister was a new woman. Come to think of it, Colin Delaney seemed pretty damned different, as well.

Everybody knew you couldn't trust what you saw on Facebook, but if Julia's timeline was any indication, she was happier than she'd ever been.

It hadn't taken her long to put their childhood home on the market and move into Delaney's place outside of Billings. The pictures she posted told quite a story: Julia moving in. Julia and Colin riding together on the Delaney property, and later, visiting her friend Mike over in Bozeman. The two of them all dressed up, attending one or another charity function. Julia and Colin visiting Cambria, and Julia being accepted into that family seamlessly—she'd even charmed Liam, as far as Drew could tell.

If you did an image search for Colin Delaney, you could see the difference in him immediately. Before he'd met Julia, he looked like a stiff—or like a Ken doll. Always dressed up, always perfectly groomed, always smiling in a way that you just knew was cultivated for the camera.

But after? Well, that was a hell of a thing. All of a sudden, his smile reached his eyes. It looked real. He looked more relaxed, too—everything from his clothes to his hair. More jeans and T-shirts, not as many suits.

And then there was Julia. She'd always been a happy, bubbly person—until their father died, and until Drew and Isabelle had their falling-out. Then, she'd seemed tense, stressed. But now, it was like the old Julia was back again. You could see the joy in her face, even through the separation of the computer screen.

Drew was happy for her, but he was also a little ashamed.

How could he not have wanted her to have this? Had he been wishing for her to stay mired in discontent the way he was? Had he wanted to pull her down with him?

And how selfish was that?

He was her little brother, and so they'd always fallen into a pattern in which she was the one who tried to take care of him, instead of the other way around.

It occurred to him now that it was time for him to do something for her.

He flew to Montana around the end of July for a visit. He told Julia and Colin that he wanted to take them out to dinner—he was wealthy now, after all, so he certainly could afford it.

They went to Jake's, a steakhouse downtown, and ordered salads and prime rib and a bottle of very good cabernet sauvignon. Drew saw that Julia's happiness hadn't been manufactured for social media. It was real. When she smiled, her face glowed. She looked at Colin Delaney the way Tessa had once looked at Drew, back in the days before everything went wrong.

They ate and drank and talked, about Drew's boats and Colin's efforts to learn how to ride as well as his brothers and his sister did. They talked about the ranch, and how Colin mostly left the running of it up to Desmond, but how Colin was learning, bit by bit, to make it his own.

They talked about Julia's business, and how she was traveling between here and Bozeman to finish the projects she'd already committed to. She was also starting to establish a client base in Billings.

When the evening was over, Drew paid the check and the three of them stood together awkwardly in the parking lot before heading to their cars.

"We should do this again," Drew said. "You two should come out to Salt Spring Island. If you want to. I mean ... I'd like that."

Julia embraced him, and he felt his eyes grow hot.

"Thank you," she whispered to him. "This means a lot to me."

He cleared his throat and released her, and straightened up. He and Colin shook hands firmly, like men who had reached an understanding.

Which, he supposed, they had.

He hung around a few more days, spending some time with Julia, and then he drove to Bozeman and visited his mother for the first time in years.

They talked, and she cried. Things weren't perfect between them, by any means.

But it was a start.

Acknowledgments

This book could not have been written without the support of many people. I'd like to thank Ken Stipanov, who taught me a little bit about wills and the law as it relates to inheritances. I'd like to thank Tara Mayberry, who understood my vision for the book's cover and fulfilled that vision. I'd like to thank my husband, John, who always makes sure I have the time and resources to write.

And most of all, I'd like to thank my readers. A book is nothing without readers to give it life. Your support has been so gratifying. You'll never know how much it means to me.

77808622R00195

Made in the USA
San Bernardino, CA
28 May 2018